MULTO

MULTO

CINDY FAZZI

ISBN 978-1-957957-09-8
eISBN: 978-1-957957-40-1
Library of Congress Control Number: available upon request

First hardcover edition September 2023 by Polis Books, LLC
62 Ottowa Road S
Marlboro, NJ 07746
www.PolisBooks.com

I dedicate this book to my literary agent, Maria Napolitano.

1

THE PRESENT

W*hat It Means To Be Undocumented In America*
If you have neither the birth certificate nor the passport to prove you belong in the US of A, you're undocumented AKA illegal. You have a visa? Lucky. But if you stay a second longer than the date stamped on it, you're illegal. Americans have many names for you: undocumented immigrant, overstaying tourist, illegal alien, migrant, deportable, removable, wetback, loser, parasite, criminal.

Frankly, those names are inadequate. They can't even begin to describe your situation. For this reason, I've invented my own special terms. First, multo, *meaning ghost in Filipino. You know why? Undocumented immigrants, like ghosts, can be invisible. Some people can see them as clearly as the little kid in* The Sixth Sense *can see Bruce Willis. Others simply can't or won't. Ghosts can appear or disappear, just like immigrants on the run.*

Second, desperate hopefuls. You desperately cling to the hope of belonging in this country someday. Maybe you've been deported before, but you came back. Most likely you'll get kicked out again. That won't stop you from trying again and again because desperate hopefuls never quit. Plain hope comes with a prayer, a sigh, and nothing more. It's a housebroken puppy, while desperate hope is a rabid dog. It knows no bounds and heeds no one.

How do I know this? I'm an immigrant like you. I'm a bail enforcement agent who catches criminal undocumented immigrants. I'm the best in the business, which means I'm your worst nightmare —or your best friend if you listen to every damn word I say.

Domingo stared at his handwriting, then at his wristwatch: five minutes before nine and already scorching. He'd parked the rental car outside the gated mansion because he'd come too early.

At least he'd made the most of it. A few more paragraphs of his handbook or memoir or whatever it was going to be. He wasn't sure yet, but he'd made up his mind to write everything he knew about illegals. Not just a diary but something worth reading and keeping. Like a self-help book or an underground guide that would be passed around in secret. A must-read for anyone planning to cross the brutal Sonoran Desert or sail across the treacherous waters of the Gulf of Mexico. It might save someone's life someday.

He wrote in a little notepad because he couldn't get used to writing on his smartphone. He was forty, old school, stubborn, and married to no one and nothing but his old habits.

Time to get to work. He shoved the pad and pen inside the glove compartment, started the car, and drove toward the gate. The property, located outside of Columbus, was secluded.

He pushed the button on the intercom. "This is Domingo. I have a nine o'clock appointment with Mrs. Reed." One call from the supermarket-chain heiress had sent him scrambling to Ohio. Money worked in not-so-mysterious ways.

"Domingo?" a woman's voice crackled.

"Sunday. It's Sunday," he corrected himself. Americanizing his name seemed the right thing to do in 1998 when he got his much-coveted U.S. citizenship. Today it sounded stupid but he was stuck with it just as Coke was stuck with its cocaine-inspired brand.

"Oh, Sunday. The bounty hunter, right?"

"I'm a bail enforcement agent licensed in eight states." As a law enforcement professional, he deserved the same respect as a cop or a sheriff's deputy. He worked just as hard and got in harm's way just as much as those guys.

The gate buzzed open.

He parked in the long driveway and got out of the car. He didn't know anybody in Ohio aside from the Reeds. He rarely met with clients, but this was a special case. He spent ninety percent of his waking hours hunting down illegals who had been convicted of crimes more serious than entering the country without proper authorization. Most of them hid in big cities, usually on either the East or the West Coast where they blended in without a problem. Ohio was a fluke. He knew the Reeds courtesy of Cutter, a military veteran who had worked a long time ago at the Clark Air Base in the Philippines. Cutter had recommended Domingo to General Leonard Reed. Domingo's reputation, a most precious commodity he nurtured, preceded him.

He glanced down at his black blazer and khaki pants. Too hot for a jacket in the summer heat, but he wanted to look professional.

He strode toward the huge colonial-style house. He ignored the brass knocker and pressed an inconspicuous doorbell instead. A rotund woman opened the door. "Hello, Sunday. Come in. Remember me?"

"Rosie? How are you?" He shook her hand. She'd been part of a cadre of helpers since 1998. Her face now bore some age spots. Her hair had turned gray, though her smile remained warm. She'd always been friendly.

She opened the door wider. "I'll let Mrs. Reed know you're here."

Inside, he gawked at the ceiling that climbed at least thirty feet. The house never failed to impress, then and now. He scanned his surroundings. The décor had changed since his last visit nine years ago. The sea-green sofa, matching chairs, and bright blue curtains were new.

He perched on a wingback chair, feeling like an intruder in some high-end interior decorator's showcase. Only the gilt-framed antique map of the thirteen American colonies circa 1775 revealed a hint that a four-star general used to live here. The map rested above the mantle where a painting might have hung, as if to say history trumped art in this home.

He never doubted General Reed's patriotism. In the end, Reed's egotism and greed eclipsed his many accomplishments, though only Domingo and a few other people were privy to the old man's *one* sexual indiscretion that hounded him to his deathbed. The public, especially military vets, continued to hold the general's memory in high esteem. If only they knew.

Rosie had returned. "Mrs. Reed is ready to see you now."

"How long have you been working here?" he asked.

"Twenty-five years. How time flies!" She motioned for him to follow. "My daughter, Tracy, also works here, but it's her day off today."

"Twenty-five years, wow." He trailed her until they reached a spacious room with the air of a cottage—botanical prints on the wall, a vase of fresh roses, and pots of indoor ivy with vines spilling onto the floor. A pair of wooden Chinese screens, the kind that folded into several panels, depicted rustic sceneries.

The last time he'd seen Mary Reed, she'd been a well-coiffed blonde. Today, the vibrant room was a contrast to the sight of the old lady propped up on the bed. Mary looked shrunken, wilted, and plain spent up. A scarf covered her head.

Hair loss, chemo, radiation, breast cancer. The thoughts came in a quick succession. "Good morning, Mrs. Reed. How are you feeling?"

"Tired. Always tired." She gestured for him to take a seat. "I appreciate your coming. You'll be compensated for this meeting, naturally, and all your expenses will be reimbursed."

"Thank you."

In the past, Mary Reed was always well-groomed, one of those rich ladies who seemed always prepared to have their pictures taken. Her husband had the medals and the prestige, but she had old money, thanks to her great-grandfather who started a successful chain of supermarkets in the 1920s.

"It's good to see you again, Mrs. Reed. It's been a while since...you know." He groped for the right words. He was never good at small talk. "I remember reading in the newspaper about the general's passing."

"He's been gone nine years."

Domingo sat in an armchair close to Mrs. Reed. "I'm sorry for your loss."

"Are you? My husband almost killed his own daughter. If he had succeeded, you and I would have shared the guilt, if not the prison sentence." Her blue eyes, washed out from age, moistened with tears. She breathed through her mouth, laborious and noisy. "I won't beat around the bush. I need you to find Monica before I die. I want to ask for her forgiveness."

He sighed. *Monica Reed.* He'd caught—and lost—Mary's stepdaughter twice. He called her *Multo* with a capital M. There were many undocumented immigrants who could be as invisible as ghosts, but no one quite like Monica, the Mother of all Ghosts. "I understand, ma'am, but maybe you're better off with a private investigator. I handle deportation cases. This case is not for me."

"No PI can find Monica. Cutter hired three already, and they all failed. They even looked for her in Manila. She's not there."

He nodded. Back in 1998, Monica had traveled from the Philippines to America to find her white father, the high-and-mighty Leonard Reed. The general had promptly hired Domingo to get rid of his illegitimate daughter, the product of Reed's sexual indiscretion involving a Filipino woman. Monica had overstayed her tourist visa—such an easy case. Indeed, Domingo had caught her on the same day he'd accepted the job. She "escaped" a few hours later.

In 2008, the general had asked him to find Monica for the second time. Not to deport her, but to seek her help on a matter of life and death. Domingo had caught her again, but she'd vanished several weeks later. Could he find her a third time?

Domingo cast his glance down, aware of Mrs. Reed's eyes on him. A knob of discomfort nudged his heart. She reminded him of Mamang, who lived in a nursing home. He couldn't take care of his own mother. Shame on him.

"Sunday?"

Here we go. He made eye contact despite his apprehension.

"Will you humor an old woman with one foot already in the grave?" A sad smile flickered across her chapped lips. "Please find Monica."

"What if I can't find her?"

"But you will because you know her."

"Mrs. Reed—"

"Monica could have been the daughter I always longed for, but I was too proud to accept her. She belonged to another woman. Meanwhile, I couldn't have a baby. I was too bitter about the injustice of it all." She extended her frail arm toward him. The veins on her translucent skin bulged. "I've been horrible to Monica. I want to make amends before I die."

He held her hand but kept mum. A good bail enforcement agent, like any professional, would never promise anything. He doubted Mrs. Reed's doctors had assured her of a cure or more time on this earth or a painless death. Only a fool made promises.

"Please help me." She clutched his hand with both of hers. Her tears fell. "Help me correct my mistake. It's the right thing to do. I'm going to give her everything I own. And you will find her so she may at last receive what's rightfully hers. I never needed *one* cent of my husband's assets. I should have transferred them to Monica."

So, the Reeds didn't have joint wealth, unlike regular couples. "The general left Monica his money?"

She nodded. "Most of it. A portion went to Cutter. Leonard and I agreed on the change in his will before he died, but I was angry and jealous. I didn't look for Monica. I gave Cutter his money but withheld the rest from Monica." She withdrew her hand and covered her eyes with it.

"Mrs. Reed, please don't cry." He got up and picked up the Kleenex box from the night stand. Mamang also cried at the drop of a hat. Any news of floods, earthquakes, and the demise of old Filipino movie stars sent her weeping.

Mrs. Reed's tear-streaked face lit up with gratitude as she plucked a tissue. She blew her nose like a child, loud and without embarrassment. "You're my last hope. This is the last thing I'll ever ask from you."

He sat back in the chair. "I understand." The air-conditioner hummed. The odor of something medicinal clung to his nostrils, though no bottles or containers were in sight. "And if I fail?"

"You won't."

"I appreciate your confidence in me, but—"

"You found her twice." Her faded-blue eyes bore into him—a death stare, a dwindling ember. She was dying.

"I also lost her twice," he reminded her.

"No, not lost." She didn't blink. "It's not like you misplaced her."

So, she'd known all along. His chest compressed, anticipating what she would say next. He shifted his gaze to the Chinese panels, where the strong odor came from. Her drugs and medical paraphernalia must be hidden behind them.

"Sunday, you're too good to lose anyone."

The sound of his name startled him. He turned his gaze back to her.

"You disliked being her jailer," she added.

"That's one way of putting it. Or I lost her, plain and simple." Unwelcome emotions rushed through him: regret, longing, sorrow. No words to describe them.

"You let her go."

There. The other shoe had dropped. His face grew warm. He gave her a small smile, but he couldn't deny it. He couldn't lie to a dying woman.

"Promise me you'll find her." Her voice wavered. Her eyes brimmed once again. "Please promise me, son."

Son. Just like Mamang. "I promise." He patted her hand.

Her face opened into a beatific smile. "I'll always be grateful."

He nodded and got up. He headed for the door, because what else was there to say? He'd just promised to find the Ghost. He might as well have promised to chew *and* swallow a razor blade. What a sucker for fragile old ladies! He was his mother's son. Damn it.

2

October 1998

Domingo panted like a dog as he jogged up the steepest street in the world. Who knew Pittsburgh was so damn hilly? It was just his luck to end up in this impossible terrain for naught. The undocumented Somalian immigrant he meant to catch had left a friend's house three hours ago. By all accounts, the bastard who had robbed pawnshops in Newark hadn't known Domingo was on his tail. The scumbag got lucky since he'd booked a flight back to New Jersey this afternoon.

At last, Domingo reached his Camaro. He'd parked on a hill for lack of any other parking spot. He placed his hands on his knees, his chest heaving, as he looked down at the yellow house he'd just come from. A cool breeze kicked up the dust from the ground and shook dried leaves from the trees.

After his heart rate calmed down, he got in his car and drove away. He needed a pay phone so he could check in with his boss. He owed everything to Joe Medina, a former cop in Manila and owner of Immigrants Bail Bonds in Brooklyn.

"You're young, brown, and fresh off the boat. You look, think, and act like the illegals you'll be chasing. All you need is a gun and a license," Joe had said in offering him a job.

The man was right. Domingo blended well with undocumented immigrants, given his thick Filipino accent, his undeniable *foreignness*. Americans called Filipino women *exotic*, but men like him were simply *ethnic*.

Bail enforcement suited him, not that he had other job options. His college degree from a diploma mill in Manila impressed no one. His work experience? Hauling produce as a stevedore at the pier and bootlegging Betamax tapes were best excluded from his résumé. Those jobs had paid for his useless college diploma and nothing more.

He pulled into the parking lot of a strip mall and called Joe from a phone booth. Even though he'd failed to catch his perp, Joe seemed happy. He had a new case for Domingo, right in Pittsburgh. "An old buddy of mine, Cutter, called on behalf of General Leonard Reed. You heard of the name?"

"No. Who's he?"

"Reed is a highly decorated, highly respected retired Air Force general!" Joe sounded downright giddy. "Just this morning, I heard on the news that the Senate is about to confirm his appointment as CIA director. You understand how important this is?"

"Yeah, of course."

"We're talking about the top dog of the C-I-fucking-A. This is a priceless opportunity."

"Got it."

"I need you to pay attention. You can't screw this up."

"Hey, I can still catch my Somalian perp—"

"Forget about it. Victor can handle it from here. I want you to focus on Reed's case."

"Copy that."

Domingo used to shadow Victor and other experienced bounty hunters. He tried to absorb their good habits while tossing out their emotional garbage. He couldn't believe how many bullies and psychopaths were in the ranks, Victor included.

"Listen carefully," continued Joe. "You need to catch a half-breed Filipino girl who claims to be General Reed's illegitimate daughter. This morning, she showed up at Reed's house in Columbus, Ohio. Mrs. Reed is devastated and can't stop crying. The general is furious."

Domingo cradled the phone receiver between his ear and his shoulder as he pulled a pen and a little notepad from his pocket. He began taking down notes. "What's the girl's name?"

"Monica Reed. Biracial—looks more white than brown. Early twenties. The general kicked her out after ten minutes of conversation. Cutter thinks she's here on a tourist visa and most likely overstaying, but he has no proof whatsoever."

He glanced at his wristwatch: five o'clock sharp. "So, Monica was in Ohio this morning...but she's in Pittsburgh now?"

"Not yet. She'll be there tonight. My contact at Greyhound in Columbus said she bought a one-way ticket to New York City. The bus is going to stop in Pittsburgh. When that happens, grab her and take her to INS."

"Got it."

"Also, the general wants to talk to you."

"Really? Why?"

"Reed is a general! Don't ask why. Just call him."

"Okay."

Joe Medina gave him the general's phone number and ended the conversation on that note. Thank goodness his boss wasn't pissed about the Somalian perp. Once again, his chest swelled with gratitude. He was lucky to find a mentor like Joe who taught him all about guns and helped him secure a bail agent's license. With the help of Joe, he learned self-defense: kung fu, judo, and wrestling.

On Joe's advice, he frequented target-shooting ranges, boxing gyms, massage parlors, and bars where law-enforcement types hung out. Talk about networking. He nurtured his relationships with other pros. In this business, everyone relied on everyone for information. Trading favors was the norm.

The strip mall buzzed with teens hanging out in a yogurt shop, moms with their kids dashing inside Great Clips, and what looked like a construction crew invading a pizzeria. The smell of greasy food wafting from the restaurant reminded him of pepperoni and sausage. But first, the general.

After one ring, Reed himself answered. Domingo managed to introduce himself before the man interrupted him.

"I have no goddamned daughter in any goddamned Third World country!" the general screamed. "I haven't set foot in that godforsaken country in God knows how long. She has no right to call herself a Reed, goddamn it!"

Domingo flinched but said nothing.

"Do you have any qualms hunting down one of your own?" asked Reed.

"Qualms? I eat qualms." A pause on the other end of the line. The general was not in the mood for jokes. "Sir, I'm a professional. I don't care what nationality my subject is."

"Good. I want to make sure about that. How does five grand sound to you?"

"Sir, I don't handle payments. My boss will draw a contract—"

"Cutter has paid Joe Medina in advance. The five grand is your bonus. It's on top of whatever Joe pays you."

"Oh." Five thousand American dollars could buy a decent house in the Philippines. Even after one year in America, Domingo still thought in terms of pesos, always calculating the exchange rate in his head. He agonized over every dollar he spent on a cup of coffee because that would have cost him *forty* hard-earned pesos. What kind of idiot squandered that kind of money on coffee? "That's very generous of you, sir." He forced himself to sound nonchalant, like someone used to getting bonuses. "I'll take care of Monica Reed. You won't hear from her again."

"I expect nothing less. From here on, call Cutter if you need anything."

"Yes, sir." He said goodbye before the man realized that such an easy task didn't merit a bonus, certainly not five grand.

Six hours later, he waited for Monica Reed amid empty benches at the Greyhound station. The ceiling light flickered. The bus arrived thirty minutes past schedule.

The driver came out first and yelled, "You all have fifteen minutes. Let's go, folks!"

A pit stop on the way to New York City. The bleary-eyed passengers disembarked, scattering like ants after being stepped on. He spotted Monica—jeans and sweatshirt, young, tall, brunette, puppy-dog eyes. She was a bona fide beauty. A tote bag hung from her shoulder like deadweight.

To make sure he had the right person, Domingo introduced himself in Tagalog.

She answered with a yawn. It was almost midnight, after all. She was about five nine, several inches taller than him. To be born a short man sucked. A short woman could be *petite*, meaning attractive, but a short dude was simply a hideous midget.

"*Kumusta ang biyahe?*" he said. How was the trip?

She appraised him with suspicion, her glance resting on his long-ish hair.

He patted his hair, held together by super-strength styling gel, which he fancied pretty cool, thank you. "I happen to know you're illegal. I'm here to arrest you." He flashed a fake badge, a trick he'd learned from Joe. It always worked. It jolted Monica out of sleepiness.

"Since your current address is in New York City, that's where I'm taking you, to INS in Manhattan." He'd switched to English for good measure.

Her New York address came from Cutter, but Domingo had bluffed about the rest. It was up to him to make sure he could indeed turn her over to the Immigration and Naturalization Service without getting sued by the ACLU.

Monica's reaction reassured him. She bowed her head as though she was unworthy of occupying the same space as him. Moments like this, he thanked the heavens for his American citizenship courtesy of his white stepfather. Domingo and his mother had immigrated to this country with legitimate papers. He could look anyone in the eye and say, "Yeah, I'm a naturalized citizen of the US of A."

"Any luggage?" he asked.

She shook her head.

"Let's go. Don't make a scene," he warned her.

She followed him to his Camaro like a scared child. Desperate hopefuls had no legal status in this country, no presence, no voice. They were *nothing*, as the Republicans and the neo-Nazis would say.

His car was parked on the side of the street, sandwiched by two trucks. He maneuvered out of the tight spot and onto the quiet streets of Pittsburgh. The arrest was so quick and easy, he worried a bit. By picking up someone like Monica who was not a convicted criminal, he risked a civil rights lawsuit. Anybody could report undocumented immigrants to the authorities, but arresting them was another matter. He apprehended people with deportation orders, not just because they were in the country illegally, but because they'd committed other, more serious crimes.

Here was how it worked. First, the cops arrested the sons of bitches for some badass shit, like a drive-by shooting or smuggling drugs across the border or armed robbery. Their illegal asses then sat in jail while waiting for a chance to face a judge. Those who could afford it paid cash bail to the court, or put up a house or a car as collateral. They got their cash or assets back if the case concluded without any violations of the bail conditions.

Most desperate hopefuls, however, had neither cash nor property, and so they went to businessmen like Joe Medina, who provided the cash on their behalf. He charged ten percent of the bail amount, regardless of the person's guilt or innocence. Some of them disappeared as soon as they were bailed out. Agents like Domingo then entered the picture to capture the fugitive, or Joe Medina would lose his money.

Nabbing a hapless girl like Monica, whom the INS had no idea existed, violated Domingo's professional standards. It was her bad luck to have messed up with the wrong white man, a four-star general about to become the CIA director. Leonard Reed couldn't afford a scandal. Domingo understood that much. Most of all, Domingo knew he could get away with Monica's arrest.

He maintained solid contacts at the INS. He'd granted huge favors to those guys by delivering criminal undocumented immigrants—drug dealers and gun smugglers who had eluded the federal government for years—right into their offices. He'd saved those lazy bums countless man-hours, not to mention thousands of taxpayer dollars. INS agents were happy to process his fugitives as long as he didn't interrupt their lunch break or the occasional office party. "Sunday, you're the man," they liked to say with a high-five. Of course, they would take Monica Reed without any questions.

The girl might be harmless, but she wasn't stupid.

"How come you arrested me? Shouldn't the police arrest me?" she asked, her eyes alert now.

Bingo. The dark streets of Pittsburgh made it seem like a ghost town. He should bluff some more to scare her, but the stillness of the night made him falter. "It's your old man."

"What?"

"It's the general." He glanced at her sideways. "He wants you out of his country."

She grimaced as though he'd hit her, followed by a torrent of tears and gulping sobs. He said nothing, just kept driving through a long tunnel. They emerged from it and continued onto an even longer stretch of pitch-black highway. Still, she cried.

"Hey, it's okay. Nobody's going to hurt you. It just means you're going back home." He hadn't known until now that the sight of a weeping woman cut right through him. "Monica, listen. You're young...how old are you?"

"Twenty-five."

So, she was four years older than him. "It's not the end of the world. You have your whole life ahead of you."

"No, I don't. I'm finished." She was sniffling and rooting through her bag for something. "All my life, I wanted to come to the States to find my dad. My mother worshipped him. He was a Wild Weasel pilot, a big hero in the Vietnam War." She found a tissue and blew her nose. "He got injured in Vietnam and was sent to Clark Air Base to recover. That's where he met my mother. He was a pipe dream."

At least she'd stopped crying.

"What's Wild Weasel?"

"An elite group of fighter pilots. They destroyed surface-to-air missile sites in Vietnam. My father brought down many MiGs. President Ford awarded him the Medal of Honor."

"No kidding!" No wonder Leonard Reed seemed full of himself. A big shot who liked to use big words like *qualm*. He probably seduced Monica's mother, the poor woman, and knocked her up. His imagination worked double time, picturing a handsome fighter pilot partying nonstop at the intersection of *Top Gun* and *Caligula*. Perhaps there had been many women, maybe even drunken orgies. Why not? He was an American hero. He could do whatever he wanted to do and still get a medal.

"What should I do?"

"Huh? What do you mean?" He'd lost track of what she'd been saying. He'd gotten worked up over the image of Leonard Reed's debauchery in the Philippines. He didn't know the real story, but Monica's gut-wrenching weeping seemed proof enough of injustice. Even just the possibility that Reed had toyed with an innocent woman without any consequences pissed him off. The man didn't deserve to become CIA director. Perhaps the scandal about his Filipino love child should be exposed.

"What should I do?" Monica repeated. "About INS, my life, everything." She was staring at the dark road ahead. Empty and endless like her future.

His heart stung, just a pinprick, but enough to make him step on the gas. *Never feel sorry for an illegal.* That was Joe Medina's rule number one, except Monica was unlike other undocumented immigrants. She hadn't stolen anything or killed anyone. Having a jerk for a father was her only crime. Fuck his Medal of Honor.

Monica turned to him, fear clouding her pretty face. "Am I going to jail?"

"I'm taking you to INS for processing. Then you'll end up in a holding facility." *Processing* was less harsh than *interrogation*; *facility* better than *jail*. While she chewed on those vague words, he directed the conversation back to what mattered most. "About Leonard Reed...forget about him, okay? He's an asshole. Meanwhile, you can appeal to the court."

"Appeal?"

"Sure. To drag out the deportation process. But you'll get kicked out eventually."

"Why? I didn't hurt anybody."

"That's true. You're just one of the millions of desperate hopefuls who bought into the American Dream."

"I just wanted to meet my father."

"What for?"

"I thought maybe I could live here. That he would help me. I'm too white, yet too poor for any white person living in the Philippines. I'm neither here nor there, neither a Filipino nor an American. I'm a Filipino-American bastard."

Her father was the bastard, but he bit his tongue. "What did you do in Manila? Maybe you can go back to your job or school or whatever."

"I used to be a movie extra, then I worked as a PAL flight attendant."

"Philippine Airlines? A movie actress *and* a stewardess. How about that?"

"*Extra*, not actress. I quit my job at PAL and used all my savings to come here. There's nothing waiting for me in Manila. My father was my only chance, or so I thought."

"Leonard Reed is your American Dream, all right."

"It's not a crime."

"Nope. For a desperate hopeful, it's always a technicality—not following what was stamped on your passport. How long are you supposed to be here?"

"Three months tops. My visa expired already."

Just as Cutter had guessed. "So you shouldn't be here."

She dropped the bag at her feet. "You know the worst thing about meeting my father?"

"That he shooed you away?"

"No. That I look so much like him. I'm a younger female carbon copy."

He'd never heard of anybody, man or woman, complain

about one's good looks. And yet, she was right. Perhaps Leonard Reed couldn't stand seeing himself in the girl's eyes, a living and breathing reminder of his sexual indiscretion twenty-five years ago.

He turned up the heater. The temperature had dropped. "Hey, it could be worse. You could be short and dark like me—"

"You know what else?"

"What? Don't tell me there's something worse than being pretty like your father."

"He told me the truth about my mother."

"What do you mean?"

"I always thought my mother worked at the air base as a maid, and that's how she'd met my father."

"She wasn't a maid?"

"She was a whore."

"Oh." The image of Tom Cruise from *Top Gun* having sex with several women straight out of the B movie *Caligula* popped up out of the blue, his imagination in overdrive again. A hot bubble of anger rose in his chest.

Monica shifted her gaze back to the canopy of trees swaying and beckoning in the darkness. It took a moment before Domingo realized she was crying again.

He fidgeted with the car radio, because what else was there to do? He was used to arresting thugs, not stray puppies. He'd never encountered so much crying before.

After a while, she blew her nose again. "I can understand why General Reed hates my guts, but it really hurt to know that my mother had lied to me all these years. I can't go back to Manila. I don't want to see her again."

On the radio, the late Freddie Mercury wailed and hit a high note. He knew the song—"Love of My Life." It filled him with an unexpected sadness. He wasn't sure what depressed him, the melancholic tune itself or the thought that Freddie had died of AIDS.

The Camaro glided at eighty miles per hour in a world devoid of joy. In the wee hours, there was nothing but Monica on his side and a risky thought worming through his head.

The exit sign for Irwin, Pennsylvania loomed ahead like an omen. He swung to the right lane and got off the highway.

About a mile later, he spotted a Shell gas station. *Open 24 Hours,* according to the sign. He turned off the radio and pulled over at the small parking lot. An SUV was gassing up.

"Can I go to the restroom?" Monica unbuckled her seat. Her wide eyes were puffy, her hair tousled.

"*Malaya ka na, kagaya ng multo.*"

"Huh?"

"You heard me—you're free as a ghost. Go before I change my mind."

"Domingo."

She said his name as though she'd only just realized who he was—her father's thug, a mercenary, her enemy. Did she regret opening up to him? She clutched her tote bag close to her chest.

He inhaled the whiff of gas so powerful and satisfying. Damn, he might get high just sitting here. The SUV roared away, startling him. At last, Monica scrambled out of the car. Whatever she'd meant to say never saw the light.

He glanced at her. Under the feeble glow of a nearby lamp post, her mirthless expression seemed as hard as a diamond, like someone who had steeled herself to the reality of being illegal. From here on, she would forever be hiding. *Tago nang tago*, or TNT, as Filipinos would say. But she would be fine. She would survive Leonard Reed and his America. Her demeanor told him as much.

He nodded. What else was there to say? They were strangers who happened to speak the same language, both of them unwanted and unwelcome in America. The biggest difference between them—he was legal and she wasn't. He chased while she hid, but he would turn a blind eye just this one time.

The gas smell, his decision to let her go, her fortitude, and everything else wrapped him in a strange buoyant sensation. It wasn't pleasant like being high on drugs, but surreal, as though he was trapped inside an elevator cut loose at the top. One moment he was floating, the next moment he was falling fast. His heart pumped hard.

She flicked her hand in a quick goodbye. No smile. He gunned the engine and drove away.

3

THE PRESENT

ow to Assimilate Successfully
Let's be clear about one thing—there's no shortcut to assimilation. The sooner you start, the better. First, speak English. Learn how to think in English, and soon you'll be dreaming in English. Second, work hard. Don't rely on handouts. It's the surest way to piss off the native-born citizen. Third, be loyal to your new country. America is now your mama, and your old country is your favorite auntie. If both of them were drowning, who are you gonna save? It better be your mother. Start calling yourself Filipino American, Chinese American, Mexican American or any other type of American pronto, so you'll get used to your "American-ness."

Fourth, play nice to native-born Americans. Remember, they were here first. Show your damn gratitude. How? Pay your taxes, don't break the law, respect everyone, and vote when you become a full-fledged citizen, but not if you're only a green-card holder. Last, get a flu shot every year. Don't spread no nasty virus or cause anybody any grief. Practice these five little steps, and you'll do just fine.

A STRIP CLUB wasn't the best place for writing, but Domingo had to make do. He could barely hear his own thoughts against the blasting techno music. At seven thirty in the evening, there was just one guy sulking at the bar and no strippers.

The joint looked like an old warehouse with a fashion runway, where he expected young women would be modeling their tits and booties later on. Large-screen plasma TVs adorned the walls for watching sports.

The crazy light from the disco ball was insufficient. He illuminated the notepad with a pen light and read what he'd written. *Not bad.* He set the flashlight, the pen, and the pad aside.

He took a sip of Budweiser. After he'd accepted Mary Reed's gig, he'd spent most of the day driving from Columbus to Chicago. He should have known Cutter would choose a joint like this as a meeting place. The dude must be a hundred years old now, but still fond of strippers. Cutter had been Leonard Reed's sidekick, not like Watson to Sherlock Holmes, but more like Chewbacca to Han Solo. Cutter had Chewie's size, all right, but without the hair. He lived in Chicago, but he was never too far when the Reeds needed him.

A bald man waved at Domingo. Charles Cutter in the flesh. His stiff gait reminded Domingo that Cutter was a former Air Commando pilot who'd flown covert missions in the early part of the Vietnam War until an enemy mortar shell struck his plane. Shrapnel wounds had left him with a bad hip.

In spite of that, the old dude still cut a striking figure even in his loud Hawaiian shirt and grandpa jeans. The Chewbacca height was imposing. What Domingo wouldn't give to be a few inches taller than his five foot five. He rose and extended his right hand. "You look great, man. Do you work out?"

Cutter shook Domingo's hand with vigor. "Damn right, I do. Tell me, how old do you think I am?"

"Ninety?"

"Fuck you, Sunday. I'm seventy-two." Cutter's golden hoop earring shone against the reflection of pulsating lights.

"No kidding!" Domingo slapped him a high-five. "Who's your personal trainer? You look great."

Cutter pulled out a chair and fell on it. "I work out on my own. You think social security will pay for a personal trainer?"

Domingo summoned a waiter with a wave before sitting down. "Man, whatever it is you're doing, keep at it. You don't look a day older than the last time I saw you nine years ago."

When the waiter came, Cutter fist-bumped the guy. "I want the coldest Budweiser you've got, buddy." He turned to Domingo. "You paying? Because I'm craving a juicy prime rib right now."

Domingo nodded. "Go ahead. Order whatever you want." *Courtesy of Mary Reed*, he almost added. So, Cutter was still broke. Money, or his lack of it, was the glue in his lasting bond with the Reeds. He owed them a bunch because of multiple alimonies and failed investments.

Cutter ordered a big steak dinner, while Domingo chose steamed lobster. After the waiter left, Cutter leaned closer just to be heard over the music. "This is the only strip club in the Midwest that serves great food. Trust me, I've been to every single one of them. Here you'll feel satiated in more ways than one."

Domingo chuckled. He looked forward to ogling topless chicks after the depressing meeting with Mary Reed. "You still work? Aren't you a manager at Mrs. Reed's supermarket?"

"It's called Save and Save. It's not a mom-and-pop grocery— more than two hundred stores in a dozen states."

"Right. So, you still work there?"

"Not anymore. I used to manage the fleet of delivery trucks and vans. I retired five years ago. I got sick of dealing with lazy drivers and punk mechanics. What is it with young people today? They expect to get paid without lifting a finger. And they have an opinion on every-goddamned-thing. Just because they know Twitter, they think they know everything. Goddamn millennials."

"You got that right."

The waiter returned with Cutter's beer. Cutter raised his glass. "Here's to you finding Monica Reed."

"Amen." Domingo clicked his glass with Cutter's in a toast.

Come to think of it, Monica was Cutter's fault. He'd been instrumental in bringing Solina Morales, Monica's mother, and General Reed together. Cutter had been the aide to the commander of Clark Air Force Base back then. When Leonard was recuperating at the base, Cutter had been in charge of providing him the special treatment befitting a war hero. Solina Morales had been Cutter's Christmas gift to Leonard.

Domingo sipped his beer. "Tell me everything you've got. You hired the three PIs that Mrs. Reed mentioned?"

"Useless sons of bitches who charged an arm and a leg. One of them went on a junket to Manila and came back with nothing. Zip. Zilch. Zero."

"There's gotta be something useful."

"Well, they found out that Monica and Mr. Up-My-Backside recently split up. Remember him?"

"Christian Price. Of course."

Christian must be forty-four now, same age as Monica. A software developer with a Brown University diploma and a six-figure job as a consultant. He lived in a posh apartment on the Upper West Side in New York City, hence the Mr. Up-My-Backside nickname. Christian could have been Monica's prince charming, except he was married with two kids. That made

Monica his mistress. Christian couldn't give her the prized US citizenship by virtue of marriage. It surprised Domingo the affair had lasted this long.

The waiter served their food. Cutter tucked the cloth napkin into his shirt like a bib. A large group of young guys swaggered in. The arrival sent the waiters scrambling.

"What's this?" Cutter gave the men the stink eye. "A bachelor party? Guys with a lot of cum and no balls—just what the world needs."

Domingo shook his head at Cutter's youth envy. The hoop earring and the fist bump were meant to show Cutter's coolness. Indeed, he was the youngest-looking septuagenarian in the world.

"So, what did Christian say?" He shoved a piece of buttery lobster in his mouth. "Come on, help me get a jump-start."

"Christian claimed he bought a one-way plane ticket to the Philippines for Monica after she decided to go back home. The cocksucker sent my guy on a merry chase in Manila. It was a dead end. Monica wasn't there."

"I could have told you that."

Cutter wiped the grease from his lips with the napkin. "You think the cocksucker lied?"

"I don't know, but I'm pretty sure Monica will never go back to Manila." Desperate hopefuls clung to the American Dream with all their might. They would rather be a discard in America than return home. Being illegal was a privilege compared to the prison of poverty, violence, and despair in their old countries. Freedom, even just a crumb, tasted sweetest to the palate of the deprived. A native-born citizen like Cutter would never understand it.

More young guys arrived. Definitely some kind of a party. Lots of bro hugs and high-fives.

Domingo had finished his lobster. He tackled the heap of wild rice and steamed veggies. "What else you got for me?"

"I have a bad feeling about Christian Price."

"What do you mean?"

Cutter spoke with his mouth full. If the music hadn't stopped, Domingo wouldn't have understood a thing. "The cocksucker kept an affair for nine years. Suddenly, he sent her packing to Manila. Only she's *not* there. It seems to me he made his mistress disappear. How convenient is that?"

"You think it's foul play?"

"All I'm saying is..." He took a long swallow of beer. "Monica seems to have vanished, and Mr. Up-My-Backside was the last person to know her whereabouts. He's got a motive to make her disappear, too."

"Speaking of motives. What's yours?"

"Fuck you, Sunday. I'm helping Mary. You saw how sick she is. She relies on me to do stuff for her."

Domingo raised his palm. "I know, I know. You certainly deserve to be included in General Reed's will."

"Damn right. I was loyal to him. I would have taken a bullet for him. I was his friend."

"Hey, nobody's questioning your loyalty. I'm just wondering why you can't buy your own steak if you've got inheritance and all."

"The money's gone, okay? It went to Peachy and the kids."

Peachy must be wife number three or four. He was married the last time Domingo had seen him.

Cutter plowed through his steak with alacrity. "Are you married?" He wiped his plate clean with a bread roll before popping the bread in his mouth.

For crying out loud. The old dude looked like he hadn't eaten in three days. "Never been married. Why?" The music came back on, and the flood lights danced.

"That's smart. Don't ever fall for the ball and chain."

"You want dessert?" asked Domingo.

"I want a cigar. I'd kill for a Double Corona right now."

"Sorry, but I can only offer you dessert."

"You mean in addition to those sugary little things?" Cutter nodded at the stage.

Five women in cowgirl attire and boots strutted onto the runway. The young guys hooted. Cutter stopped a passing waiter and asked for another beer, but Domingo declined. He had work to do and a flight to catch in a few hours.

The chicks danced to a disco remix of a Shania Twain country tune. More men streamed into the club. Cutter got his drink, and they watched the show.

Domingo would fly back to New York at the crack of dawn. The first thing on his agenda back home—Christian Price. Was the guy capable of hurting Monica? She was in love with him, that much was clear. When Domingo caught Monica for the second time, she'd willingly traveled to her father's house in Ohio to spare Christian the trouble. Domingo had threatened to inform Mrs. Christian Price about the illicit affair unless Monica cooperated. Theirs was a classic case of adultery—a handsome rich dude banging the gorgeous babysitter under the nose of his slightly older wife.

Did the Price family still live on the Upper West Side? Only one way to find out. He would pay the man a little visit.

The cowgirls on stage had stripped down to their G-strings and boots. Cutter applauded. "Shake it for me, baby!" he yelled.

Domingo's dick stood at attention, but unlike Cutter, he couldn't enjoy this shit. His brains were such a killjoy sometimes, reminding him that nature couldn't possibly have made boobs as large as bowling balls. Grotesque, not sexy. On top of it, the thought that Monica might be in mortal peril kept creeping into his head.

One of the young bucks got up and tossed something onto the stage. A coin? No, a ring. His posse guffawed and howled.

The women turned around, flashing their ample booties.

The spotlight dimmed and the curtains came down. "More! More! More!" the guys chanted.

Alas, the topless cowgirls didn't return for an encore. The DJ or emcee or whoever was behind the curtains announced: "Gentlemen, when the clock strikes twelve, you can get the privacy of a champagne room with the company of two hot ladies for the price of one."

Cutter turned to Domingo, mouth agape. "You heard that? Let's do the champagne room!"

"Nah. Not me." Domingo gestured at their waiter for the check.

"Why not? You can charge it as an expense. Don't tell me you didn't get a hard-on."

When the waiter arrived, Domingo handed him his credit card. "Cutter, don't worry about my hard-on, okay? Just take care of yours." He pulled three hundred dollars from his wallet and set it on the table. "Enjoy the champagne room. Maybe get a cigar later. Anything else I need to know before I go?"

Cutter snatched the cash. "Tell Christian Price he better produce Monica Reed unharmed or he's going down."

Domingo smirked. "You really think the guy's a murderer?"

"*Any* guy can be a murderer. He happens to have a good reason to kill her."

"You sure about that?"

Cutter nodded, pocketed the money, and reared back in his chair. Smug as hell. He must have been a piece of work during his Air Force days.

"Just like you're sure that those dudes over there are having a bachelor party, right?"

"Damn right."

"Wrong. Those guys are not having a bachelor party."

They both craned their necks to watch the men make a toast with their beer glasses.

"What the fuck are you talking about?" said Cutter. "One of

those motherfuckers is about to get tied to a ball and chain, but he's too stupid to know it."

"Actually, one of those guys just *escaped* a ball and chain. He's the one who tossed out his wedding ring. It's a divorce party, Chewie."

"What?" Cutter's expression changed from bewilderment to puppyish. "Well, I'll be damned. This is why Mary Reed pays you the big bucks."

The waiter came back with Domingo's credit card. He got up. "Nice seeing you, man." He picked up the notepad and his other stuff. "I'll be in touch."

"Do that. Call me anytime." Cutter gave him a fist bump.

You bet he would. Cutter might have missed the reference to Chewbacca, but he must have realized that if something terrible happened to Monica Reed, he was likely to be a suspect as much as Christian Price.

4

July 2008

L etting Monica Reed go had caused endless teasing from Domingo's close-knit circle of bounty hunters, cops, private investigators, and INS agents. To save his ass, Domingo had made up a story of how he'd "lost" Monica.

Here was the official fake story. He'd apprehended her without any hitch and intimidated her out of her wits, driving her to escape at the first opportunity. At a gas station in Irwin, Pennsylvania, she'd gone to the restroom, where she presumably split through a window. There had been a freight truck and a minivan leaving the parking lot at the time. Domingo had sensed children inside the minivan with tinted windows. On the other hand, the truck had carried two middle-aged men who looked like suckers for young chicks. He'd chased the truck, but Monica had not been there. By then he'd lost the minivan.

Leonard Reed had been outraged, but it never bothered

Domingo because he'd never met the general. He'd let the man simmer in fury five hundred miles away. What hurt Domingo was the loss of Joe Medina's confidence. He had to work doubly hard to regain his boss's trust.

Today, ten years after he first met Monica Reed, he was looking for her again. The place: a second-rate hotel in New York City where she worked as a maid. The joint teemed with undocumented workers from all over the world, a poor man's United Nations. Employees like Monica, who had no social security cards, were paid in cash every week.

Domingo never thought General Reed would hire him again. Apparently, the man believed Domingo's fake story about losing Monica. Domingo's reputation as the catcher of the most elusive undocumented immigrants in America also helped. Even the Bureau of Immigration and Customs Enforcement, or ICE for short, hired him in special investigations. ICE replaced the old INS after the September 11th terrorist attacks.

Domingo could have turned down the general, but truth was, he couldn't. Monica Reed haunted him. She was number one on his list of illegals—the first subject he'd set free and his one big mistake. He might have never set Monica free if he'd known any better. Since that fateful day in 1998, he kept a notebook of names of undocumented immigrants he'd apprehended. *The Book of Illegals* if ever there was one.

He glanced at his wristwatch—11:11. He strolled down the hallway on the second floor, passing by the laundry room. Two crew members chatted in Spanish. No Monica. She started her shift at nine o'clock in the morning, usually helping out with the laundry. He timed this visit so she would be cleaning rooms alone by now, but which floor?

He took the stairs to the third floor, then the fourth. No sign of Monica. Could she have called in sick today? No way. He'd stalked her just yesterday and she'd appeared healthy. He took the elevator to the fifth floor, then the sixth.

At last he spotted Monica pushing a cart of dirty sheets and towels. She wore a red blouse and black pants, the housekeepers' uniform. He could have identified her from a mile away. Her mixed race, an accident of nature, gave her a singular beauty that stood out.

"*Magandang umaga*, Monica." Good morning, he said in Tagalog.

She stopped dead in her tracks, her eyes bugging out. She toppled the cart and ran to the nearest stairway.

The overturned cart stopped him for a few precious seconds. *What a bitch!* He stumbled into a sprint on the narrow corridor and through the exit door, spiraling down the stairs, all the way to the ground floor. The girl seemed to have grown invisible wings.

He burst out of the packed lobby with his heart pounding and his lungs burning. Only an illegal like Monica could match Domingo's speed. Desperate hopefuls evaded authorities better than rats escaping the train on the subway tracks. He could tell she'd had practice. Every now and then, the cops raided hotels to target whores and drug dealers. If the raid also yielded undocumented immigrants working in the kitchen or cleaning rooms, so much the better for New York's finest.

"Excuse me! Out of my way!" Domingo shoved the Asian tourists in the hotel lobby as he chased Monica out of the building and onto West Fifty-Seventh Street.

Pedestrians swarmed the sidewalks like flies. *Shit!* July was peak tourist season in the Big Apple, the time when hundreds of fanny-pack-wearing people walked willy-nilly, either undecided about their destination or plain lost. "Move it!" He pushed people left and right.

His spirits sank, though adrenaline primed his body for the hunt. Why had Monica behaved as though he was her enemy? Didn't he deserve a little courtesy after he'd set her free before? He'd be damned if he let her escape this time.

He expected her to dash to the nearest subway station, but instead of heading east toward Fifty-Ninth Street, she was heading south. Where the hell was she going? Then it hit him. *Times Square. Port Authority. A bus ride to New Jersey.*

He scurried across the street, drawing honks from irate taxi drivers. Monica glanced over her shoulder and saw him veer away. *Good.* Let her think he'd given up. He took another route to Port Authority. If he couldn't catch a subject by virtue of speed, he would do it through cunning.

Desperate hopefuls focused only on one thing—running away. Like other types of prey, fear dictated their actions. Domingo had the advantage of a plan. He'd followed Monica for a week before pouncing on her. He knew about the love nest in New Jersey set up by her married lover, down to the nine-digit zip code and the fastest route to get there.

While she concentrated on outrunning Domingo, he went straight to his contact at Port Authority. He got the schedule for the next bus to Hasbrouck Heights and located the driver. He set up his next move, put on his sunglasses, and waited for her.

The doors of Port Authority never actually closed for longer than a few seconds because of the steady flow of people who were coming and going. It was packed with people standing in long lines before the ticket windows, gliding upward or downward on the escalators, browsing or shopping in shops, buying lottery tickets at the newsstand, and just milling around.

Effective surveillance required endless patience, something he'd developed. Hidden amid the crowd on the second floor, he watched the automatic doors, just waiting.

Finally, Monica Reed staggered inside, panting and wet as a mop from running. She'd left the hotel in haste without a purse, but she'd arrived at the bus depot carrying a tote bag. She must have retrieved an emergency bag from a friend, perhaps another illegal, working or living in the area. Again, it told Domingo that she'd had experience dodging authorities.

She proceeded to the restroom before picking up a slice of pizza, which she ate while waiting for her ride. Lunch on the go.

When the bus began boarding passengers, she scanned the environment like someone bracing for the worst. She was thirty-five now, but still the same scared girl. Only the hardened criminals got over their fear of authorities. Most undocumented immigrants, like Monica, would never even dare to jaywalk or cut in line to avoid attracting attention. It was ironic how illegals turned out to be the most law-abiding citizens you would ever meet, something rabid anti-immigrant politicians and pundits refused to admit.

The bus closed its door and rolled toward a queue of other buses leaving Port Authority. Domingo stared at his wristwatch. After fifty-seven seconds, the line of buses inched forward, then halted. They must wait for their turn, a process that took about ten minutes, tops. Perhaps Monica had just settled in for the one-hour commute. The brief pause—an element of surprise— was important during a hunt, but especially when the quarry had a head start.

On the sixty-second mark, Domingo bolted in front of Monica's stopped bus and waved at the driver, who opened the door as part of their agreement earlier. He clambered up the bus and clapped the driver's shoulder. "Thanks, boss." Joe Medina's rule number two: always call a man "boss" or "chief" to stoke his ego, which was necessary when asking a favor.

All seats were taken, so Domingo stood behind the driver, assessing the situation. Monica sat along the aisle, beside an old lady, at the back of the bus. Monica was gazing outside the window, the tote bag on her lap. Across from her, a young man tapped the keys of a laptop computer.

At last, the bus drove out of Port Authority and onto the streets. Domingo strode toward Monica and stopped beside her. *"Kumusta ka, Multo?"* Tagalog for How are you, Ghost?

She looked up, stunned.

He removed his sunglasses and gripped her seat's headrest. "Remember me?" Not that he expected any response. She'd frozen, her face drained of color.

He snatched her bag and rooted inside. No pepper spray or knife or weapon of any kind. One could never be too careful. Joe Medina's rule number three: intimidate the illegal from the get-go to gain the upper hand. What better way to scare Monica than by searching her bag *without* her permission? Such violation in front of so many people ought to remind her of the inalienable truth about being an illegal. She had no right to be on this bus, in this city, in this country.

He dropped the tote on her lap. "I'm pissed that you're running away like a subway rat. Haven't I been good to you before?"

The old lady beside Monica adjusted her hearing aid. "This bus is full. Why do they let people stand in the aisle?" she harrumphed.

"It's an emergency, ma'am. I hope I'm not bothering you." Domingo flashed a deferential smile at the witch.

She frowned and turned to the window, her hearing aid humming faintly.

Monica stared daggers at Domingo. "What do you want?"

"Your cooperation." He lifted the side of his shirt to display the butt of his Glock sticking from the waistline of his pants. He continued in Tagalog. Speaking in a foreign tongue afforded him privacy even in public places. "I thought you would have returned to Manila already or, at least, you might have done something about your status in this country. But instead, you chose a married man. Unless Christian Price divorces Emmy Price to marry you, there's no way he can make you a US citizen. So why are you wasting your life with him?"

She opened her mouth, but nothing came out. Too shocked for words. He'd flaunted his knowledge of her dirty laundry.

She swallowed hard. "What the fuck do you want from me?"

"Wow. Where did that cuss word come from? You never said *one* bad word when I first met you. What happened to you? This is what America has done to you?" He lowered himself into a squat to meet her eyes. "Now, listen. I won't repeat this. Your father is very sick. He needs you. To be exact—he needs one of your kidneys. In return, he'll do everything in his power to make you a US citizen. In fact, just consider yourself an American citizen already."

"What?"

"You heard me." He glanced to his left and right. The young man? Still glued to his laptop. The old witch had closed her eyes.

Monica clutched her bag close to her chest. "What if I don't want to do it?"

"The general never said anything about that. I don't think it's an option."

"Why me?"

"His wife donated one of her kidneys to him, but his body rejected it. He needs a kidney from a *blood* relative. You're the only one left in the world."

"It's ridiculous!"

"He's your father and he needs you."

The bus ran smoothly, the cool blast of the air conditioning lulling everyone into silence. "I need time to think about this," said Monica.

"I'm not going anywhere, and Hasbrouck Heights is an hour away."

Her face was tight with fear. "I need more than an hour."

"What is there to think about? Like I said, I don't think it crossed the general's mind that his only daughter—his only child—would turn him down."

"This is too much. He kicked me out ten years ago. Now you

expect me to hand him my kidney?"

Good point. "Consider this a blessing in disguise. You have an extra kidney you can do without, which you can exchange for American citizenship, plus your father's undying gratitude. Isn't that what you want? Leonard Reed's acceptance? It's your one true American Dream. Grab it while you can."

She exhaled a deep sigh and slumped back in the seat. "I need some time to process this."

Body language always told him everything he needed to know. As expected, an illegal's ancient fear of deportation and utter displacement had overtaken the fight in Monica. He sniffed her distress as though she'd lit an incense stick.

"How much time do you need?" he asked.

"I don't know."

"Twenty-four hours."

"What?"

He pressed his lips to her ear, as intimate as a lover, and there was nothing she could do about it. "I know where you live. I know where you work. I know where Christian and Emmy and their two children live. So don't force me to do anything that you'll regret later on."

He rose to force her to look up at him. "You have twenty-four hours to think about it. I will *not* let you go this time."

The bus slowed down before pulling over to the side of the road. Union City, New Jersey—the first stop for the bus.

He glanced at his watch. Twenty-five minutes. *Not bad.* "Until tomorrow, then."

"Where will I find you?"

"No worries. I'll find *you*, I promise." He put his sunglasses back on and turned around. Another passenger disembarked first.

And just like that, he'd ensnared Monica Reed for the second time. Catching her was not a problem. Keeping her was another matter.

5

July 2008

Domingo fingered the Glock 19 in his blazer pocket and liked its smoothness. It also fit his hand better than a Glock 22, which most cops and bail agents carried. "It's time to go. Chop-chop! It's a long way to Columbus." He stood in the middle of the tiny living room. Monica's bedroom door was open. He could see her stuffing clothes in a duffel bag.

"I'm not finished packing," she murmured. She wore a pair of jeans and white T-shirt. No make-up, no jewelry, just a wristwatch.

He swaggered into her room. "You have ten minutes."

"You're not the boss of me."

"Let's get this straight—I'm in charge. I call the shots."

She arched an eyebrow. "And why is that?"

"Because I'm legal, and you're not."

That shut her up. She continued packing without a peep.

Joe Medina's rule number three always worked: intimidation terminated any discussion.

Domingo went back to the living room and appraised the framed images of plum blossoms on the wall. Instead of overhead lights, an elegant Japanese paper lamp hung from the ceiling. A beige-and-white throw on the couch showed the Hermès tag. Soft and expensive-looking, but it sounded like a disease.

Christian Price's love nest exuded an Upper-West-Side elegance in a neighborhood for the cubicle-dwelling class. Its residents were office workers who commuted to Manhattan every day. They wore JCPenney suits and battered sneakers, perfect for chasing a New Jersey Transit bus. And when they arrived in their office cubes, they changed into their faux-leather shoes. None of them could afford to venture into Christian Price's Hermès-draped world. They couldn't possibly know any of his friends. His secret was safe here.

Monica emerged from the bedroom with her duffel and tote bags. "I'm ready."

"Let's move it."

Domingo would have preferred a quick flight to Ohio, but Monica didn't have the necessary ID to fly. He'd rented a car courtesy of the Reed family for the trip—537 miles, according to the map. No need to subject his personal vehicle to unnecessary wear and tear.

They traveled under the blazing blue sky of New Jersey and across the green expanse of Pennsylvania. No small talk, just a couple of stops with ten-minute breaks and McDonald's lunch on the go.

The sheer size of the states they traversed amazed Domingo. America unfurled before him without boundaries. Could you blame immigrants for believing they could find a little corner of their own in this endless landscape?

They arrived at the Reeds' mansion at eight o'clock in the

evening. Photos of a dashing fighter pilot decked the walls of the grand house, but the man in the sick room was a far cry from those glory days. General Reed's cadaverous color, sunken cheeks, and skeletal frame shocked Domingo. Monica winced at the sight.

"Well, sir, I'll let the family talk." Domingo turned on his heel. After delivering the daughter, he'd expected to call it good. "I'll be in touch."

"No, no. Please stay." The bedridden general sat up and motioned for him and Monica to sit down.

"You two must be famished," Mary Reed said. She was in her sixties, slender and elegant in a designer outfit and chiseled hairdo. "I'll make some sandwiches and salad for you." She smoothed the quilt covering her husband's lap before leaving the room.

Domingo moved a chair closer to the general's bed and offered it to Monica. He perched on a stool by the door.

"Monica, I can't thank you enough for coming, especially after we started off on the wrong foot so many years ago." Leonard Reed's eyes radiated hope. "I trust that you're doing well. In New York, right?"

"Yes. I work in Manhattan and live in New Jersey." She sat on the edge of the chair as though she might bolt at any moment. Her hair and T-shirt were disheveled from slumping all day long inside the car.

"What's your job?"

"I clean hotel rooms."

The general's thin eyebrows creased with concern. "There must be other opportunities out there—better jobs. You're college-educated, aren't you?"

She nodded. "I'm also illegal."

"I can help you with your legal status. You're my daughter. You can become a US citizen." The old man inhaled noisily through his mouth. "I almost died fighting in Vietnam. I've served this country all my life. Surely I can make you a citizen. It's only a matter of paperwork."

"And in exchange you want me to donate one of my kidneys?" Monica had entered the house as sharp as fangs. The weepy girl from a decade ago had toughened up.

"That's entirely up to you. Whether you do it or not, I will file a petition for your citizenship."

"Why?"

"Because…just look at me. I'm dying. And I want to do right by you." The general locked eyes with his daughter in that rare moment of truth and intimacy.

Domingo cast his gaze down to hide his discomfort. What could be more personal than admitting one's imminent death and irrevocable defeat? Once he'd wanted his daughter deported, but it never happened. Worse, his life suddenly depended on her.

Leonard pulled the blanket up to his chest. The AC was blasting arctic air. "It's true when I first called Joe Medina and Sunday, I was looking for a kidney match."

Domingo refrained from moving or uttering a word to make himself as inconspicuous as possible. Still, Monica glanced at him when his name was mentioned. She raised an eyebrow, like, *Sunday? Seriously.*

"A blood relative like you is an ideal candidate. You're the only one I have left. I admit, I wanted your help," the general continued. "But while Sunday was looking for you, everything changed. You see, for someone like me, one day feels like a month. One week feels like a year. I can't move around without a wheelchair. I'm so weak it requires all of my strength just to put on my pants. One leg in and I have to rest. The other leg in and I need a nap. That's about all I can do. It used to be I was on dialysis twice a week. Now I'm on dialysis *seven* days a week."

Monica turned her face aside in a pointed manner, but General Reed touched her arm, forcing her to look back. "I longed to see you…a hopeless longing of a father for his child, his own flesh and blood."

Monica held the general's hand. One, two seconds passed before she let go. Leonard Reed sobbed. No longer the fighter-pilot hero and top dog at the CIA, but a diabetic dying from kidney failure. Ten years ago, the general had sworn he didn't have a daughter in any "goddamned Third World country." Who would have guessed the man would one day eat his own words? There was no sorrier sight than a mighty rock crumbling into dust.

Domingo rose to fetch a tissue box from a side table. "Kleenex, sir?"

"Thank you." Leonard blew his nose, and after a moment, he rested his back against the headboard. "Two years ago, I was diagnosed with type 2 diabetes, then chronic kidney failure—a double whammy within the space of a few months. Suddenly, our life revolved around doctors and hospitals. Mary wanted to stop all that, and so she gave me one of her kidneys. But my body rejected it almost immediately. Mary felt—"

"How can you be sure that I'm your daughter?"

"What?" The general dropped the used tissue.

Domingo picked it up and tossed it in the trashcan, wishing he could disappear. He'd never been privy to his clients' drama before. Why had Leonard asked him to stay?

"My mother…" Monica swallowed as though trying to compose herself, her eyes brimming.

"She was just twenty when I met her," Leonard said.

"I'm assuming there were other men. So how can you be sure I'm your daughter?" She blinked her tears away.

"Oh, I'm certain of it. After your mother and I met, I made sure there were no other men." The general's lips curled into a sad smile. "When you look at yourself in the mirror, don't you see *my* eyes, *my* nose, *my* skin color? I have no doubt, sweetheart. None whatsoever."

"I want to be sure."

"About what?"

"That I'm your daughter and a good match for a kidney donation."

"Ah." The old man shook his head. "You don't have to do anything for me. Your coming here is enough. My lawyer will meet with you for the paperwork, so I may petition your US citizenship."

"And in return, I'll donate my kidney."

"No, sweetheart—"

"But first, I want a DNA test."

"Monica, sweetheart—"

"I want to be sure you're my father. And then, I'll give you my kidney."

Holy crap. The woman had become Americanized, businesslike. No polite bullshit, no beating around the bush like most Filipinos.

The general heaved a weary sigh and closed his eyes. Monica glanced back at Domingo with a hard expression. Truth was, he'd expected her resistance, a flat-out rejection. Tit for tat.

The room was so still that both he and Monica perked up when Leonard Reed stirred and opened his eyes. After just a few minutes, he'd grown weaker than a twice-brewed tea, his breathing more laborious.

"Sunday?" the general said. "Please take Monica to the Lawrence Memorial Hospital for a DNA test. Go there tomorrow morning. It's the best in the state. It's named after Mary's great-grandfather. Her family has a wonderful tradition of philanthropy."

"Yes, sir."

"I'm extending your contract. You're going to stay in Columbus for as long as Monica is here...to help her out, drive her around. After the DNA test, take her to Gary Wilcox's office downtown. He's our lawyer. He's filing my petition for Monica's citizenship."

"Very well, sir."

The old man patted his daughter's hand. "Thank you, sweetheart." He smiled and lay down.

"You can thank me after the DNA test."

Leonard Reed nodded. He could not have been certain that his bastard would agree to give up a body part for him after he'd tried to deport her, but he'd been one hundred percent sure she was a blood relation. And he'd always known she would do anything to become a US citizen.

That was why he'd wanted Domingo's presence—to bear witness to a deal. The visit wasn't the tearful reunion it appeared to be, but a business transaction, a win-win for both father and daughter.

6

THE PRESENT

L *ist of Undocumented Immigrants*

```
Monica Reed
   25
   Philippines
   Father seeks deportation
   10/1/1998-10/1/1998
   Last seen in Irwin, PA


35
   Philippines
   Father  needs  kidney  donation  7/9/2008-
```

7/16/2008
   Last seen in Columbus, OH

44
   Philippines
   Stepmother seeks reconciliation
   8/12/2017-XXXXXX

JESUS QUINTANA
   22
   Mexico
   Grand auto theft (5x)
   5/12/1998-5/15/1998
   Delivered to INS

AMADOR de los Santos aka El Rapido
   40
   Mexico
   Drug smuggling
   5/15/1998-5/30/1998
   Delivered to Essex County (NJ) Sheriff's
office

MIKHAIL GOLOVKIN aka Baltika the Crusher
   (DECEASED)
   29
   Russia
   Homicide, gun smuggling, APO
   5/16/1998-6/6/1998
   Died in car crash during chase

. . .

Hassan Najafi
  27
  Iran
  Money laundering, battery
  6/1/1998-8/5/1998
  Delivered to INS

DOMINGO USED to keep paper files. Now he worked on Smartsheet, a project-management software application. He stared at his laptop, at number one on his list and the multiple Xs under Monica Reed's name. Those were meant to be filled out after he closed the case.

He could count on his fingers the undocumented immigrants he'd hunted down more than once. Multiple hunts implied failure. Imprisonment or deportation was the endgame, the only acceptable result in his job. Sometimes an injury or death was unavoidable. He vowed to make the current search for Monica the last one, especially because he planned to include the list in his book.

"Yo, dude, how you doing with Smartsheet? Everything cool?" Inday rolled over to his desk. They both sat on wheeled chairs in the office of Immigrants Bail Bonds.

Inday, Joe Medina's twenty-one-year-old niece, was the office manager, IT Department, researcher, and all-around person. In other words, she was her uncle's only office employee. She was a part-time engineering student at New York Institute of Technology. The kid knew how to dig up information and hack systems if necessary.

"I love Smartsheet." Domingo raised his arm for a high-five.

Inday slapped his palm in return. "Welcome to the Digital

Age. Now you can work even when you're out in the field, as long as there's an internet connection."

"How are you? How's school?"

"I'm trying to search my soul, dude. I've decided to drop out of school. For now. After I fix all my personal bugs, I'll be ready for some major enhancements. I'll be the Next-Gen Me."

"What are you talking about?" The kid thought of herself as a software application. Talk about smart but weird.

She shrugged and rolled back to her own desk. Her real name was Alexandra. She worked hard using her brains, but don't ask her to get off her butt. She could lose twenty pounds, at least.

"Don't waste too much time searching your soul or debugging your noggin or whatever it is you're trying to do. You better get that diploma sooner than later. You deserve a better job than this." Domingo turned off his laptop, unplugged it, and put it inside a drawer. "Before I leave, you got anything else on Christian Price?"

"Everything's in my report."

Inday's research included credit card purchases, license plate number, and latest income tax return. It confirmed that Christian had paid for a one-way ticket to Manila in the name of Monica Reed. If she had indeed used it, she would have revealed herself to immigration authorities. She would never again set foot on American soil—at least not using her real name. That would be the end of her American Dream. Would she really have given it all up after everything she'd been through? Knowing Monica, she would never steal or buy a fake identity. Therefore, she must not have used the plane ticket. She must still be in America. So why did Christian buy the ticket in the first place?

Inday pointed the remote control at the TV on the wall. Amaury Penn's face materialized on the flat screen. "Let's talk immigration crackdown, my friends! Is ICE tough enough, fast enough, and smart enough to round up the bad hombres invading the southern border? I say no, no, and no. What do you think?" A teaser for *The Bull Penn Show*, the anti-immigrant hate fest that captivated millions of viewers.

"Do you really watch that crap?" Domingo indicated the TV with a tilt of his chin.

"Penn's entertaining. He dictates the latest anti-immigration buzzword."

"Which is?"

"Mass deportation."

"Meaning?"

"Expansion of round-ups of illegals. Penn is urging ICE to arrest illegals anywhere, anytime—even in churches and schools."

"The guy sounds charming."

"He has a personal hotline to the White House. Given his popularity, he could be living there someday."

"That's scary."

"Not any scarier than the dude who lives there now."

"I hate that you're always right." Domingo rose. "I better go and have a little chat with Christian Price." He patted her back on his way out. "Good job on your report."

At nine thirty in the morning, the coffee shop overflowed with customers. Domingo sat at a small table outdoors and waited for Christian. If not for the railing that enclosed the space, he'd be sipping espresso on the sidewalk amid harried pedestrians.

Most of the time, finding a subject was easier and simpler than what movies and novels portrayed. In the case of Christian, Domingo had simply called and invited him for a cup of java at his favorite cafe in his neighborhood on the Upper West

Side. They'd met once before, so they were not strangers. Nine years ago, Christian made an unexpected trip to Ohio to see Monica. He'd met Domingo at the time.

Today, Christian was immaculately groomed in a navy-blue suit. Then and now, he looked like he'd stepped off a *GQ* cover. Everything he wore was in shades of blue. Any other guy would look like a pompous asshole, but with Christian, the outfit appeared elegant and effortless. A computer bag hung from his shoulder. Domingo raised an arm to catch his attention.

Christian approached and extended his right hand. "How are you?"

Domingo rose to shake hands with him. Damn, it emphasized the disparity in their heights. He was an ethnic midget, while Mr. GQ was a towering prince. They sat at the same time. Christian put his bag on his lap.

On reflex, Domingo glanced down at his black blazer and khaki pants. Today he'd also worn leather shoes because he knew Christian Price's good looks would squash his self-confidence faster than Shrinky Dinks in a burning oven. Tall, beautiful people did that to him. Monica had the same effect on him, stirring awe and embarrassment every time he stared at her.

He slid the extra Styrofoam cup across the table. "I took the liberty of getting you coffee—macchiato, double shot. Otherwise, you have to line up for half an hour."

Christian questioned him with a look: *How did you know what to order?* He nodded. "I forgot...you're some kind of a private investigator, right?"

"A bail enforcement agent."

"A bounty hunter, that's right."

For crying out loud. "The ladies inside know you. All I did was ask for your usual order."

"Thanks." Mr. GQ took a sip. "So, how can I help you?"

"I'm looking for Monica. Her stepmother is dying and she wants a reconciliation before it's too late."

"I know. I've been through this with a PI...Damon something or other."

"James Damon."

"That's it. I already told him everything I know. You can talk to him."

Mr. GQ sat in perfect composure, courteous but impassive. Up close, his eyes were bluer than he remembered.

Domingo sipped his espresso. "If you don't mind, just tell me what you know about Monica."

Christian glanced at his wristwatch, a sleek black band. Cartier? Rolex? He could certainly afford it. He'd developed an innovative quality-control software for Big Pharma and sold it to a Canadian start-up for big bucks right around the time he'd met Monica. Now he consulted for companies that used his software.

"I have a meeting with a client downtown in an hour. Traffic's bad at this time," Christian said.

"Ten minutes is all I'm asking. What happened between you and Monica? Why, when, and how did you dump her?"

His eyes flashed, hostile. "Excuse me?"

Good. People tend to talk when they're pissed. "You kept an affair for nine years, and just like that, you sent her home packing. What happened? You got tired of her? Cutter thinks you wanted her gone."

"Who?"

"Charles Cutter, General Reed's best friend."

Christian narrowed his eyes before a glint of recognition changed his expression. "From what I remember, Cutter wasn't exactly the general's best friend but more of hired help. A jobless veteran the Reeds keep on their payroll. Monica hates his guts."

"Well, Cutter thinks you have a good reason to make Monica disappear."

A flush spread across his face. "Disappear? What are you implying?"

Domingo raised a palm. "Hey, not me. Cutter is the suspicious one."

"*I* should be suspicious of Cutter and *you*. The fiasco nine years ago...you were both part of it, right?" Christian scoffed. "Didn't Cutter make all the arrangements in Columbus? Didn't *you* bring Monica to Ohio so she could donate her kidney, which would have killed her?"

The mere mention of the kidney donation transported him back to the hospital. The narrow hallways, the commotion, and the announcement of a lockdown. Monica had escaped just minutes before going under the knife.

Regret fell upon him like a boulder. He flinched. *Focus*, he commanded himself. "This isn't about me, okay? We're talking about you because you're the last person to see Monica. Why did you let her go?"

"It was *her* decision, not mine, to leave. Her mother died, and she was heartbroken. There was nothing I could do to stop her from going home. She was finished with this country."

"You didn't tell Damon *that*."

"He didn't ask. All he wanted to know was *when* Monica left and *where* she was going. Well, she left New York on June fourteenth en route to Manila. She texted me twenty-four hours later to say she'd arrived safely. I haven't heard from her since. Not that I expect to. Everything between us is over." He drank his macchiato. "Now, excuse me, but I have to get going."

"How do you know she's in Manila?"

Mr. GQ pulled a five-dollar bill from his wallet and left it on the table. "I told you. She texted me." He slung his bag over his shoulder and turned on his heel.

Domingo stood up and walked beside him on the sidewalk. "Monica could have texted you from anywhere."

"Maybe. But she didn't text me from this city." Christian waved at a cab without breaking his stride. The taxi zipped by.

"How do you know she's not here?"

At last, he paused. They stepped aside and out of the way of commuters hurrying into a nearby subway station.

Mr. GQ looked Domingo in the eye. "I drove her to La Guardia and said goodbye to her in person. I saw her enter the security checkpoint for departing passengers."

"She's illegal. How can she travel by plane? She has no ID."

"Wrong. She has an old passport. Expired, yes, but it was all she needed. She had a one-way ticket to Manila—she was self-deporting, or whatever you call it. You really think anybody would stop her from leaving the country? ICE wants undocumented immigrants like her to go back where they came from. That's what she did."

Mr. GQ was right. Of course, Domingo knew that anyone could self-deport, especially someone like Monica who had no criminal record. The United States didn't require formal exit papers or departure stamps. Uncle Sam cared only about a foreigner's entry, not exit.

Christian waved vigorously at a cab, a tad impatient now. "Cutter has no right to disparage me. He's the one who inherited money from General Reed. Don't you think he has the motive to get rid of Monica? No Monica means more money for him."

The taxi pulled over. Mr. GQ ducked inside.

"Thanks for your time." Domingo shut the car door for him.

Christian pushed a button and the glass window came down. "When you find her, will you please call me? I just want to make sure she's okay."

"What for?"

He curled his lips into a sad smile. "Have you been in love before?"

"I don't know. Maybe."

"I care about Monica very much, but our timing was off. She came into my life too late. I'm always going to care about her no matter what happens. You won't understand the feeling until you fall in love yourself."

The car window went up. Domingo watched the cab merge into traffic with a sinking feeling in his chest. Day three of this case and still no promising leads. Was the Ghost in hiding or permanently missing?

No Monica means more money for him. Mr. GQ was right. Money could drive foolish old men with too much time on their hands to do stupid things. Cutter was as much a suspect as Christian Price, if not more.

The memory of the hullaballoo at the hospital came back. Metal gates coming down from the ceiling to prevent people from leaving. Employees rushing everywhere. A door left ajar had caught his eye. Inside the room, he'd found Monica hiding under a bed. She'd bolted from the operating room because she'd sensed danger in the very hands of her own father. She hadn't blamed Domingo for any of it. His complicity, unintentional as it was, had never been as clear. It had been a rare moment of clarity.

Now he wished for a similar gift of insight, a direction, even just a hunch. He stood on the sidewalk amid the morning traffic, the clock in his head ticking without mercy. *Multo.* The Ghost continued to haunt him after all these years. Monica was getting farther and farther away with every passing minute.

7

July 2008

Domingo wished his clients would spare him the drama. Alas, no such luck in the case of Monica Reed. He was her driver, bodyguard, water boy, whatever—he had no choice.

"This is surreal." She turned to him with the DNA report in her hand. They were sitting on the sofa, waiting to be summoned by the general. A cacophony of noises filled the Reed household. A vacuum cleaner growled upstairs, while a lawn mower roared outside.

"What does it say?" he asked.

Her pinched expression told him she might just cry. She handed him the two-page document.

The report showed a table of genetic systems tested and analyzed. Strings of letters and numbers marked "systems/chromosomes" made no sense, but the summary was clear.

Single Parent-Child DNA Paternity Test.

Final Certificate of Analysis.
Alleged Father: Leonard Robert Reed.
Child: Monica Reed.
Probability of Paternity: 99.999%.

"So it's official. He's your father." Domingo replaced the document in the manila envelope. "Congratulations. This is a vindication for you."

She shook her head. "All my life, I believed that Leonard Reed was my father. But in the past week, I hoped I was wrong."

"What?"

"I'm scared about giving up a kidney. It would be easier to say no if he's not my father."

"You don't have to do anything for him. Remember what he said?"

Rosie's footfalls interrupted their conversation. She motioned for them to follow her to the general's bedroom.

The sight of Leonard Reed slumped in bed shocked Domingo. The old man appeared exponentially sicker than he was only twenty-four hours ago. He sat up with great effort. His face was pale, his eyes sunken. He barked a rattling cough.

"General, are you all right?" Domingo asked.

"I had a bad night."

Monica sat on the edge of the bed. "What happened?"

"I didn't sleep at all…a headache that won't go away."

"Can't you take ibuprofen?"

Domingo stepped back farther, closer to the door, to let father and daughter talk.

"It's not that kind of headache," Leonard croaked. "I have anemia."

"Anemia?"

"My kidney has stopped producing the hormone that keeps the blood healthy." He made gasping noises and clutched his chest, as though he would rip his polo shirt off.

Monica rose. "We should get help."

The general latched onto her arm. "I'm all right. Don't be afraid."

She perched back on the bed. Her eyes had grown moist.

"Enough about me. I'm glad you insisted on doing the DNA test. As it turns out, we need it for the US citizenship petition. The lawyer also needs your birth certificate. Do you have it?"

"It's in my apartment in New Jersey."

"Sunday? Do you mind flying to New Jersey to get Monica's birth certificate?"

Domingo stepped forward. "No, not at all. When should I go, sir?"

"Now. You should catch the next flight to Newark."

"Yes, sir."

The general coughed again, a terrible hacking that seemed to suck the life out of him. "My dear, I want to make sure you get your US citizenship before I die. It's the least I can do." He sank in exhaustion.

Monica looked stricken, tears streaming down her pretty face. Domingo understood. She'd just found her father—not the nasty, powerful general who'd attempted her deportation, but the fragile, repentant old man. How ironic if she lost him so soon after she'd found him.

"Now look what I've done. Sweetheart, please don't cry." Leonard extended his brittle-looking arms.

She buried her face in his chest and he wrapped his arms around her. After her sobs abated, she pulled away from him and reached for a tissue to wipe her face. "I've decided. I'm going to donate my kidney."

"Sweetheart—"

"I want to do it as soon as possible. I won't let you die, Dad."

Dad. A one-hundred-eighty-degree turn. She held her father's hand. He smiled and heaved a deep sigh. A picture of reconciliation and peace. Domingo made his exit and got back to work.

From his motel, he booked a flight for the following morning. While eating dinner that night, his mind raced a hundred miles per hour. *Leonard Reed. DNA paternity test. Kidney donation. Things were moving faster than a whirlwind. What was Cutter's role in addition to hiring Domingo?*

Earlier that day, Cutter had let the cat out of the bag. On the phone, Chewbacca had pretended to be in Chicago, but he'd also said, "Keep an eye on Monica at all times. Make sure she stays here."

That night, Domingo wracked his brains while driving around Columbus. He checked out a couple of bars where Cutter hung out whenever he was in town. He visited another night club frequented by military vets. Cutter always picked up the trail and followed his pack. Domingo even asked around, but no sightings of the man.

Around midnight, on the way back to his motel, he passed by the Lawrence Memorial Hospital, where Monica had the DNA test. The hospital was named after Mary Reed's great-grandfather. This little nugget of information piqued him just then. He stopped by for no good reason other than to kill time and satisfy his restlessness.

The hospital might as well have been a five-star hotel, with its shiny glass façade and a sky-lit atrium lobby. He picked up a pamphlet, strolled down to the cafeteria, and settled in a corner with a cup of java as he read the pamphlet.

The hospital was famous for its transplant center—heart, lung, liver, kidney, bone marrow, or any given combination of transplants. Monica and her father both would be admitted to the facility for the general's kidney transplant. He imagined a roomful of solid organs, freshly harvested, dripping with blood, displayed as in a butcher's shop. *Want a heart? Coming right up. Need a liver-and-kidney combo? No problem.* He caught himself, disgusted by his macabre thoughts.

He turned his attention back to the pamphlet. A brief

history of the hospital said the six-story building was built for forty million dollars and renamed in honor of Mrs. Reed's great-grandfather. *How did it feel to hand out a cool million, much less forty?* The very wealthy always amazed him.

After finishing his coffee, he stood up and made a beeline for the lobby. Four women in blue scrubs were exchanging niceties. The night crew saying goodbye or the overnight crew saying hello? Could be both. The night crew passing the baton to the overnight crew.

Not more than twelve feet away, a familiar bald figure was talking to a young guy in scrubs. Cutter!

Domingo pivoted to hide his face. *What the fuck was Cutter doing in the hospital? Who was the dude with him?*

A wailing ambulance arrived. Employees rushed to meet the patient and put him in a wheelchair, causing a minor commotion in the lobby and sending Cutter and his buddy outside. Domingo hurried after the duo. They headed toward the parking lot.

They stopped for a moment before separating. Cutter climbed inside his Toyota 4Runner, while the guy in scrubs approached an old sedan. Before Domingo could decide what to do, the SUV pulled away. *Damn it!*

Cutter had left, but Mr. Scrubs was still in sight. Domingo half jogged to his rental car. When the battered sedan rolled out of the parking lot, he followed it.

The air reeked of conspiracy. Nothing could stoke his anger faster than deception. Cutter and Leonard Reed had been using him, but he vowed to get to the bottom of it all.

8

THE PRESENT

*A*ssimilation in America: You Are What You Eat

If you are what you eat, you must learn to like what native-born Americans eat. Mac and cheese, hot dogs and hamburgers, pizza, snickerdoodles and cupcakes, mashed potatoes, and lots of cereal. Mind you, I didn't eat any of these things while growing up in Manila. Mamang still refuses to eat them even after two decades in America. She's seventy years old; it's too late to teach her new habits.

Unless you're as old as my mother, your assimilation should include eating like an American. If you want to be accepted, you must embrace the norm. Appreciate the abundance around you. We're lucky to live in the present America where a halal market sits next to an Italian bistro and an Indian restaurant, where you can buy hard-to-find sauces and spices in a Chinese or Mexican or Filipino store. Once a week, I buy a loaf of bread as heavy as a cinder block from a Russian supermarket, though I've never been to Russia and the only Russians I ever encounter are undocumented immigrants with names like Baltika the Crusher and Babuska the Bookie. Baltika is now dearly departed, unfortunately, but I digress. We're talking about food.

Here's my advice: feed yourself and your family tikka masala, falafel, burrito, or whatever your ethnic heart desires, but also french fries, fried chicken, apple pie, and donuts. Now that you live in the great US of A, do as the customers of Golden Corral do—eat all you can! You'll probably pick up an American-style muffin top and high cholesterol. The secret to consuming a carb fest without getting fat is exercise. Take up jogging, twerking, or whatever will get you off your ass. In assimilation, as in everything in life, keep the good stuff and toss out the bad stuff.

TOO MUCH COFFEE, not to mention talking to Christian Price, had left Domingo with a bitter aftertaste. The meeting had yielded zero leads and bad vibes, but at least it had given him a chance to scribble a few paragraphs for his book during the subway ride to Times Square.

Now he stood on the sidewalk, outside a nondescript Midtown building, waiting for Tess Chua, Monica Reed's best friend from Manila. Tess worked on the tenth floor as the manager of a small leather-goods export business. Her family owned the company, which explained her late arrival this morning. She could come and go as she pleased. The woman who answered the office phone assured him Tess was due any minute now.

Domingo slipped his sunglasses on to protect his eyes against the sun. Across the street, a few people lined up at a storefront with a psychic sign on its glass window. Really? Only tourists would consider fortune-telling as an adventure in the Big Apple.

The "don't walk" hand signal at the crosswalk lit up, but a throng of jaywalkers darted across the street anyway. Now they streamed toward Domingo. A familiar woman in a flowing yellow dress and strappy sandals caught his eye. She strode past him.

Tess Chua's dark hair showed blondish highlights. She wore dark-rimmed eyeglasses. Other than that, she hadn't aged one bit or gained one pound since the last time Domingo had talked to her nine years ago.

"Tess!" He walked beside her. "Hello, Tess."

"Excuse me?" She paused, her eyes narrowing.

"It's me, Domingo...Monica's friend."

"The bounty hunter?"

Oh, for crying out loud. "That's me. How are you?" He extended his hand, which she shook. "Do you have a minute to talk?"

"Sorry, but I'm running late." She proceeded toward her building.

Domingo kept up with her. "I'll just walk with you, if you don't mind."

"Okay."

They both joined the line at the reception counter, where a security guard inspected IDs and purses, a post-9/11 practice in many buildings in Manhattan.

"Do you know how I can get in touch with Monica?" asked Domingo.

"No."

"I haven't even told you why I'm looking for her."

"I don't need to know because I have no idea where she is." Tess pulled a tissue from her shoulder bag and patted the sweat on her nose and forehead. Summers in New York City were a killer. The weak air conditioner failed to alleviate the humidity. Domingo's armpits felt sticky, but he refrained from fidgeting.

He removed his sunglasses. "When was the last time you talked to her?"

"I can't remember. We had a falling out, you know?"

"Sorry to hear that."

"Yeah, I'm sorry, too. But I can't condone her relationship with a married man. Not anymore. I really tried to be understanding, but I'm married myself. What if someone like Monica screws my husband? I would kill the woman, whoever she is." She stuck the used tissue in her bag.

The line moved an inch. A dude with a big backpack took his sweet time unzipping the gazillion pockets. The lone security guard looked overwhelmed inspecting the bag.

"I heard Monica's mother died," said Domingo.

"That's right. She died in an accident."

"Really? I didn't know that."

"She was in a freak jeepney accident. Everyone was injured, but only she died. A bus lost control and plowed into the jeepney that wasn't even moving. It was stopped outside of Quiapo Church, waiting for passengers."

He could almost hear the clanging of church bells, the jangle of the market at the plaza. The image of diesel-guzzling, fume-spewing, retrofitted Jeeps bloomed in his mind. Filipinos relied on jeepneys as their primary means of public transportation. The vehicles clogged the streets and heeded no traffic rules. They were an environmentalist's worst nightmare.

Domingo clucked his tongue. "That's terrible. How did Monica take the news?"

"I don't know. Like I said, we don't talk anymore."

The line advanced faster after a couple of women realized they were in the wrong building and left.

"If you were to make a wild guess, where do you think Monica is?" he persisted.

"No clue."

They were eye to eye, her expression revealing nothing. She

would make a great poker player. "Christian said Monica went back home to Manila—"

"I don't wanna hear about that man, okay? He's been using her all these years and giving her false hopes. He'll never marry her."

"I agree."

It was their turn for a security check. Tess showed her employee ID and thrust her bag at the guard.

Afterward, the man turned to Domingo. "May I see an ID, sir?"

"I'm not going in." Domingo stepped outside of the line. "Thanks, boss."

Tess also stepped aside, while the woman behind her moved forward.

"Sorry I can't help you," Tess told Domingo.

"I'm having trouble locating Monica. Aren't you afraid something bad happened to her?"

She shrugged. "I'm done worrying about her. She's a grown-up. She can take care of herself."

He pulled a business card from his wallet. "Please call me if you hear from Monica. Her stepmother is dying and she's leaving all her assets to Monica." He handed her the card. "This is going to change Monica's life for the better."

"Oh yeah? Will it make her legal?" She accepted the card and shoved it in her bag.

"Yes. She'll be able to afford the best lawyer in New York to get her an EB-5 visa."

"What's that?"

"It's for investors and the super rich who want to stay here."

"I didn't know US visas are for sale."

"Everything has a price."

"I gotta go." She waved her hand in a quick goodbye and scurried off.

Domingo watched the ripe color of her billowing dress

disappear from his view. Tess knew too much. Not even Christian mentioned the details of the accident that killed Monica's mother, yet Tess had spilled it just like that. The more she feigned nonchalance over her friend's whereabouts, the more he was convinced that she knew. Of course, she was protecting her best friend by claiming to be estranged from her.

Now what? He glanced at his wristwatch. Almost eleven in the morning. He could follow up with James Damon, the PI who traveled to Manila. Perhaps the dude could tell Domingo about Cutter's real interest in the case. Chewbacca had been too eager to point a finger at Christian Price.

His phone trilled. He answered it as he strode out of the building and into the sultry morning. "Hello, Mamang."

"Oh, good! You still remember your mother."

"What's wrong?"

"You're too busy to see your mother, that's what's wrong."

He sighed. She was as dramatic as the soap operas she watched. "I just saw you last week." He headed toward the subway station.

"What could possibly be so important that you can't stop by every couple of days?"

"Every couple of days? Come on, Mamang."

"I have heart palpitations! I can barely breathe. But do you care? Of course not!"

"What? Did somebody call an ambulance?"

"I don't want an ambulance. I want my son."

He could almost see his mother growing teary. She had too much time on her hands at the nursing home and nothing to distract her but television. "Okay, okay. I'll stop by tonight. You want Chinese takeout for dinner?"

"Pork dumplings and lo mien."

"You got it."

"You need a wife, *hijo*."

"What?" His mother tended to go off on a tangent, making

their conversations unpredictable. "What does my love life have to do with anything?"

"You have *no* love life. That's the problem."

"Mamang, give me a break. I'm going to hang up now. I'll see you later."

"You should go to the church potluck. You'll meet young ladies there."

"I'm going to hang up now, okay?"

"You should get married soon. I want a grandchild."

"Unfortunately, they don't sell those in Chinese restaurants, so you'll have to make do with pork dumplings and lo mien. Bye, Mamang." He hung up before he lost it.

He paused and stepped aside at the top of the narrow stairs leading down to the subway station so other people could go first. Tess's words crept back into his mind. *She died in an accident.* Why did Christian skip the most important detail about the death of Monica's mother? Something was amiss, but Domingo couldn't put his finger on it.

He glided down the stairs and onto the airless subway platform before realizing he'd taken the wrong entrance. James Damon's office was located downtown, but the approaching Number 1 train would take him uptown. In that fleeting moment right before the train screeched to a stop, he'd decided to go back to the Upper West Side and dig deeper into Christian's lies.

9

THE PRESENT

Assimilation in America: *What's in a Name?*

If a Shakespeare wannabe asked you, "What's in a name?" the answer is EVERYTHING! In this country, you will be judged by your name, as much as your skin color and legal status. Why do you think I endure people calling me Sunday? Because it makes native-born Americans more comfortable. They can't remember Domingo. They don't like the way it sounds, looks, or smells. Sunday, on the other hand, reminds them of lazy mornings and Lionel Richie crooning, "I'm eaaasy...eaaasy like Sunday morning..." Remember that song? Of course, you do. And that's why Americans remember my name.

If you're called Rigoberto in your country, do me a favor and change it to Bob. Wang Li, you're Wanda now. Ibrahim should be Abe. Mikhail should be Mike. Hinata could be Helen or Helena. Giulia should be spelled Julia, for crying out loud! And don't even think of keeping a name like Abejide. Choose Abe, instead. For those of you with names like Aaban, Aayan, and Aalam, you could all be Abe, too. So what if it's common? Better to be common and acceptable than original but suspicious—as in, "Does his name sound Muslim?" Trust me, you'll want to be Abe when that happens. It will make your life so much easier.

ANOTHER SUBWAY RIDE, another couple of paragraphs for his book. Domingo took pride in being efficient and productive. He emerged from the subway station and walked toward Riverside Park, debating whether to eat an early lunch. His stomach twitched with a pang of hunger at the whiff of greasy meat from a food truck. But, no, he had work to do.

His phone rang—it was the PI who traveled to Manila. He sat on a bench facing the Hudson River. In spite of the heat, joggers of all ages straddled the pathway along the river. "Hey, James. Thanks for returning my call."

"No problem. Any luck finding Monica Reed?"

"Not yet. Listen, I'm curious about Cutter. What's his deal?"

"He wants money, of course."

Sultry breeze kicked up from the murky river, blowing his hair. He brushed his bangs away from his eyes. "Yeah, but Leonard Reed left him an inheritance already."

"All I know is he's negotiating with Mary Reed to get more," continued James. "He has a lawyer talking to the Reed family's lawyer."

"Negotiating? Like a contract?"

"I have no idea. I just know about the negotiation because his lawyer was the one who hired me."

"I didn't know that." Cutter, always broke, would never pay for a lawyer's services unless the stake was substantial. What could he be negotiating with Mary? "Who's the lawyer?"

"Gus Patterson. He lives in Chicago. Don't even bother

asking him about Cutter because of attorney-client privilege and all that crap."

"Yeah, right."

"Hey, Sunday...you're Filipino, right?"

"Yep."

"Filipinas are hot, man! I had a great time in Manila. I'm really into Filipino chicks right now. Do you happen to know any *magandang* ladies? How's my Tagalog?"

Maganda meant pretty. He'd give the PI an A for pronunciation and F for creepiness. He'd met more than a few dudes with a similar fetish. They ate up Asian women the way they'd devour food in a buffet restaurant. "If I know a beautiful, single Filipino woman, you can bet your ass I'll keep her for myself."

The PI guffawed. "In Manila, I watched a DVD of Monica Reed's film. It's called *Mahal*...something. Man, she's quite a looker. Is she still hot today? I mean, that movie's old."

"The movie is called *Mahal Kita*, meaning I love you." Possessiveness engulfed Domingo. Monica had that effect on him. "Yeah, I've seen it, too."

Monica had played the younger sister of an A-list Filipino actress because of their uncanny resemblance. Monica could have given the actress a run for her money, but the gig turned out to be a dead end.

"I don't have the guts to take my clothes off in front of the camera," Monica had told Domingo when he asked about her acting ambition. "Every part I was offered, no matter how small, required wearing skimpy clothes or getting naked. Sex—not religion—is the opium of the masses. Boy, did Karl Marx get it wrong." Her trademark deadpan expression could never hide the bitterness.

Filipinos obsessed over fair-skinned good looks, thanks to hundreds of years under white colonizers. White was superior to brown. And yet for Monica, the currency of her pale-skinned beauty had failed to catapult her to stardom. It was a liability. If her skin had been dark, her legs short, and her face blemished, she might have landed the role of a funny sidekick or the wise-cracking best friend. Nobody would want to watch her nude on the silver screen if she had been fat.

"Is Monica Reed still hot today?" James the PI persisted. "Because I might just help you find her. For free! And when we find her, I'll ask her out."

A seething bubble rose in his throat. The guy just wouldn't let go of the subject. He swallowed hard. "Dude, you're beginning to sound like a perv. I've got work to do. I suggest you get busy with your own job. Thanks for returning my call." He hung up before he lost it.

He sauntered out of the park and toward the residential area, where leafy trees shaded old brownstones and elegant townhouses. Cars lined the streets; parking space in this neighborhood came at a steep price. He stood at a crosswalk on Riverside Drive, trying to catch his bearings. He had no plan. He'd followed his instinct to venture uptown without giving it a thought.

Across the road, a young woman with a Maltese on a leash emerged from Christian's apartment building. She chatted with the doorman while the dog barked up a storm at passersby. A maid? A dog walker? Most residents in that building would toss a polite good morning to the doorman and nothing more. A sense of déjà vu came upon him. In the name of duty, he'd stalked Christian Price and his family more than he cared to admit.

He crossed the street, walked past them, and took a left on Seventy-Fifth Street. With any luck, he could befriend the doorman or any hired help who lived in the building. They were observers, neither seen nor heard in the lives of those they served. He identified with them. He found comfort in blending into the background.

He glanced at his wristwatch. Noon. A thick blanket of

humidity lay upon the city. A sports car, a Jaguar, skidded as it turned a sharp corner on Broadway. The other cars honked. He went back to Riverside Drive.

A surge of pedestrians greeted him there, the lunchtime crowd scurrying to and from the park. He lingered outside Christian's building. The heat seemed to have sucked even his saliva, his mouth now parched. He ought to stop for lunch, or at least a cold drink, but he'd just made eye contact with the doorman, who nodded. Too late to avoid him.

Domingo approached him at the entrance. "How's it going?"

"Not bad." The man eyed Domingo, neither suspicious nor friendly. Talking to strangers was part of his job, no big deal. "A cool river breeze would be nice, though."

His hair had been razored close to the scalp, like most Black guys Domingo knew. In this heat, he wished he had the same haircut. He needed a trim, especially his bangs.

The glass door behind them flew open. A well-dressed, gray-haired woman stepped outside. The doorman turned to her and said hello.

"I need a cab," she responded.

Just as Domingo had expected, no unnecessary chit-chat between the rich residents and the doorman, who said, "Yes, ma'am," and bustled down the street in search of a taxi. Only then did Domingo notice the sandwich board sign in the lobby, visible through the glass door.

Co-op for sale. 1233 Riverside Drive, Apartment #6A. Sterling Associates Real Estate Co., (212) 923-5610.

His gut tingled. He knew the address. Yes, it was Christian's apartment. For sale. Something was up.

The doorman let out an ear-piercing whistle, and a cab pulled over. He opened the passenger door for the lady. As soon as he'd shut the door, Domingo walked over to him. "Is Christian Price's apartment for sale?"

The man glanced over his shoulder at the sign. "Oh, that?

Maybe. There might have been some change. I'm not sure. Do you know Mr. Price?"

"Yes, I do. I'm here to see him."

"He's not home."

"Are you sure? I'm supposed to see him." He bluffed on the fly. "He had an appointment downtown this morning, but he should be back right around now."

"I haven't seen him come back."

"Okay. Well, let me give him a call and see what's up." Domingo retrieved a phone from his trouser pocket.

The doorman nodded, backing away, perhaps to give Domingo some privacy. He went inside the building for good measure.

Domingo punched some keys on his phone, aware of the doorman observing him from behind the glass door. He wasn't calling Christian Price, but the realtor selling the apartment. He wasn't even using his regular phone but a cheap burner he could toss away if necessary.

A woman picked up after one ring. He asked to see the Price apartment. The first available slot was tomorrow at two p.m. Too long a wait. His impatience flared up. "I'm right outside the building. I'm really hoping to see it today."

"I'm sorry, but that's not possible. We need a couple of hours' notice, at least, before we can show you the apartment."

"I actually know Christian Price, and that's why I'm doubly interested in the property. I love the view of the Hudson River from his living room. Can you tell him I want to see the place as soon as possible?"

"Certainly. I didn't catch your name—"

"Frankly, I'm wondering why it's still on the market. I thought it would sell overnight."

"We removed it from the market for a while, but there's been a change. Mrs. Price put the listing back on two days ago."

"Oh, is Emmy in charge of selling? I thought she'd be the

one who would have a hard time giving up the apartment." The information from Monica ages ago came in handy. Christian would rather move to the posh outskirts, like Westchester County, but Emmy clung to her Manhattan roots.

A pause at the other end of the line. The realtor seemed surprise that Domingo was on a first-name basis with the Prices.

"It's the divorce, I understand." Another bluff. Once he got started, he couldn't get off the snooping train. If he got burned, he would simply hang up.

"Pardon me?"

"It's okay. I understand about the family problems and all that."

Another pause. "Um, I believe everything's fine now."

"Oh, good! That's wonderful news. So why does Emmy still want to sell?"

"She wants a change of scenery, I believe. A house outside the city."

"That's what Christian always wanted."

"Sir, I'm going to need your name and contact number—"

"You know what? I'm going to call Christian myself. Thanks." He hung up, the rush from the revelation ratcheting up his heart rate.

The doorman continued to eye him, so he waved goodbye before crossing Riverside Drive. As his mind churned through bits and pieces of information, he headed toward the park. The realtor had confirmed his wild guess. The on-again, off-again listing of the Price apartment meant Christian and Emmy Price had come very close to a divorce. Now they were back together again, and they wanted a fresh start in a new house outside the city.

Two decades of hunting down undocumented immigrants had taught him how to deduce the truth even from the scantest of facts. His previous experience snooping on Christian Price, his mistress, and his family also helped. Cutter might be right. Mr. GQ appeared to have a good reason for making Monica Reed disappear.

Every fiber of his being was alert. Every subject or suspect was a jigsaw puzzle to be assembled and completed. He loved his job! He lived for the moments when serendipity and logic crossed paths. Most of all, his blood sang with every chase.

"I care about Monica very much, but our timing was off." Oh yeah, he was going after Christian Price.

10

July 2008

On the afternoon Domingo resumed stalking Mr. Scrubs, he went straight to the apartment building within a shopping complex that had seen better times. He didn't understand why a young hospital professional would want to live in such a place.

He waited in his rental car in the parking lot. Fifteen minutes later, Mr. Scrubs left his apartment. This was the intoxicating part of his job, when a new piece of the puzzle presented itself.

The dude lived in a low-rise building surrounded by shuttered shops. He was young, Caucasian, red-haired, no taller than Domingo, but thinner. Most likely single and living alone. This afternoon, he wore mesh shorts, a T-shirt, and rubber sandals.

As soon as Mr. Scrubs left in his brown Honda Accord, Domingo climbed to the second floor of the two-story building to check out his apartment number: 220. Then he went downstairs to the wall of mailboxes and found number 220, owned by M. Gray.

Domingo hurried to the leasing office before the dude returned. The woman in the office wore a frilly pink dress, too tight for her generous proportions. The name plate on the desk said: *Courtney, Manager.*

He approached her and turned on the charm. "I was hoping to catch my buddy at number two twenty to ask him about the apartments here, but he's not there. I guess I should have called him before stopping by."

"Who are you looking for?" Courtney asked.

Damn, he didn't know the dude's first name, but at least he knew the last name and where he worked. "Well, I like to call him the Graymeister because all he does is work all night long at the Lawrence Memorial Hospital."

"Oh, Max Gray! Yes, he does work long hours, the poor thing."

Bingo—Max. "I thought he'd be at home sleeping, for sure. But he's not home."

"Did you say you wanted to ask Max about our apartments?"

"Yes. He recommended this place, so I thought I'd check it out."

"Do you work at the hospital, too?"

"Not yet. But I'm hoping to get a job there."

"So you're a lab tech, too?"

"Lab tech? No. I'm not as smart as the Graymeister. I'm hoping to get a position in security."

"Like a security guard?"

"Yes."

Courtney giggled, complete with eyelash batting. "I bet you security guards have a nicer-looking uniform. Better than the scrubs Max wears."

"I agree. Those scrubs look awful. But don't tell him I said that. He loves his job, you know."

"Oh, you're fine. Max is pretty laid back. He can talk all about bacteria and specimens, if you let him, but he knows how to chill out."

His heart thumped in excitement as Courtney revealed more information without knowing it. He pushed further. "I don't really understand his work, do you?"

"I think he performs tests on specimens from hospital patients."

"Like blood and shit?"

Courtney broke into another fit of giggles. "I think they call it stool."

"For me, shit is shit."

"Oh, you're funny!" Her dark eyes sparkled, her moon face blushing. She grazed his arm with her fingers in a flirty way. "I'm sorry, but I didn't catch your name."

"I'm Christian." The name had spilled out of him without any effort. Boy, he'd been too preoccupied with both Monica Reed and her lover.

"What a lovely name. Christian, would you like to see one of our apartments?"

"I would love to get a copy of your brochure. I'll come back when Max is here."

Courtney's lips dipped in disappointment, but she handed him a brochure and a business card.

"I'll see you when I come back." He smiled and winked for good measure. That was the extent of his flirtation, hence, his zero love life.

"Yes, do that. I'm here nine to five. I'm usually free after work."

An invitation to go out on a date if ever there was one. Domingo skedaddled. Whew! If he'd been less of a doofus, he could have taken advantage of the offer and enjoyed a one-night stand.

Instead, he went back to work and called Vilma in Washington, D.C. to dig up some information about Max Gray. The woman he called Tita Vilma, or Aunt Vilma, was a Filipino friend of his mother's. Whatever he said to her would surely reach his mother's ears. She was his primary contact at the IRS.

After the call, he waited in the car. His job required long intervals between chases, as though he was born to wait. He'd learned to appreciate the downtime as a chance to meditate with his eyes closed or open, depending on where he was.

Max returned to his apartment at around five p.m. He then emerged from his door in his scrubs. Domingo tailed the dude's battered Honda. He thought lab technicians earned good money, but judging by Max's car with its missing hubcap and a dent on the side, it could not have been much.

Domingo anticipated following the car to the hospital, but nope, Max Gray stopped at Olive Garden. He joined a chick at a cozy table. She was blonde, of the Clairol variety, and on the wrong side of forty when a mini skirt appeared pitiful. A cougar. Not a relative, but maybe a friend or a date. Light makeup, a wicked cackle. Charming in her own way. What could Max have said to make her laugh *that* much?

Domingo's snooping was interrupted when Mary Reed summoned him back to drive Monica to the mall. She was moving into the Reeds' guest house and needed some stuff.

Several hours later, he returned to the Lawrence Memorial Hospital to stalk Max Gray. At around eight p.m., Max would have been at work already.

Domingo entered the lobby, wandered the hallways, and observed. The hospital was abuzz with people coming and going. The security guard stopped a couple with *Get Well* balloons. "No latex balloons allowed inside," the guard said.

Domingo went up and down the different floors, locating all the important areas—the emergency department, the surgery suite, the ICU, the rehabilitation center, and the dialysis center. Monica and her father were scheduled for the kidney transplant in four days. Domingo's knowledge of the hospital's layout should come in handy.

After almost an hour at the hospital, still no sighting of Max Gray. He hadn't seen any room that looked like a lab. In the hallway, he stopped a man whose ID card hung from a lanyard around his neck.

"Boss, can you direct me to the lab?" Domingo asked.

"Which lab?" the man responded.

He was stumped. If he name-dropped Max Gray, it might get back to the dude, so he shrugged. With his brown skin, he would sometimes pretend not to understand English, and he'd always gotten away with it.

The hospital employee eyed him. "Microbiology? Toxicology? Blood bank? Unless someone sent you to a lab, you won't be able to get in, anyway. Are you a patient?"

"I'm a visitor."

"Sorry, but no visitors are allowed in the labs."

"Okay, boss." Domingo turned around in haste before the man became suspicious. He continued wandering until he reached the cafeteria. He flowed with a stream of people lining up. Chow time for the night crew.

His phone trilled. "Hello, Tita Vilma. You found out anything about my boy?"

"Where are you? It's very noisy," she harrumphed.

"Sorry. I'm in a cafeteria." He was at the tail end of a long line. In as much as he wanted a cup of java, he'd been waiting all afternoon for Vilma's information, so he left the room and hurried back to the atrium. He plopped down on one of the couches where families and other visitors waited. "Is this better, Tita Vilma?"

"Yes. You're going to need a pen and paper. I have some numbers for you."

"Oh, good." He took out a gas receipt and pen. "I'm ready."

"Full name—Maximilian Gray. Twenty-seven years old. Laboratory technician at Lawrence Memorial Hospital's microbiology and immunology lab. Last year, he made thirty thousand and two hundred dollars."

"Isn't that pretty low for a lab tech?" Domingo asked.

"If Max Gray had been a lab *technologist* instead of a technician, he'd be making upward of forty grand," Tita Vilma said.

You could expect an IRS employee to know the nuances in pay grades. She was a reliable and prized source for Domingo. He maintained ties with several people at every key government agency in D.C. Joe Medina paid their sources or traded information, whatever was necessary in any given situation.

In parting, Domingo asked Tita Vilma for Max Gray's social security number, always helpful in digging up criminal record, if any.

After hanging up, Domingo strolled back to the cafeteria. No wonder Max Gray lived in a blighted mall-turned-apartment complex and drove an old car. The new information about Max reinforced the impression that he was cash-strapped in spite of his hospital job, but it didn't tell him anything about the dude's relationship with Cutter or Leonard Reed. What could someone like Max have anything to do with Monica Reed? Still, he was pleased at the few pieces of the puzzle at hand.

He passed by a group of scrubs-wearing men and women chatting in the lobby. They spoke at the same time, their voices cascading, laughter rising. He took a double glance at a cackling chick. Blondie! Max Gray's dinner date.

The woman had traded her mini skirt for frumpy scrubs. He wondered whether she was in cahoots with Max and Cutter. He had to find out, so he retraced his steps back to the lobby.

Part of the boisterous group had dispersed, but Blondie

remained gabbing with another woman. Both of them had their ID cards hanging from lanyards.

Domingo slowed down as he walked past them, surreptitiously raising his cell phone to snap a photo of Blondie. He made a quick beeline for the exit and drove to the nearest Walgreens.

At the drug store's photo center—just a counter, really—he asked a young man to help him upload a picture from his cell phone.

"Is this all you have?" The clerk stared at Blondie's photo on the computer screen. He couldn't have been a day older than twenty. A day's growth of beard hadn't camouflaged his youth. It only made him look like he wasn't used to shaving yet.

"Yep, that's it," said Domingo.

The clerk stuffed a piece of gum in his mouth before asking, "You want four-by-six or five-by-seven? Glossy or matte finish?"

"Can you zoom in and make the image larger?"

The kid zoomed in on Blondie's face.

"I'd like to see this part, too." Domingo pointed at the space below Blondie's neck.

The kid blew a bubble with his gum. "Sure thing."

The image of the ID materialized, but was impossible to read.

"What's your name?" Domingo asked.

"Kevin."

"Kevin, here's my situation. I saw this woman at the hospital, and bam! I'm hypnotized. Can't get my eyes off her. You know what I mean? I'm dying to find out her name, which is on that ID right there. Can you enlarge it so I can read her name?"

"You're in love, bro."

"I'm afraid so. Of all places, a hospital."

Kevin clicked on icons, and Blondie's ID had gotten bigger and clearer. *Savannah Sorinski. Emergency Department.*

"Savannah." Domingo exhaled in relief and gave Kevin a high-five. "Let me order a print—a nice five-by-seven, glossy."

"Come back in an hour, and I'll have it ready."

Domingo paid for the photo and wandered the aisles of the drug store. *Max is a lab technician. Savannah works at the emergency department.* He processed the thoughts. She must be a nurse, otherwise her scrubs would have identified her as a doctor.

He was getting more excited as he turned over the facts for a possible connection of the duo with Cutter and Leonard Reed. *Damn, I love my job.*

11

THE PRESENT

Assimilation in America: Socializing and Dating
You don't trust nobody, and nobody trusts you. Sound familiar? Yep, that's Taylor Swift for you. It's also every undocumented immigrant's reality. Lack of trust means zero social life and love life. Living in a new country can be extremely lonely. Take it from me, a naturalized US citizen who has no significant other. I'm legal, but I'm just as preoccupied as you are in finding my place in the sun. I didn't come to America to waste my time.

But I digress. We're talking about you. So what if you're undocumented? Stay within your safe circle—your church choir or Bible study group, your coworkers, friends of friends—you get the point. A Catholic church in New York City that shall remain nameless has a special once-a-month Mass for immigrants, legal and illegal alike. They hold a potluck after Mass, a dance on Valentine's Day, and a picnic on Labor Day. The first thing anyone asks anybody during an introduction is, "What's your case?" Let's just say no ICE employee will ever be invited to their socials.

If you don't belong to a church, no problem. There's always online dating. The internet has neither borders nor an immigration department. At last, a place where you're NOT illegal. Flirt all you want. Re-invent yourself. Hell, replace the ugly mug in your profile with your good-looking cousin's picture. Trust me, you can get away with it. That is, until someone asks to meet you in the flesh. When that happens, beware of ICE agents running a sting. They sometimes organize a party or a bingo social to ensnare criminal illegals.

Speaking of criminals, I'd like to take my word back. If you have a criminal offense or conviction, plus you're illegal, forget about socializing and dating. If ICE considers you "removable," your problem is much bigger than being lonely. Don't go crashing the church potluck or the summer picnic. Just fuck off. This book is not for you.

DOMINGO SHOVED the little notepad in the glove compartment. He swept the packed parking lot with a glance. He hated to keep his Pontiac GTO idling, but he needed the AC to fight off the muggy heat while he scribbled a few paragraphs for his book. He glanced at his wristwatch. Six twenty in the evening. He turned off the AC and the engine. Time to bring Mamang the Chinese takeout. He picked up the plastic bag of food and got out of the car.

Choosing the Vista Nursing and Rehabilitation Center on Coney Island was one of the best decisions he'd made. When his mother slipped on the stairs at home and fractured her hip, she'd undergone a hip-replacement surgery, followed by four weeks of physical therapy. He'd expected everything to return to normal, but she'd healed slowly. Two months after the surgery, she remained in pain, unable to walk on her own. A nursing home had been the only option, and this was the best place for her. The facility's proximity to the beach gave the illusion of a resort. It almost made up for his inability to care for her at home.

Inside his mother's room, Domingo found her chatting with Lulu, a Filipino nursing assistant.

"You're late. I like to eat at six o'clock." Mamang sat on the bed, while Lulu occupied the wingback chair. They both faced the TV.

"Sorry." He kissed his mother on the forehead. Today she'd worn a pink cotton blouse and brown slacks. Her gray hair had been cut short, like a military crew cut for women.

Lulu turned off the TV. "Mamang was about to call you, but I told her to give you another half hour in case you were out with a girlfriend, and maybe you were in the middle of something romantic." She smiled, saucy as hell. The heavy makeup overwhelmed her small face. The fake eyelashes reminded him of Halloween décor—rubber spiders. She was in her forties, divorced, and hunting for a new husband.

He might as well have worn a red target circle on his chest. "Well, nothing romantic. It's just work as usual." He set the plastic bag on the floor and pulled his mother's wheelchair from the corner. "I better take you to the dining hall now." He helped his mother get up.

She leaned on him and slid into the wheelchair.

He turned to Lulu. "I can handle this one. Thanks."

"All right, you know where to find me." Lulu scowled. "My days off are the same, Sunday and Monday."

Oh, for crying out loud. He ignored the open invitation for a date and handed the takeout bag to his mother, who put it on her lap.

At last, Lulu stepped out of the room. He sighed in relief.

"Don't you like Lulu?" His mother looked wounded, as though she herself had been rejected. "She adores you and she's very sweet to me. She keeps me company long after her shift is over, unlike the other aides. They fly out the door the very second their shift ends."

"I like her just fine." He pushed his mother's wheelchair out of the room and into the hallway.

"Why don't you ask her out on a date?" she asked.

"Why should I?"

"Because you're forty and unmarried. At your age, you should have a wife and several children. You need to start building a family or you'll be alone when I die. Who knows how much time I have left? Who knew your father and your brother would leave us so soon?"

Here we go again. Domingo's father had died of tuberculosis, then Domingo's twelve-year-old brother had caught the disease from their father and died soon thereafter. All of this happened when Domingo was just ten.

They got inside an empty elevator. "When was the last time you went out on a date?" Mamang continued.

"This is the reason I don't stop by every couple of days. Can we please not talk about this?"

She sulked. He let it slide. He knew how her mind worked. A daughter-in-law, preferably a Filipina like Lulu, would mean an in-house caregiver. She could go back home instead of staying in this nursing home.

A bell pinged, and the door opened. The dining hall was only a floor below his mother's room. He wheeled her out of the elevator.

Mamang herself had been the caregiver for Roger, her second husband and passport to the USA. They'd met through an agency that matched lonely Americans with Filipino women. Unlike most American men, Roger Ronan hadn't picked a young hottie, but a mature and responsible woman he could trust. He was a male spinster who'd worked all his adult life as a Sears repairman. Mamang was forty-seven years old and Roger seventy-two when they got married in a hurry in Manila.

Domingo was seventeen, with just one year left in his status as a minor. If Mamang had waited any longer, Uncle Sam might have rejected the petition for Domingo's US citizenship. He would have been left behind in the Philippines for good instead of the three years while he earned a useless college degree from a diploma mill. Mamang prized a diploma, and so he'd obtained it for her benefit.

On the way to the dining room, a couple of nursing aides called out, "Hello, Mamang!" Did those people think Mamang was her first name? It meant *mother* in Tagalog. Nobody here ever called her Aurora or Mrs. Ronan.

They entered the half-empty dining room. Most of the old folks ate between four and five in the afternoon. By this time, they watched TV in their rooms or at the recreation center. Some were probably in bed. Indeed, why stay up late?

He parked the wheelchair at a table near a large window, overlooking the sea. No need for her to get up.

She opened the Styrofoam boxes and sniffed the dumplings and lo mien. "You want some, *hijo*?"

"No, it's for you. I'm not hungry yet." He took in the sunset, diffused in a bronze sky. He welcomed the torpor and hushed conversations after a full day of the big city's swirl and noise. He sat there with a renewed appreciation for everything Mamang had done to secure their American citizenship. She'd been Roger's wife, nurse, and maid for over a decade. Theirs had been a contract of mutual need. Her companionship and caregiving in exchange for his petition of US citizenship and pension. After Roger died, they'd also inherited his house in Brooklyn where Domingo still lived.

He removed two water bottles from the plastic bag and uncapped them. He slid one across the table for her and sipped the other one.

Mamang slurped the noodles, licking the brown sauce off the plastic fork. "What case are you working on this week?"

"Same as the last time I was here."

"What kind of a criminal are you chasing? I wish you'd find another job, even if it pays less. How many bullets in your body do you need to learn your lesson? And don't tell me you survived because you're such a tough guy. You survived because God was trying to teach you a lesson, but it's clear you haven't learned a thing."

"Don't get started on that again."

"I can't help it. I worry about you. Why can't you get a normal job and get married? That's all I want for you."

"I've been doing this job for nineteen years. I'm not going to quit now. You might as well accept it."

Another resident, a lady who wore a thick cardigan in spite of the crackling heat outside, said hello.

"Leila, this is my son, Domingo," chirped Mamang. "He brought me Chinese. I'm sick of eating tuna sandwich and pickles."

"Oh, you're the agent who arrests illegal aliens." Leila bared her teeth when she smiled, displaying a pearly set of dentures. "I've heard so much about you. May I see your gun?"

"Excuse me?"

"Your mother said you're always armed and ready." Leila glanced around in a conspiratorial manner. "I've always wanted to touch a real gun."

"I don't have it. Weapons are not allowed in this place." He extended his hand. "Call me Sunday. Pleased to meet you, Leila."

They shook hands. After the exchange of niceties, Leila shuffled along.

"Why do you tell people I'm always armed?" he asked his mother.

"Because it's true. You're Mr. Tough Guy, aren't you?"

"You make it sound like I'm a terrorist."

"You *could* be. I imagine the job description is quite similar."

In spite of the sarcasm, she must be proud of him. Why else would she tell the old folks about his job? How many people in this nursing home could claim a son who kicked ass for a living? Who had survived three forty-five-caliber bullets in his body? Courtesy of a bad hombre who had sprayed Domingo's old Camaro with gunfire in a chase on a highway outside of Washington, D.C. during the wee hours of the morning.

A surgeon had removed the bullets and stapled closed the holes in Domingo's intestines. Since then, Mamang never missed an opportunity to remind him just how close he'd been to joining his father and brother in the afterlife.

"You haven't answered my question." Mamang cracked open the fortune cookie that came with the takeout. She'd finished her food.

"What question?"

She shoved the cookie in her mouth. "What kind of a criminal are you chasing?"

"Not a criminal for a change. I'm looking for a Filipina, the daughter of a general, someone I know from a while back." A familiar ache filled his chest. The first time he'd told Mamang about Monica, he'd been a blustering rookie. He could not have known Monica would be his *Groundhog Day* of a nightmare that would keep on coming back to haunt him.

"A Filipina...hmm." Mamang's eyelids drooped, which always made her look sleepy. "Why, it should be a piece of cake, then."

No hint that his mother remembered Monica Reed. No point in re-telling the saga. He finished his water in one long gulp. "So far, it hasn't been easy. I haven't found her."

"She's illegal?"

"Yes."

"She's Filipino, so you'll find her."

"That's the most illogical thing I've ever heard."

"Filipinos can't hide from other Filipinos."

"You're still not making sense."

"Just because you don't understand something doesn't mean it's not true."

"You just muddled this conversation further."

She frowned. "You'll find her, believe me."

He sighed. His phone rang—it was Inday. "Tell me you have good news. Otherwise, you shouldn't be working at this time. Your uncle doesn't pay you enough to work overtime."

"I'm at home, actually. I'm on Twitter. Did you talk to Christian Price this morning?" she asked.

"Yes, but I think he was lying to me."

"Do you want to talk to him again?"

"Yes. Definitely."

"His wife just tweeted a picture. They look great together. They're attending a fundraiser at The Plaza."

"The Plaza." He glanced at his watch. Given the traffic, it would take him an hour, at least, to reach Manhattan.

"It's a party. They'll be there all night long. If you go now, you'll catch him."

"Thanks, kid." He slipped his phone back in his pocket, gathered the empty Styrofoam boxes, and shoved them in the plastic bag.

"Who was that?" Mamang slugged the water. "Are you leaving?"

"That was Inday. Yeah, I have to drive back to Manhattan." He got up, picked up the empty bottles, and tossed them in the recycling bin. The plastic bag with the Styrofoam boxes went into the regular trash can.

When he faced Mamang again, she flashed an expectant smile. "Are you going back to the city because you found the Filipina?"

"Nope. I'm going to talk to someone who might have more information."

"It's Monica Reed, am I right? The bastard daughter of that big-shot general."

"Yep." Warmth rushed to his face, as though his mother had caught him lying. He dared not ask how much she remembered of the woman's life story. He swiped a small strip of paper on the table that he'd missed. The fortune from the cookie.

"You're not going to rest until you find Monica, are you?"

"It's my job to find her." He rolled the paper into a tiny ball and stuck it in his pocket.

She waved away his remark. "I'm not stupid. I remember Monica Reed. You call her *Multo*. She's the one you've *always* been looking for."

The hair on his neck prickled. Some sentiments burned too brightly to hide from his mother. "Okay, let's go." He sidled behind her and pushed the wheelchair. At least this way, he didn't have to look her in the eye. She might read his thoughts and see the anxiety weighing him down. Day three on the case and no solid lead. The Ghost was the hardest, damnedest case he'd ever handled. He might never find her again. Not this time.

12

THE PRESENT

From a fortune cookie: You will find what you're looking for.

Domingo left his notepad in his car, so instead of scribbling a line or two for his book, he fidgeted with the strip of paper from Mamang's fortune cookie. Maybe he would include it in his book as an advice to illegals. *When you find hope, even if it's just a fortune from a free cookie, hang on to it. Half of the battle for survival in a country where you are unwanted is to keep your spirits up.*

Yeah, perhaps he would write that bit of advice. The uncertainty of his search for Monica Reed had reduced him to a superstitious fool. The woman had no electronic trail. She knew enough never to use credit cards, own a cell phone, or hang out on social media. A smart, undocumented immigrant was as cunning as any dangerous fugitive. Without an electronic trail, Monica remained a ghost.

He glanced at the fortune cookie again before pocketing it. Somehow its positive prediction galvanized his hope that he would find her. Still, unless he acted within the next five minutes, a security guard or someone else might find him suspicious and kick him out of The Plaza. He'd been loitering outside the Terrace Room for twenty minutes.

When the door opened, he intercepted a young waiter.

"Boss, I need to speak to one of your guests. It's an emergency. He's attending the dinner party—" He glanced at the sign. *Welcome to the Mercer School Annual Fundraiser.* "He's a Mercer parent. His name is Christian Price. If you can just let me take a peek inside, I'm sure I'll be able to spot him."

The guy appraised Domingo's black blazer and khaki pants and frowned. "Sorry, but it's a five-hundred-dollar-a-plate event? You can't go in there unless you're invited?"

He was one of those kids who put a question mark in every sentence, as though being young meant being unsure of everything.

So, Domingo's jacket and slacks from Target didn't pass the fashion test for this joint. "Five hundred dollars, wow. What are you serving tonight—gold nuggets a la carte?"

The waiter chuckled. "Tell me about it."

"If I write a note, will you give it to Mr. Price?"

The kid shook his head. "I don't think so. There are two hundred sixty people inside. I might as well be looking for a needle in a haystack." Another waiter emerged from the door, waving the young guy back inside. "Sorry, I gotta go."

Domingo glanced at his wristwatch. Nine p.m. sharp. He could wait it out. When the dinner party ended, he would see Christian come out the door. Somehow he doubted Mr. GQ would agree to chat with him over coffee again. Domingo had used up Christian's goodwill. He couldn't afford to squander this opportunity for a face-to-face talk.

The last time Domingo saw Christian's kids, they were

babies. The boy must be about twelve and the girl nine or thereabouts today. So, they were attending one of the priciest schools in New York City. Five hundred dollars a plate just to get invited to a party where the parents pledged even more donations to the private school.

Every time someone opened the door, Domingo glimpsed the vaulted, gilded ceiling and the massive crystal chandelier inside. Laughter rang out. Inaudible conversations buzzed. The smoky aroma of grilled steaks from a waiter passing by sent his empty stomach growling. He should have eaten dinner with his mother at the nursing home.

A group of women in cocktail dresses and stilettos emerged from the Terrace Room. Their toned legs, alabaster complexion, and self-assured air spoke of their class. *The golden people.* The young mothers who lived on the Upper East Side or Park Avenue, whose darling sons and daughters attended the elite Mercer School as a prerequisite to Harvard or Yale or Princeton. Christian himself had graduated from Brown University.

"Oh, Ems! That's way too funny." A brunette elbowed the blonde beside her. They both laughed.

Ems. Could that be Emmy Price? A tiny muscle in his calf twitched even before his mind clicked. He followed the women until they entered the restroom.

He prowled back and forth in the hallway. It had been nine years since he'd laid eyes on Christian's wife, but he remembered the longish face, like a beautiful, expensive racehorse.

What could Domingo tell Emmy to compel her husband to come out and speak to him? *Excuse me, but your husband's mistress is missing. Do you, by chance, know if he killed her?*

Damn it. He stopped pacing and fumbled in his pocket for a pen. No paper other than the fortune from the cookie and a McDonald's receipt. He placed the receipt against the wall, with the blank side up, and wrote. *It's me, Sunday. Pls talk to me now and I'll leave you alone for good.* Would that be enough to convince Christian to come outside?

Before he could decide, the women emerged from the bathroom. The brunettes led the pack. The one called Ems, with buttery-blonde hair, trailed behind.

He fell in step beside her. "Mrs. Price?"

She turned to him with a questioning look. Bingo. It was indeed Christian's wife.

"Mrs. Price, I need to speak to your husband."

She stopped walking and looked him up and down, not hostile, but curious. "I'm sorry...but who are you?"

"My name is Sunday. Christian knows me. I actually spoke to him this morning. I need to follow up on something."

One of the brunettes touched Emmy's arm. "Let's go, or we're going to miss the bidding on the Hitchcock chair."

Emmy's gaze darted to her friend and then back to Domingo.

"Mrs. Price, if you can give this note to your husband, I'd greatly appreciate it." He folded the receipt and handed it to her.

She accepted it with a nod.

"I'll be waiting here." He exhaled in relief and paced the floor again.

Back in 2008, Emmy Price had been a stay-at-home mom overwhelmed by the stresses of motherhood. She'd hired Monica Reed to watch her kids three days a week so she could see her shrink, work out in a gym, shop with her girlfriends, and spend money on whatever her heart desired. Now that her kids were older, perhaps she was making use of her Vassar education and had resumed her career in marketing. Did she still hire Filipino help?

Men in tuxedos and women in pink sleeveless gowns came out of the Grand Ballroom. A wedding party must have just ended. Guests snapped photos of each other outside the room. Old ladies exchanged hugs as they said goodbye.

When Domingo switched his gaze back to the Terrace Room, the doors flew open. Christian Price hurried toward him.

Domingo waved. "Hey, man!" He let his hand fall to his side when he recognized the fury in Christian's red-faced, tight-lipped expression.

"What are you doing here? You have the nerve to approach my wife!" He jabbed his forefinger at Domingo. "I already talked to you. What the fuck do you want from me?"

Domingo stepped back. "Whoa, whoa...calm down, man. I'm here because we need to talk about Monica." He motioned for Christian to follow him, away from the wedding party. They stopped near the men's room. "You lied to me. You didn't tell me you're selling your apartment."

Christian's imposing height, not to mention his impeccable dark suit, gave him an imperial air. He'd changed into different attire for the party.

"Why should I tell you anything? You have no right to my personal information." He balled his fists, as though he was this close to slugging Domingo. "Who do you think you are?"

"I'm interested in the reason you're selling the house. Did Emmy find out about your affair with Monica? Did she threaten to divorce you?"

"Fuck you! You're out of line. It's none of your business."

"Unless you killed Monica Reed. Then it's my goddamned business to tell the police that she's been seeing you for the past nine years, and you're the last person to see her alive."

"What?"

"She's missing! How do I know you didn't kill her?" If the bluff sent the man ballistic, so much the better. It would be easier to nail down the philandering bastard.

But, no. Christian heaved a sigh and loosened up his fists. "What do you mean she's missing? I told you she's in Manila."

"And I'm telling you she's *not* there. Nobody has seen her since June."

"Why don't you ask Cutter? He's going to inherit more money from the Reeds if Monica is out of the picture."

"Let me worry about Cutter, okay? I want to know what really happened between you and Monica."

He grunted. The men in tuxedos streamed past them on the way to the restroom. Domingo motioned for Christian to walk with him. They ambled side by side in the hallway.

"What really happened between you and Monica?" Domingo repeated.

"One of Emmy's friends saw me and Monica in ShopRite in New Jersey. We were grocery shopping like a married couple. There was no way I could lie my way out of it."

"So what happened?"

Christian paused, his shoulders drooping. He rested his back against the wall. "I confessed everything to Emmy before her friend could rat me out. My wife gave me an ultimatum—dump Monica or get a divorce. So I broke up with Monica. Emmy and I are trying to start over. Can you *not* fuck this up for me, please?"

Domingo stood before him. How he hated having to look up to the guy. "Did you know how Monica's mother died?"

"A terrible jeepney accident, yes."

"Did you find out about the accident before or after you broke up?"

"After."

"Go on."

"I bought the one-way plane ticket to Manila so she could attend the funeral." Christian ran a hand through his hair. He gave Domingo a faraway look. Was he imagining Monica? Did he miss her? After a moment, he sprung to attention and stuck his hands in his trouser pockets. "Listen, Sunday. Monica was unhappy about the breakup, but we both knew our relationship wouldn't last forever. It was just a matter of time. We didn't fight. We ended everything on a positive note. I would never hurt her, okay?"

Domingo nodded, though he couldn't have disagreed more. *Monica the Ghost.* As an undocumented immigrant, she didn't exist in the eyes of the government. Her mother was dead. Her best friend was estranged. Nobody would have guessed her rich stepmother would be looking for her after all the bad blood between them. She made the perfect victim for someone like Christian Price. The man was physically capable of strangling or smothering her.

Domingo eyed Christian's crisp suit and shiny, lace-up leather shoes. "Nice shoes, by the way. What are they?"

"Armani."

Domingo clucked his tongue. "Wow, Giorgio Armani." Mr. GQ had too much class to get blood on his hands. If he had killed Monica, it wouldn't involve gore or anything messy.

"Let's go back." Christian turned in the opposite direction. "Emmy will be looking for me soon."

They loped toward the Terrace Room. Scenarios ran in Domingo's mind like a movie trailer. Where would an upstanding citizen like Christian Price hide a body? What happened to the love nest he'd been renting in New Jersey for Monica?

"Well, here we are," declared Christian.

They lingered a few feet from the Terrace Room. The wedding guests loitered throughout the hallway, their laughter and banter overlapping.

Domingo extended his right hand to Christian. "Thanks for talking to me."

Mr. GQ glanced down at Domingo's hand, but didn't touch it. He wore the mien of an aristocrat who'd been interrupted by a servant. "Please don't approach my wife again. In fact, please don't contact me again. I've told you everything I know. Monica and I are history now."

Domingo withdrew his hand. "Now you're acting guilty. What are you hiding?"

"I'm trying to save my marriage!" The flush on Christian's cheeks spread to the tips of his ears.

"Well, good luck with that. I can't promise you I won't be in touch again."

"You said in your note you won't bother me again."

"That was *before* I learned the circumstances of your breakup with Monica." He turned on his heel before Christian could say anything more. He could feel the heat of Mr. GQ's stare on his back. If the man had plugged Monica Reed, Domingo would stick to him like gum under his very expensive Armani shoes.

13

July 2008

On the day before Leonard Reed's kidney transplant, Cutter ended Domingo's services over the phone. Chewie continued to pretend to be in Chicago, though Domingo had seen him at the hospital. Leonard and Cutter wanted him out of the picture. Why?

Domingo drove to the Reed mansion to deliver Monica's birth certificate and other belongings, which he'd fetched from her apartment in New Jersey. He tried not to gawk at her as she lounged by the swimming pool in the backyard. She wore a one-piece swimsuit, displaying mounds and curves in all the right places. Even a modest bathing suit displayed more skin than he deserved to see. Her face glowed with a reddish tan. Her beauty made him feel meager, made him wish to be invisible.

"I have your documents." He handed her a brown envelope.

"I left your laptop, your apartment keys, and luggage in the living room."

Monica swept her dripping hair up and fastened it neatly with a hair clip. Then she looked at the envelope's contents.

He cleared his throat. "Cutter says your dad no longer needs me, so I guess this is goodbye. Everything set with the surgery tomorrow? I can't believe how fast it was scheduled."

"Yeah, we're on a fast track." She was thumbing through the contents of the manila envelope. "If not for me, my dad would have to wait for at least three years to find a kidney match. At his age, that's just too long."

"Are you ready for the surgery? I mean…" *It's been less than a week since the father who never acknowledged your existence for thirty-five long years asked for your kidney, and now, chop-chop, give it up already!* He winced, deciding against such candor.

She set the envelope aside. "I spoke to a psychologist to make sure I'm emotionally ready for this. I also talked to the doctors on the transplant team. They said the risks are minimal. I can live a long, healthy life with just one kidney. It won't stop me from any physical activities or having a baby someday."

"Sure, but what's your gut feeling about this surgery?"

"What do you mean?" She glanced up at him, hand to her forehead to protect her eyes from the sun. "I'm his only hope. I have to do this."

"I understand."

She rose and wrapped a towel around her body. She wore a determined expression. *A woman on a mission.* What was he thinking stalking Max Gray and Savannah Sorinski? His concern had been downright misplaced.

"Okay, I should go now." He took out his sunglasses from his shirt pocket and put them on. "Good luck with the surgery tomorrow."

She held out her hand, and they shook hands. "I appreciate

everything you've done for me. This is what I've always wanted —to be with my father."

"I'm glad everything worked out." He scanned his surroundings, his eyes resting on the little guest house right in the backyard, where Monica had moved in. She belonged here, not in New York cleaning hotel rooms or in New Jersey waiting in an empty apartment for a married lover. She didn't deserve to hide like a subway rat or, well, like an illegal alien. She'd found her family. A destiny gone awry had been corrected. She was a desperate hopeful no more.

He turned on his heel. "Tell your dad and stepmother I came by."

"I will."

To his surprise, she walked beside him across the lawn.

"Say thanks to Rosie for me," he added. "She's always feeding me when I come here."

"She's great, isn't she? Rosie takes care of me like she's my fairy godmother." Monica smiled. "She would have wanted to say goodbye to you, but she's off delivering cigars in Dublin."

Cigars...cigars? He stopped dead on his tracks. "Come again?"

She halted, too, giving him a puzzled squint. "What?"

"Where's Rosie?"

"She's delivering cigars in Dublin."

"Delivering to whom?" A tingle down his spine signaled his sixth sense going off.

"I don't know. She didn't say."

The image of Cutter fidgeting with a seven-inch cigar back in 1998 swept over him like a wave. They'd met at a diner where smoking was forbidden. Cutter had fancied himself a gentleman, and the cigar was his proof. "Great men smoke great cigars," he'd declared. "Winston Churchill...Douglas MacArthur...hell, even Fidel Castro."

"Don't forget George Burns," Domingo had responded, which made both of them laugh.

"What's going on?" Monica's face clouded with befuddlement.

"Nothing." Domingo shifted in place. "Did you mean Dublin, Ohio?"

"I guess. Rosie didn't look like she was traveling to Dublin, *Ireland*." She chuckled. "Not in her old sweat pants and flip-flops."

"Gotcha, Cutter," he muttered. "All right. Bye." He high-tailed it toward the wrought iron gate and out of there. No time to explain that the cigar was for Cutter. He couldn't afford to waste another minute. He needed to find out the motive behind the bastard's lies.

14

July 2008

Domingo had been waiting all night long for Cutter in the hotel parking lot. At three o'clock in the morning, the sky was pink like the face of a blushing girl, the opposite of the washed-out-looking woman with Cutter. She wore a purple tube top and fake-leather miniskirt.

Chewie draped his right arm around her shoulders as they staggered across the parking lot. The woman, tottering in red stilettos, struggled to keep the drunk bastard from falling. The sight of a whore babysitting Cutter was pitiful.

Domingo tucked the Glock in his waistband before getting out of the car. He strode toward the couple. "Yo, Cutter! Let me help you, buddy."

"Sundaaay! What the fuck are you doing here?"

Domingo acknowledged the woman with a nod. "I'm a friend. I've got this. You can go."

She slithered out of Cutter's arm. The veteran shifted and

leaned heavily on Domingo's shoulder. Up close, the woman seemed too old to be a prostitute, or maybe the cheap makeup had given her premature wrinkles.

She handed Cutter's car keys to Domingo. "I've got no ride. I need cash for a cab."

Domingo groped Cutter's trouser pocket, finding crumpled twenties and fives. "This should be more than enough."

"Hey, she's been paid," Cutter protested. "I gave her plenty already."

The woman loped away with the money.

"Bitch," Cutter murmured.

"Come on, man. You're pathetic." Domingo dragged Cutter inside the hotel. The man reeked of whiskey and cigar plus weed.

Domingo panted as they waited for the elevator. His sweat soaked his armpits from pulling and propping up Cutter. He could bench-press 225 pounds, no problem. He should be able to powerlift the old dude. He was used to loading and unloading hundred-pound sacks of rice or sugar as a stevedore. Back in Manila, he'd never heard of bench press or bodybuilding, never stepped inside a gym, but he'd always been health conscious.

When the elevator door opened, he draped his arm around Cutter's waist to steady him as they both swayed and staggered to his room. As soon as Domingo opened the door, he lifted the old man in a fireman's carry, lugging him over his right shoulder like an oversize sack of rice. He dropped the son of a bitch on the king-size bed.

"This is nice." Cutter smiled as he kicked off his shoes. "How'd you find me, Sunday?"

"I checked every hotel in Dublin." Truth was, he'd called Rosie, but he didn't want to get her in trouble. He swiped the sweat off his forehead with his sleeve. The Reeds had chosen a classy suite for their lapdog, complete with a kitchen and a whirlpool jet tub. "What are you doing in Ohio, huh? You've been lying to me all along."

Cutter moaned and closed his eyes.

"Hey, man!" The asshole snored like a freight train. "Goddamn it, Cutter." No choice but to carry him to the bathroom. He plopped the man in the bathtub and turned on the cold shower full blast.

Cutter screamed.

Domingo shut off the shower. "You awake now?"

"You're a prick." Chewie tried to sit up, gripping the sides of the tub, but slid. Tried once more, slid again. "Fuck it. I'll sleep right here." He slouched lower.

"What are you doing in Ohio?"

Cutter shook the water off his bald head, rubbed his eyes. "None of your fucking business."

Domingo turned on the water again, sending Cutter into a flopping frenzy. He cussed till he was out of breath. Although fully clothed, he shivered, teeth chattering.

Domingo shut off the shower and grabbed him by the shirt collar. "I know about Max Gray and Savannah Sorinski. They're working for you. I want to know the rest of the story."

To Domingo's surprise, Cutter yawned, his eyelids heavy. The motherfucker was about to doze off again. He banged Cutter's torso against the side of the tub, eliciting a cry. He punched him in the gut for good measure.

Cutter doubled up in pain.

Domingo's face grew slick with adrenaline. He grabbed Cutter by the shoulders. "What are you and the general up to? Are you going to tell me or shall I make you?"

Cutter's face was scrunched up. He swallowed hard before speaking. "The wheels have been greased. They're in motion as we speak. You're too late, boy. You can go ahead and kill me, but you're too fucking late. As you know, I was out all night celebrating. There's nothing left for me—or for you—to do. It's a

done deal. What do you really care? You got paid pretty well...
unless you're infatuated with Reed's bastard. Is that it? You
want to fuck the daughter of a whore?"

Domingo released Cutter with a thud. He lifted his right
foot and slammed it down on Cutter's stomach. The man
howled in pain and erupted with a gush of vomit. In an instant,
the bathroom had ripened with a sour stench.

Domingo glanced at his wristwatch: 3:50. Soon more people
in the hotel would be up. Beating up Cutter some more would
have been akin to grandpa abuse. What mattered was he knew
where to find Max Gray.

Enough with this shit. He pulled the Glock from his waistband and brought it down hard on Cutter's head.

Chewie crumpled with a grunt.

Domingo waited a moment, but Cutter remained still. A
pistol-whip executed properly never failed to silence one's
enemy.

15

THE PRESENT

Paths to US Citizenship: By Birth or Through Parents
There are only a few roads toward American citizenship. Imagine a map with only a handful of ways to get to your destination safely. Outside of these routes, anything goes.

Number one: US citizenship by birth. This is like riding a sleek, chauffeured limo to the prom. You only get to ride this limo if you were born in a nice hospital somewhere in a quiet suburb of Maine or Wisconsin, or even in a midwife's mobile clinic in a ghost town or a shitty hospital in an inner city, as long as it's in the great US of A. This is the fastest and easiest road to American citizenship. It's handed to you by God, decided by fate, and completely out of your control. Be grateful; you're the lucky one.

Number two: citizenship through acquisition. Remember when Angelina Jolie gave birth in Namibia? I don't know why the hell she chose to do it, but her daughter, Shiloh, became an American through acquisition. Both of her parents, the once golden couple known as

Brangelina, are US citizens, therefore, Shiloh is a citizen, too. In this case, she still gets to ride the sleek limo even after Brangelina hit splitsville. In short, this road isn't too shabby either.

DOMINGO DIDN'T FINISH WRITING this chapter because his plane had already landed in Chicago. Time to lock and load. Three days after he'd confronted Christian Price at the Plaza, Domingo had hit a dead end. He couldn't continue wasting time while Monica remained missing. Yes, he now thought of the Ghost as missing, though he didn't have the heart to tell Mary Reed. Instead, he'd booked a flight to Chicago to focus on Cutter.

Traveling without luggage meant a fast escape from the chaos in O'Hare International Airport, followed by a pickup of a rental car. He drove straight to the VA clinic where Cutter went for physical therapy once a month. Domingo had found this out from Cutter himself. He'd called the old dude to inform him of Christian Price's vehement denial of foul play, which made Chewie even more suspicious of Monica's lover.

During the course of their fifteen-minute phone conversation, Chewie had babbled about his bad leg and hip and how his old injuries continued to hurt. He'd also mentioned a forthcoming appointment with a physical therapist. "Every month, I go to this wet-behind-the- ears Chinaman at the VA hospital in North Chicago. Not that he's been able to cure my pain despite his fancy college degree," he'd whined.

"Nobody uses the word Chinaman anymore. In case you haven't heard, the California Gold Rush is over," Domingo had countered.

"Fuck you and the Chinaman both."

Although Cutter had said it with a chuckle, his bigotry hadn't been a joke. Domingo's suppressed outrage had inspired the idea of flying to Chicago to dig deeper into the man's motivations. He was a suspect as much as Mr. GQ. Also, Domingo knew exactly where to find Chewie in a few days—in the Chinaman's clinic at the only VA medical center in North Chicago.

In the middle of the afternoon, the hospital teemed with shuffling old-timers and younger amputees. They exuded an air of defeat, these broken military veterans. He followed the arrow pointing toward the sign: *Dr. Matthew Chu, Physical Medicine and Rehabilitation*. He'd timed the visit so Cutter would already be inside.

A current of excitement ran through his spine as he entered Dr. Chu's clinic. An ambush like this never failed to electrify him.

No Cutter in the waiting room. He couldn't risk coming here for naught, so he waved at the receptionist to catch her attention. "Hi. I'm picking up Mr. Charles Cutter. Do you know how much longer he would be in here?"

The woman appraised him. "And...who are you?"

"I'm with VTS." Veteran Transportation Services. Cutter wouldn't need the free ride for poor old vets who required assistance to and from the VA hospital, but it made for a good alibi.

The receptionist nodded. "Give it another fifteen or twenty minutes."

"Thanks." A bail enforcement agent worth his salt always came prepared with little facts and lots of lies.

He stepped outside for a quick reconnaissance. Since this was the fifth floor, Cutter would need to take the elevator located at the end of the hallway. Meanwhile, the exit door leading to the staircase beckoned about twenty feet away. Excellent.

After a two-hour flight from New York to Chicago, he

needed a pit stop. Six minutes later, he stood near the staircase and glanced at his wristwatch: 2:40 p.m.

The door to Dr. Chu's clinic swung open. A man with a cane emerged. Despite the summer heat outside, he wore a long-sleeved shirt and slacks. His navy-blue cap bore a red letter C in front. *Chicago Cubs.*

Just watching him inch by pained Domingo. The scenario reminded him of Mamang, who had complained about this sudden trip to Chicago since it meant Domingo would miss a visit to the nursing home. He ambled beside the old veteran. "May I help you, sir?"

The man smiled. "Much appreciated." He latched on to Domingo's right arm while he used the cane with the other hand. That accelerated his pace by fifty percent. Not fast enough for Domingo, who kept glancing back in case Cutter came out. The elevator bank seemed to be a mile away given the adrenaline pumping in his veins. He needed the element of surprise to confront Cutter.

"Sundaaay!" A man's voice startled him and the Cubs fan both into an abrupt stop. They looked back.

"Hey, Cutter!" Domingo replied. The prey catching the predator. *Shit, shit, shit.* He excused himself and turned around.

"What are you doing here? Playing Boy Scout?" Cutter bared his cigar-stained teeth when he smiled. He walked with a stiff gait toward Domingo. "Did you tell me you're coming here? Sorry if I forgot. I don't even remember what I ate for breakfast. Tell me you're here because of good news. You found Monica?" He stopped and groped his pockets, perhaps looking for his keys or cigarettes or cell phone.

Domingo strode fast. *Keep talking, Cutter.* In a split second, he drew the Glock from his waistband and stuck it against Cutter's side. "Play nice."

"What the fuck?" Cutter raised both arms in a gesture of surrender.

Domingo glanced at the Cubs fan, who watched them, his eyes bugged out.

"Arms down, Cutter." Domingo pressed the gun harder. "No grandstanding. Act normal."

Chewie nodded. Domingo smiled at the Cubs fan, as if pulling a gun was the most natural thing to do in a hospital hallway. He nudged Cutter toward the stairway, hiding the Glock from the view of the other old man.

Cutter waddled down the stairs, Domingo behind him.

"Stop right here." They'd reached a landing. No geriatric patients would climb down five stories to the lobby or vice versa, but the younger employees might. He would hear someone's footsteps from where they stood. Likewise, anyone pushing the door open above or below them would tip him off.

He shoved Cutter against the wall. "Don't make me use this, okay?" He tucked the Glock in his pants.

Cutter was taller, so he looked down at Domingo. Being short sucked, but especially at times like this. "I'm going to ask you a few questions, that's all," he assured Chewie.

"You flew here to ask questions?" Contempt was written all over Cutter's face.

"I want to look you in the eye, that's why."

Cutter glared. "Ask away."

A sense of déjà vu filled Domingo. It was 2008 all over again. Different time, different place, same purpose, same exercise of roughing up the old dude to make him 'fess up. He hated having to do things over and over. "I know about your lawyer, Gus Patterson," he continued. "What are you negotiating with Mary Reed?"

Cutter smirked. "That's your question? Bounty hunters are not famous for their brains, but you've gotta be so stupid to come here just for that."

Domingo kicked him hard in his bad leg.

Cutter crashed onto all fours. "You motherfucker."

Another solid kick, this time in the ribs, making Chewie double up. Domingo's heart banged. He took a deep breath of the cold air from the AC vent and puffed up his chest to calm himself down. "Say something nice."

"Fuck you, Sunday." Cutter sat up with great effort and rested his back against the wall. "You're wasting your time coming here when you should be following Christian Price. The cocksucker is the only man who has the motive to get rid of Monica."

"*You* have a motive, too." Domingo planted his hands on his hips. "If Monica disappears somehow, and Mary Reed dies tomorrow, you're bound to inherit her money. Is that what Gus Patterson is negotiating on your behalf?"

Cutter stretched both of his legs. "No matter what happens to Monica, *I'm* getting the money I deserve. That's what my lawyer is negotiating, you imbecile."

Domingo lifted his right foot, ready for another blow.

"Stop!" Cutter cringed. "Do you want answers or what?"

That was better. He squatted to bring his face closer to Cutter's. "What exactly do you want from Mary? You almost destroyed her marriage. Why on earth would she want to give you more money?"

Cutter clenched his teeth. "Mary Reed owes me at least a million dollars. That's the price of her husband's betrayal, or I will ruin Leonard Reed's reputation and legacy. I will spill the beans about his illegal immigrant bastard."

"What betrayal? You're the one who betrayed Mary's trust when you paired her husband with a poor Filipino woman, which resulted in an illegitimate child. *You* are the reason Leonard Reed had a bastard daughter."

"You know nothing about nothing." He rubbed his shiny head as though trying to erase a bad memory. He sighed. "Mary Reed owes me money because her beloved husband blocked my promotion. Forty years ago, I could have been a respectable instructor at the Air Force Academy. Guess who was the commandant at the time? Can you guess who rejected me?"

Leonard Reed. After he'd returned a Vietnam War hero, he was appointed as head of the academy, followed by a gig as director of the Joint Chiefs of Staff. His star had risen as steady as one of those F-105s and F-4s he used to fly, reaching the pinnacle when he became a four-star general and the Air Force Chief of Staff.

Domingo clucked his tongue. "If the general blocked your promotion forty years ago, why didn't you make him pay *forty* years ago? Let me guess. You just found this out recently?"

Chewie nodded. "I requested my file from the National Personnel Records Center for a loan I'm trying to get. Imagine my surprise to see my old application to the academy with a rejection stamp and the signature of the son of a bitch...the snake who claimed to be my friend." He took a deep, ragged breath, his eyes on fire. "I did everything for Leonard Reed but wipe his ass. Hell, I would've wiped his ass, if only he'd asked. I was his most loyal friend."

"I'm guessing he never really considered you a friend. He was a rock star and you were just a fan and an errand boy. You weren't good enough."

Cutter lunged at Domingo, head down, but he moved quicker. He blocked his enemy's skull with both hands. He shoved Cutter back hard and slapped his face. He jumped up, restraining himself from injuring the man further. "General Reed was out of your league, Cutter. He was the son of a triple Ace. Your father was a hillbilly mechanic, for crying out loud. Leonard Reed was a fighter pilot, a tactical aviator, with two hundred successful combat missions." He let out a low whistle. "The general flew an F-4. You flew a Flying Boxcar. See what I'm saying? You were the dog shit stuck on the sole of Leonard Reed's shoes. You were never his friend."

Instead of inflaming Cutter's anger, Domingo's mockery

seemed to have exhausted the poor old man. He slouched lower and closed his eyes. His chest rose and fell with his breathing.

When he opened his eyes, he flashed a stupid grin. "Well, yeah, but the general is dead, isn't he? What good were his pedigree and his medals and his money when he had a malfunctioning heart and kidneys? He's six feet under like a fucking buffet for the worms, but I'm still here. And I'm going to make his widow pay me a million dollars, and there's nothing he can do about it. So, fuck you, Sunday."

The door on the floor above creaked open. The voices of women echoed.

Domingo extended his hand. "Get up, Cutter. We're through here."

The scowl glued on the man's face deepened, as if he wanted to bite off Domingo's nose.

"Come on, you don't want the ladies to see you like a pathetic invalid. Save whatever dignity you have left."

Invoking Cutter's vanity and machismo worked. A reprieve from a possible charge of assault and elder abuse. The old dude gripped Domingo's hand and sprang up. When the two women came down the landing, both men said hello. The women wore scrubs and carried clipboards.

"Lovely earrings. They complement your eyes." Cutter admired the shorter of the two women. "What kind of stone is it?"

She flashed a shy smile. "It's agate."

Cutter tipped an imaginary hat. "Have a great day, ladies."

After the door leading to the hallway shut behind the women, Domingo motioned for Cutter to follow him. "Come on, I'll buy you coffee. Let's take the elevator before your legs crumble like peanut brittle."

"Fuck you."

"Yeah, yeah...I'll cut you some slack this time." Domingo

opened the door for him. "I hope you get your money. I really do. Mary has more than enough to give away, and you waited on the general hand and foot when he was alive."

"Damn right, I did."

Cutter shuffled through the door, and Domingo followed suit. He offered his arm for support, which Cutter took begrudgingly, and they walked toward the elevators. They were now one floor below where they'd started. The corridor seemed longer, the elevator bank farther, as they inched forward.

"Jesus, my leg is killing me." Cutter was panting. He held on to Domingo with both hands. "If you hit me again, I'll get you arrested. I'll sue the hell out of you."

Domingo smirked. "And if you say *Chinaman* or any racist word to my face again, I'll break your leg. If I find out that you hurt Monica Reed, I'll hunt you down and kill you."

The old dude grunted, but said nothing more.

Now they were on the same page. Still, Cutter remained on his list of suspects. This trip was just a crumb on a long trail of bits and pieces. No clear path just yet. No sure destination. He must retrace his steps back to Christian Price.

16

July 2008

Cutter talked the talk, but usually didn't walk the walk. His talent lay in finding the right people to do the walking for him. Domingo realized beating up Cutter accomplished little. The key was to find the person who would do the dirty work, either Max Gray or Savannah Sorinski, or both.

At five in the morning, nobody was up and about yet at Max Gray's apartment complex. Domingo rapped on Max's door. The lock clanked, and a bleary-eyed Max peeked out the door. Domingo flashed his fake badge and pushed the door. Within seconds, he'd handcuffed both of Max's hands behind his back. Like magic.

"Who are you?" Max screamed in a voice too shrill for a guy. "What have I done?"

"I'm a bail enforcement agent."

"A what?"

"A bounty hunter." He hated it, but no point in dwelling on semantics. He pressed the Glock to the side of Max's head.

"Okay, take it easy, man."

"On your knees."

Max complied. He wore only boxer shorts. Goose flesh covered his bare back.

"I know you're working for Cutter—you and Savannah Sorinski." Domingo walked around to face Max.

Max's head jerked up, his gaze piercing Domingo's eyes. Perhaps he was flipping over the Rolodex of his memories and wondering whether he'd met him before.

"I want to know what you're doing for Cutter. I've got Cutter in custody, so don't lie to me. I can easily corroborate it."

"Why don't you ask *him*?"

Good point, but wrong answer. Domingo smacked his wiseass face, knocking him down. He was so skinny, a puff of breath could have blown him away. Domingo propped him back up. "On your knees. Let's try this one more time. What did Cutter pay you to do?"

Max bit his lower lip. Not a peep. Another slap across the face landed him back on the floor. Domingo pushed the muzzle of the gun against his temple. "Can you feel that?"

"Okay, okay!"

Domingo pulled him up to a kneeling position. "Start talking." He cocked the gun and pressed it against Max's temple again.

"I...my job is...I'm a lab tech at Lawrence Memorial." The dude's voice was shaky.

"And?"

"And what?" Max was panting. No, hyperventilating. He reeked of sweat, drool, and panic.

Domingo shook his head in a rush of guilt. First, he'd beaten up an old man, now a fucking child. Why couldn't people just answer his damn questions? "I'd rather not hurt you, so spill the beans already. What does Cutter need from you?"

"I work at the—" He gasped for air. "At the microbiology and immunology lab."

Shit, the dude was close to swooning. Domingo tucked the revolver in his jacket pocket and unlocked the handcuffs.

Max hunched forward, as though bowing before Domingo. "Now, talk. If you make a move, I will fucking shoot you. So, you're a lab tech. What does Cutter want from you?"

"Cutter asked me to give Savannah a culture from someone infected with staph." Max's eyes grew teary.

Domingo stood over him, hands on his hips. "When are you supposed to give it to Savannah?"

"This morning. For General Reed's kidney transplant."

"A staph culture? For General Reed? You're not making any sense. You better start making sense or else." He withdrew the gun.

Max recoiled and covered his head with both hands. "Okay! The culture is not for General Reed. It's for his daughter, the one who's donating a kidney."

"What?"

"Staph infection is quite common after a surgery. Thousands of hospital patients with surgical wounds get infected with staph or other germs. Everyone who works in a hospital knows there's no such thing as a sterile room. So, if the general's daughter is infected...you know, nobody would question it."

"But why would the general want his own daughter infected?"

"What?" Max's eyes bugged out, his arms falling to his sides.

"Why the fuck would General Reed want his own daughter infected?"

"She's a bastard, isn't she? A bastard and a prostitute."

Domingo whacked his face with the back of his hand, sending Max down on all fours. "First, she's not a prostitute.

Second, yes, she's the general's illegitimate daughter, but she happens to be his only child." He squatted and repositioned the gun's mouth at the side of Max's head. "So tell me, why would the general want his daughter infected?"

Max shut his eyes. His breathing had grown jagged. "Because he needs a heart."

"Wrong. He needs a kidney." He'd grabbed the lab tech by the hair. "If you don't start making sense in about five seconds, I'll shoot you."

"He needs a kidney, yes. But also a heart."

"What?"

Max opened his eyes, tears flowing, snot bubbling. "The general needs a kidney *and* a heart. Savannah is going to assist in the daughter's operation. Instead of treating her with antibiotics to prevent staph infection, she'll give her staph bacteria. The daughter agreed to donate her body organs, so when she dies, her heart would go to her father. He's at the top of the waiting list for a donor heart."

"Tell me—" Domingo prodded Max's head with the gun. "Exactly how Monica is supposed to die from an infection." A surge of fury tore through him. He'd always known Leonard Reed was greedy, but to steal his own daughter's heart in the literal sense? Evil knew no bounds. It thrived if left unchecked, but he would squash it even if it killed him.

"All right, all right." Max clamped his eyes shut again. "After the surgery, she'll feel weak, but that's normal. Nobody will think of testing her for staph because her chart will show that she was treated with antibiotics pre-surgery. Every hour she doesn't get tested for staph, sepsis will get worse. Her organs will shut down in two days tops. They key is to prevent Monica from getting tested within the first twenty-four hours of infection. The surgery was timed so Savannah will be Monica's nurse the whole time and she can stop the testing until it's too late."

Domingo flung Max across the floor. "What the fuck is wrong with you?"

Max sat up and wiped his tears with his hand. "Savannah talked me into it. I need the money."

Domingo grabbed Max's arms and replaced the handcuffs on his hands.

"What are you doing? I told you everything."

"That's right." Domingo fished a handkerchief from his pants' pocket and tied it around Max's mouth. "And now I want you to shut up."

He glanced at his wristwatch. Five thirty already. "I will simply keep you here. If you don't show up at the hospital, then no one can give Savannah the staph culture. The general's kidney transplant will take place, but his daughter won't get infected. Problem solved."

Max made muffled noises. In resisting, he'd stumbled into a prone position, his legs flailing. Domingo ignored him. Instead, he rummaged in the drawers in the small kitchen, where he found a roll of duct tape. He tied Max's legs with the tape, but it didn't stop him from grunting and moaning through the gag.

Domingo kicked him in the stomach. "Shut the fuck up."

Max curled into a fetal position. He sobbed quietly.

Domingo sighed. "Now, if you don't mind, I'm going to make coffee. This is going to be a long morning."

In the kitchen, he found a small coffee maker, a box of coffee filters, and a half-full container of Maxwell House Original Roast. "Max Gray drinks Maxwell. How about that?" He smiled as he made coffee. Thank goodness he'd arrived in time to stop the lab technician from going to work. Monica would donate one of her kidneys, but she'd be all right. Her monster of a father would have to find a replacement heart somewhere else. Nobody would die today, not on Domingo's watch.

From the periphery of his vision, Max lay still like a sack of flour. If the dude had fallen asleep, so much the better. All he wanted was to let the kidney transplant take place safely before letting Max loose.

Domingo poured a cup of coffee and perched on a stool. He sniffed it before taking a sip. After a while, he turned toward Max. "Hey, you want some coffee?" His guilt had crept up again. Max was an unwitting conspirator. Leonard Reed was the mastermind and Cutter the henchman. Savannah was Cutter's right hand.

"You want coffee?" he repeated. "Just nod if you want a cup. I'll remove your gag for a little bit." Where Max lay, the carpet appeared dark. Wet? *Fuck.* "Did you piss in your pants? Oh, Christ." He jumped up and freed Max—gag, handcuffs, and duct tape all undone.

Max rubbed his wrists. "I was trying to tell you."

Domingo pointed to the bathroom. "Go. Take a shower. You stink."

The dude dashed inside. Domingo returned to the kitchen and gulped his coffee. Then he stood guard outside the bathroom. As soon as the shower stopped, he banged on the door. "That's enough. Come out now."

Max's hair dripped. Despite the thick bathrobe wrapped around him, he was shivering. Domingo handcuffed him again.

Max stomped like an overgrown boy. "Why do you have to do this? I don't even know who you are. Who gave you the authority to do this?"

"*This* is all the authority I need." Domingo brandished his Glock 19. "I'm keeping you here until the kidney transplant is over. You should thank me for preventing you from becoming a murderer."

Max scowled. "It's useless. If I don't show up at the hospital at seven thirty, someone else will give the culture to Savannah. Everything will proceed as planned."

Domingo placed his right palm on Max's chest heavily,

pushing him against the wall. "Why the fuck didn't you tell me?"

"Man, I tried so hard to tell you that I fucking pissed my pants."

Domingo pinned Max against the wall as he racked his brain about his next move. Max shut his eyes.

"Open your eyes." Domingo breathed down his neck. "Who's your replacement at the hospital?"

"Do you really think Savannah would tell me?"

"How do you even know she would replace you?"

"She sensed that I was getting scared. She told me if I screw up and not show, I won't get any money at all. I won't get paid even for the hours I've already put in...all those stupid meetings with her and Cutter. She said she found a backup."

"And you believe her?"

"I know the bitch. Yeah, I believe her."

They stared daggers at each other: a stalemate. The putrid odor of urine from the living room forced Domingo to act. He couldn't stay a minute longer in the pigsty, not a second more to waste while Monica faced the possibility of death.

He shoved Max toward the bedroom. "Put on your scrubs!" He glanced at his wristwatch. "You have ten minutes to do it. We're going to the hospital to kick Savannah's ass."

17

THE PRESENT

P aths to US Citizenship: Seeking Asylum
Let's talk about applications for asylum, the third path
to American citizenship. Unlike the other two we've
discussed, this road has multiple entry points. People caught in a civil
war in countries like Sudan or Syria, or anarchy in places like Soma-
lia, can apply for political asylum in America. Afghans or Iraqis who
helped the US military in their countries can apply for the same
thing.

They are refugees. Some people spit after they utter the word like
it's dirty. Those people are morons. They don't know what refugees
have contributed to this country. The next time some redneck tells
you there's no room for refugees in America, be sure to name-drop the
rock star of all refugees—Albert Einstein. Yes, the genius of the wild-
white-hair look and the theory-of-relativity fame. The dude was a
German Jewish physicist persecuted by the Nazis. He immigrated to
the United States in 1933 and became a naturalized citizen in 1940.

That will shut up any nasty, racist bastard who's obviously no Einstein.

DOMINGO WORKED on his manuscript before heading to Manhattan. Christian Price worked out at the gym twice a week and jogged in the Riverside Park on weekends. That was back in 2008 when Domingo had stalked him and Monica both. Did Mr. GQ stick to the same fitness routine today? Only one way to find out.

Well, old habits indeed died hard. This Saturday morning, Domingo trailed Christian as the dude alternately ran and jogged along Riverside Drive. Christian wore jogging pants and a T-shirt, while Domingo himself wore running shorts or he'd be soaked in sweat by the time he was done.

Yesterday, Domingo had also tailed Christian to the gym, then downtown where he'd met with clients. In the evening, the Price family had dined out in a Japanese restaurant. Nothing unusual. Today, the family would be out and about during the day while the real estate agent showed their apartment to potential buyers. Domingo knew because Inday had called the realtor and feigned interest in the apartment.

Christian typically jogged early, but today he'd emerged from his apartment building at almost nine thirty in the morning. The wife and kiddos had taken a cab to who knew where.

Mr. GQ slowed down to a trot. Domingo stayed behind other joggers and walkers with strollers and dogs on leashes. He wondered if he'd see anything useful today. Most of the time, surveillance yielded little, especially the type of information Domingo sought. If Christian had killed Monica, would he return to the crime scene? How likely was it for the dude to incriminate himself?

And yet, Domingo must keep close tabs on Christian.

Perhaps nothing would happen today, but maybe tomorrow or the day after. No way to guess when a perpetrator would make a mistake and reveal a secret. Hence, snooping could last for days or weeks. Only a client's inability to pay could end it. At the very least, Domingo got to work out this morning while also getting paid by Mary Reed. He couldn't complain.

Right around Eighty-Ninth Street, the circular top of the Soldiers' and Sailors' Monument loomed above the trees. A white temple-like structure made of marble and granite. A couple of tourists were taking pictures.

Christian glanced at his wristwatch and strode at a brisk pace toward the monument. Why? Perhaps he wanted to catch his breath.

Mr. GQ stopped at a bench. He looked around. Domingo ducked behind a tree. The dude paced back and forth like he was waiting for someone. He paused, his gaze trained on a woman from about thirty feet away. She wore jeans, a white blouse, and huge sunglasses. It wasn't Monica Reed. A new paramour? The philandering bastard not only had one mistress, but apparently *two* mistresses.

Christian ambled toward the woman, meeting her halfway. Dark-haired, slim, about five four. Asian. *Tess Chua? What the fuck?*

Christian and Tess strolled toward a bench. They chatted, but no display of affection. Not a peck on the cheek, no holding hands. They both sat on a bench facing the monument so their backs were to Domingo. Tess seemed to be doing all the talking, while Christian nodded once in a while.

A man pulling a flat dolly brimming with folding tables and chairs blocked Domingo's view for a moment. Women carrying big crates and boxes followed. More people with banners and balloons. Within minutes, a small crowd had descended on the area. Geez, where did they come from? People were setting up tables in front of the monument. A couple of women unfolded a banner and hung it from a low branch of a tree nearby. *MOMMYPALOOZA! Arts & Crafts. Games. Free Lemonade & Cookies. Come Join Us!!!*

Some kind of a fair for mothers and tots. The vicinity buzzed with energy. Tess and Christian got up, still chatting. They could have fooled Domingo into thinking this was a casual tête-à-tête. They shook hands. What had they talked about? Only five days ago, Tess had refused to even utter Christian's name. *"I don't wanna hear about that man."*

The two drifted away from the crowd. They paused for a moment, then Tess bustled out of the park toward Riverside Drive. Christian resumed a slow jog.

A slight thrill sparked inside Domingo. Should he follow Tess or Christian? Moments like this, a bail enforcement agent must think on his feet. The body language of the two told him they were not lovers. Who possessed a greater motive to get rid of Monica? The best friend and compatriot? Or the married lover?

Domingo glided into a run after Christian. The sun was high now. A warm breeze coming from the Hudson River across Riverside Drive rustled the trees. More people coming and going. A young woman in shorts and a bikini top, teenagers on skates, old women with small dogs.

A crowd like this could be a deterrent, but, this time, it might just work in Domingo's favor. When he got closer to Christian, he faked a stumble. They bumped and fell together, walkers and joggers parting for them. They rolled onto the grass, Christian face down and Domingo on top of him.

"What the hell?" Christian exclaimed. He couldn't see who or what had hit him.

Domingo straddled him and pinned down both of his arms. "What did you talk about with Tess Chua? I'm pretty sure it has something to do with Monica."

"What the fuck, Sunday?" Christian croaked. "This is harassment."

"This is *nothing* compared to what I'm capable of doing to you." Domingo wrapped an arm around Mr. GQ's neck in a chokehold. A few people tossed them an irritated glance. Two guys roughhousing. "Are you gonna tell me? Or shall I make you?" he whispered in Christian's ear.

An old couple exchanged glances and smiled. Did they think Domingo and Christian were gay lovers fooling around? Like hell.

"All right, all right," squealed Christian.

Domingo released him and sat on the grass. "What did Tess want from you? Where's Monica?"

Christian coughed, still lying on his belly. "The next time you touch me, I will press charges." At last, he sat up. His face had turned red, his hair tousled.

Instead of looking like a spineless ninny who had been subdued with a single hit, Mr. GQ seemed even cooler in an insolent way. Women passing by eyed him. The dude's good looks grated on Domingo's nerves.

"Go ahead and report me to the cops—I *will* tell Emmy Price that you're looking for Monica because...*I care about Monica very much.*" Domingo mimicked Christian in a theatrical manner, complete with hand gestures, to remind him of their conversation five days ago.

Mr. GQ scowled. "What do you want?"

Christian's polite upbringing prevented him from throwing a punch or making a scene in a public place. Domingo was right to confront him here. "What's your business with Monica's best friend?"

Christian let out a big sigh. "Tess told me she's been in touch with Monica."

"What?" Domingo straightened up.

"You're right. Monica's still here in the States. Even though I dropped her off at the airport and everything, she never went to Manila. She got off the plane during a stopover in San Francisco and just disappeared. I can't believe she lied to me." A small frown materialized on his face. He rubbed his neck. "Monica called Tess regularly, then the calls stopped. It's been two weeks since the last call. Tess is beginning to worry."

Thoughts swirled in Domingo's head. "Tess is worried, but you're not?"

Christian shook his head. "Monica's silence just means she no longer wants to be in touch. First, she cut ties with me. Now she's doing the same thing with Tess." He looked away toward the direction of the river across the street, his expression wistful or maybe resigned. After a moment, he turned his face back to Domingo. "I can't help you. You should talk to Tess." He got up and brushed a dry leaf off his pants. "I've given you all the information I have. That's it for me." He walked away without waiting for Domingo's response.

He rose and caught up with Christian. "I just want you to know I appreciate your help." The latest information had confirmed that Monica remained in the US. *Alive.* It changed Domingo's perspective, made him grateful, even.

"And I'd appreciate it if you'd stop harassing me." Christian resumed jogging.

Domingo did the same. "If I find Monica, you still want me to let you know?"

"Why do I feel like you're manipulating me?"

"Hey, I'm just trying to be nice."

"Well, *don't.*" Mr. GQ sprinted like a man running for his dear life.

Domingo didn't bother following him. He veered toward Riverside Drive and farther from the growing crowd at the monument. He rested under a tree to savor the view of the Hudson River, so vast he could pretend it was Manila Bay. White sailboats dotted the water.

Nineteen years had gone by since the last time he'd seen Manila, the bay or otherwise. His heart twitched. Overcome by a sudden sadness, his breath shortened in his throat. He hadn't meant to turn his back on his native country. He had neither the time nor the money for a trip halfway around the world. His entire time in America was spent earning a living and trying to belong.

He would find the Ghost, no matter what. She was a link to his past and a reminder of where they both came from. Yes, he could at least make himself useful to Mary Reed and bring home her stepdaughter. He gave the river a last glance before walking to the subway station.

18

THE PRESENT

Paths to US Citizenship: Joining the Military

Foreigners have been enlisting in the military to gain citizenship since the American Revolution. It used to be a fast track to US citizenship. Not anymore. In fact, there are no guarantees you'll become a citizen even after risking your neck in Afghanistan or Iraq.

It's never easy to hunt down an illegal military veteran for deportation because I believe those guys are true Americans by virtue of their sacrifices. A lot of them get deported for little mistakes. One dude lost his birth certificate required for the citizenship application. Another got caught in a brawl that led to an arrest. Some of them got nailed for drug possession or DUI. Not that I condone those things, but they don't justify erasing the path to citizenship. There's something very wrong about a society where OJ got away with murder and a poor veteran got deported for pot possession.

Over the years, I've escorted illegal vets to the southern border *because ICE couldn't be bothered to deport them. Those guys grew up in the States and have never been to Mexico before. It broke my heart to drop them off like trash on garbage day. They were willing to do what most of us have no guts to do—kill and die for the great US of A. They got injured or captured or tortured. They all came home damaged. Then they got deported.*

When I deport a veteran, I apologize. It's the only time I apologize for my job. I tell them I'm sorry this country is blind. Why else would it kick out people who have proven their love and loyalty by losing their limbs and risking their lives? Why banish Americans from their country?

DOMINGO FOLLOWED Tess Chua to church Sunday morning. She'd taken the subway to St. Patrick's Cathedral in Midtown Manhattan, except she didn't go inside. She crossed Fifth Avenue and joined the crowd outside Rockefeller Center.

Dreamers Not Criminals! Build Bridges Not Walls! #Defend-DACA. The placards bloomed above the throng gathered at the famous Atlas statue. What on earth was Tess doing with a bunch of protesters?

Some dude thrust a flyer in his face. *Deferred Action for Childhood Arrivals.* DACA, as he knew it. That was the name of the program protecting about half a million young immigrants from deportation. They were called Dreamers. They came to this country illegally as children, through no fault of their own.

The flyer blamed a Republican White House for emboldening the bigots in this country. The administration wanted to kick out the Dreamers. It had banned travelers from certain Muslim countries and restricted the number of foreigners who received worker visas. It had begun building a wall outright to shut the southern border from migrants.

How fitting that the Dreamers protested underneath the

bronze Atlas statue carrying the world aloft. Even the Greek god, or giant, or whatever Atlas was, appeared to buckle from the sheer weight of this country's immigration problems.

A young woman was speaking without the benefit of a bull-horn, so Domingo couldn't follow it all. He stood across the street, watching Tess, while blending in with gawking tourists. At nine in the morning, the sun blazed and the air hung heavy. The DACA supporters high-fived each other and sipped their coffees. Some talked to passersby. If not for the signs and the flyers, Domingo could have mistaken this bunch for just another group tour in New York City.

A few things nagged at him. Why were the DACA activists demonstrating *here*? Why now? Most of all, what was Tess doing protesting? She was legal, thanks to her American-born Filipino husband. Her two teenaged sons were US citizens. A house in a decent neighborhood in Queens. A steady, comfy job as manager of a small export business owned by her family. So, why would a middle-class, forty-something woman with no apparent connection to the Dreamers demonstrate on a Sunday morning?

Tess mingled with a group of women below the massive Atlas. She wore a cotton blouse, brown slacks, and flat shoes as opposed to the shorts and flip-flops worn by the protesters. Her eyeglasses had turned dark, those transition lenses that auto-matically adjusted in the sun. Tess and Monica's friendship went all the way back to Manila. Monica had dated Tess's cousin. The relationship had ended, but the two women's friendship lasted through their separate journeys to America.

Domingo took in the nervous energy in the air and racked his brain. Why was Tess protesting? And why on earth did the Dreamers choose this place at this time for their rally?

He could just ask the protesters why they were there, but it meant getting too close to Tess. He couldn't risk being spotted. The answer to his second question came in the form of a placard waved by a guy. *Fire Amaury Penn!* Someone else raised a sign. *Xenophobic Penn Must Go!*

Amaury Penn was the loudest voice of the right-wing, anti-immigrant forces in this country. Inday had described him as entertaining, the guy who made "mass deportation" the latest media buzzword. His live talk show, *The Bull Penn*, aired right about now in one of the studios in Rockefeller Center. No wonder the DACA people had chosen this place at this hour. That part of the puzzle was solved at least. Still, it didn't explain Tess's presence.

A police car slowed down, as though assessing the crowd. The protesters waved. The car left, eliciting applause and whistles.

Two muscular men emerged from Rockefeller Center. Domingo glanced at his watch. The talk show must have ended, and these must be Penn's bodyguards. Penn's bigotry had earned him many enemies and death threats.

"Fire Amaury Penn! Fire Amaury Penn!" the crowd chanted.

A black Lincoln Continental and a silver SUV pulled up. The glass doors of the building swung open and out came another big guy, followed by the talk show host himself in a blue sweat suit. Geez, how many hired thugs did he need? The man was famous for being paranoid. People joked about his multiple failed marriages. They said he changed wives before any of them could plot to kill him.

Amaury Penn was tall and sleek as a shark, like someone who took serious care of his body. He wore his full head of dark hair like a helmet. The inflated self-confidence came across as a distinct swagger.

Penn was whisked away by his entourage with military precision. The crowd grew louder with their placards, banners, and signs aloft. Tess slinked away. Domingo followed her.

She took the subway, but, to Domingo's surprise, she was

headed downtown instead of back home to Queens. What was she up to?

Tess hopped out of the R train on Canal Street. Domingo barely made it out before the train door closed as boisterous teenagers rushed on board.

He emerged from the subway platform and onto the street. He kept a comfortable distance from Tess. Tribeca buzzed with hipsters coming out of their apartments and old folks walking their dogs. The sweet smell of pastries, or maybe pancakes, bloomed around him as he passed by outdoor cafes.

He gazed up at the old factories and warehouses that had been converted into apartment buildings—a landscape of bricks, glass, and wrought iron. The area was no longer an industrial neighborhood, but home to expensive boutiques, art galleries, and restaurants. He would never be able to afford to live here.

Tess stopped outside a gym called Brisk. Domingo crossed the street so he could observe her from a distance. He'd heard of Brisk before because of its popular Instagram posts of its famous clientele—movie stars and fashion models.

Two familiar-looking guys rounded the corner and approached the gym. Amaury Penn's bodyguards. One was tall, big, and bearded, while the other was short and built like a John Deere tractor. Tess seemed to recognize them as well because she bolted for the gym's door. *Damn.* Was Tess stalking the TV host? Why?

The bodyguards lingered outside the building. The tall one was on the phone. What now?

The clammy summer air made Domingo itch, driving him to scratch his armpits. Walking helped him focus, so he strolled the length of the street, all the way to the sign pointing to the Holland Tunnel entrance where cars inched along, waiting to go through the tunnel.

From his vantage point, he had a clear view of Brisk's glass doors. The short John Deere-like bodyguard strode inside, while the other guy continued to jabber on the phone.

Domingo ambled down the sidewalk and paused across from the gym. Tourists wearing New York Yankees shirts and caps asked him where the Tribeca Sheraton Hotel was. He gave them the directions even as he kept his eyes on the bearded bodyguard.

The doors flew open. Penn's squat bodyguard emerged, dragging Tess by the arm. The Sasquatch stuck his phone in his pocket and jumped in front of Tess.

"Let go of me!" She snatched her arm away and staggered backward.

"Excuse me. Gotta go." Domingo brushed past the tourists and dashed across the street. A car honked at him.

"Tess! What's going on?" He stood between her and the two thugs.

Her eyes widened. "What are you doing here?"

Mr. John Deere looked Domingo up and down. They were eye to eye. "Get this woman out of here before we call the cops. She's harassing Mr. Penn."

"I just want to talk to him," yelled Tess. Her eyeglasses had slid down her nose. Her face shone with sweat.

Sasquatch stepped forward, like an overlord looking down on Tess and Domingo. "Mr. Penn doesn't want to be bothered. Leave. Now. Or else."

Domingo put his palm up. "It's all right. This is a misunderstanding. We're getting out of your hair." He attempted a smile, but the two guys just stood there stone-faced. Mercenaries were not famous for their charm. "Have a nice day, guys." He turned to Tess, whose mouth hung open, her fury soundless.

He touched her elbow. "Let's go. You don't want to be arrested for disorderly conduct."

"What do you think you're doing?" she said through her teeth. "This is none of your business."

"If you really want to talk to Penn, I'll help you make an appointment in his office during business hours." He grabbed her arm and led her away.

"Why are you here? Are you following me?" she asked.

"Yes, I am. And I just saved you." He didn't dare glance back at Penn's thugs. "Without me, you could be sitting in jail for at least fifteen days for disturbing the peace."

"What do you want from me? Let go of me!"

He tightened his grip on her. "I want you to stop lying. You *do* know where Monica is. Tell me where she is."

"Let go of me!" she repeated.

"First, answer me. Where's Monica?"

"Ask Amaury Penn. Why do you think I want to talk to him? You idiot."

"What?" He released her. They both paused on the sidewalk amid pedestrians scurrying around them. His heart pumped faster, his mind swirling. "What's Amaury's connection with Monica?"

"That's what I'm trying to find out. The last time I spoke to Monica, she wanted to see Amaury Penn. Out of the blue, he agreed to meet her. They were supposed to meet on August sixth. And now she's gone." She was panting. Her body seemed to vibrate with tension and fear, so strong that Domingo couldn't help but absorb the negative vibes.

"Okay, slow down." He stepped to the sidelines, under the trees that lined the street and away from pedestrians. "Is Monica here in New York?"

"No, she's in San Francisco."

No surprise there. Christian Price had revealed the information yesterday. "What's she doing in California?"

"Christian bought her a one-way ticket to Manila. The plane made a layover in San Francisco. Monica got away there."

"Okay, fine, but what is Monica's business with Penn? How

can she be talking to Penn in California when the guy is right here in New York?"

"If I tell you, will you help me find her?"

"It's my job to find Monica. Her stepmother is dying. I told you that last week."

"I don't care about Mary Reed. I'll tell you everything I know on one condition."

"What's that?"

She pressed her lips together, her expression tight. The woman looked like she would burst into tears at any moment. "Will you help me hide Monica?"

"Listen, Tess. She doesn't need to hide anymore. Like I told you before, her stepmother is giving her everything she's got, and we're talking loads of cash and assets. Monica is going to be very rich. She'll be able to hire the best lawyer in the world to get her US citizenship. Her father was American, after all."

"No. I'm not handing her over to Mary Reed." She resumed walking, almost bumping into a young couple's baby stroller.

"Tess." He caught up with her. "Will you listen to me, please?"

"No. If you can't accept my condition, then leave me alone." She hastened her pace.

"Okay, I agree," he called out. What choice did he have? He half jogged to keep up with her. "I will help you hide Monica and not tell Mary Reed about any of this." He would find a workaround, a compromise. Everyone wanted the best for Monica. That was more than enough ground for all of them.

She glanced at him sideways. Her eyes had grown steely. "I'll kill you if you betray my friend."

At that moment, he didn't doubt her ability to murder anyone. "You have my word."

"Okay, let's talk." She made a beeline for a coffee shop.

He stood there, watching her scuttle away and trying to process the new facts. *Amaury Penn.* The man had changed the entire paradigm of this search. Was he Monica's lover? If not, what could she have possibly wanted from him? What on earth was the connection between a bigoted zealot on the East Coast and an undocumented immigrant on the West Coast? The questions bombarded him, made him gasp for air out loud.

The chorus of honks from the street snapped him out of his thoughts. Some jaywalker almost got hit by a car and drew the ire of drivers.

He entered the café and joined Tess.

19

THE PRESENT

The triangular shape of the café meant there wasn't much space inside and the tables were smacked close to each other. Domingo wiggled in his seat, trying to get comfortable, as he read the menu. Nothing but fancy crepes, French toast, frittata, and more froufrou. Tess ordered avocado toast and iced coffee from a young waiter who used the word *super* to describe everything. *Super* hot outside. *Super* busy. *Super* delicious.

Domingo ordered the same as Tess, just to accelerate the process.

"That's a *super* choice. I'll be back in a jiffy," said the waiter, who looked too young to be working. He could have been thirteen or fourteen.

Domingo turned his attention to Tess. "Please start from the beginning. Did Monica mean to go back to Manila?"

"Yes, at first." She took a big gulp of water before continuing. "She was depressed about her mother's death and she wanted to go back home. But she changed her mind. She's been living here for nineteen years. This is her home now. She didn't tell Christian because she wanted a clean break from him. She wanted a fresh start in California."

"Why San Francisco?"

"Because it was the layover city for her flight. It helped that she knows a Filipina who knows another Filipina who needed workers in a nursing home in Hayward."

"Monica works in a nursing home?"

She nodded. "She's a caregiver. She feeds the old folks, cleans up after them...you know, helps them in any way they need help."

"What's Monica's connection with Amaury Penn? Why on earth would there be a connection between the two of them to begin with?"

She sighed and removed her eyeglasses. She used the cloth napkin to wipe the lenses. The coffee shop, packed to capacity, catered to people who could afford to waste ten dollars on avocado toast. No plastic silverware or paper napkins here. A pink fabric covered the table, complementing the red rose in a vase at the center.

Tess put her eyeglasses back on. "Monica said the residents at the nursing home liked Amaury Penn. His bullshit entertained them. She mentioned Penn almost immediately after she started working at the nursing home."

"When did she start working?"

"The day after she arrived in San Francisco."

"That fast?"

"Well, someone's got to change adult diapers and clean up after other people's vomit." A shrug accompanied her bitter tone.

He understood. Like him, she'd seen and heard enough about the plight of illegals, who took the filthiest, lowliest jobs nobody wanted. "Monica was on the way to self-deportation. How did she get the job?" he asked.

"The same way she's gotten all her previous jobs. Through other Filipinos."

"What I mean is, *who* gave Monica the job?"

Their order arrived. The kid served their food with an aggressive sort of enthusiasm, like someone trying too hard to please.

Domingo took a bite of his toast. "So, who's the person who hired Monica?"

To his surprise, Tess sliced her toast with fork and knife. Was that how other people ate toast?

"You want a name? Why?" she asked. "This person took a chance in hiring an undocumented immigrant. I don't want to get anyone in trouble."

"Come on, give me some credit. I'm not going to snitch."

"Sorry if I don't buy that. You're a bounty hunter who deports illegals." She forked a small piece of toast into her mouth. "I'm not comfortable naming names."

Now he got it. She used a fork to avoid making a mess of the mashed avocado atop the bread. He himself had green shit all over his fingers. He wiped his hand with the napkin. "I made a promise that I'll help you hide Monica. But first, I have to find her. It means I have to get my ass on a plane to San Francisco and talk to someone in that nursing home who can tell me everything about Monica's work there before she disappeared."

"Actually, the nursing home people don't think Monica has disappeared."

"What?"

"They think she quit, but I'm not convinced. She never told me she was going to leave the job, which she enjoyed. Besides, she can't afford to quit. Christian's no longer supporting her."

"Did the nursing home tell you when she allegedly quit?"

"August seventh. One day after her dinner date with Amaury."

"A dinner date?"

"Okay not a *date*, but just dinner."

He picked three packets of sugar from a bowl of condiments and dumped the sugar in his iced coffee. He stirred it with a teaspoon before taking a sip. "Let's go back to Amaury Penn. What's his business with Monica?"

"I'm not clear about it. First, Monica said she helped an old lady write a letter to Penn. You know, like fan mail? There might have been more than one old lady...yeah, maybe a couple of others, too. Then she said she helped them contact Penn. I'm assuming they wanted his picture or something. Later on, she was trying to meet him. I really didn't pay any attention to it. There were many such stories about the old people she cared for." She cut the tomato slices to smaller pieces before eating them. "Many of the residents suffer from dementia or Alzheimer's. An old guy showed Monica a leather watch, which was supposedly a gift from Elizabeth Taylor, whom he claimed to have dated. Seriously! Monica's stories didn't seem all that important. Frankly, I can't remember all of them. I was more worried about Monica getting back together with Christian."

"You said she wanted a clean break."

"Well, she also misses him. She's always tempted to call him. And I always play devil's advocate. I wanted her to leave Christian a long time ago. You know that already."

"Let's go back to Amaury Penn. How can he be in Hayward—?"

"Not Hayward, but San Francisco."

"Okay, but how can he live in San Francisco—?"

"He doesn't. His wife does. He commutes back and forth between coasts. Apparently, that's how rich people live."

He hated it when people wouldn't let him finish a sentence, but he was at her mercy for information. He ate the second piece of toast from his plate in two big bites, while rearranging the facts in his head. *A geriatric fan of Amaury Penn. Nothing wrong with that. But Monica having dinner with Penn out of the blue?* It made no sense.

He locked eyes with Tess. "Maybe Monica quit the nursing home and decided to cut off ties with you, just like she's left Christian. That's what he thinks, anyway."

"You talked to Christian?"

He nodded. "Yesterday. Right after you met him at the Soldiers' and Sailors' Monument." He'd wiped his plate clean, but his stomach still rumbled. This restaurant was one of those places that left him hungrier than before he'd eaten, making him crave a hamburger or something he could sink his teeth into.

Her face clouded over. "I don't appreciate you stalking me."

"I don't like doing it either, but you should have told me about Monica when I went to your office last week." He finished his coffee, chewing the ice cubes. "I'm going to need names and addresses." He took out his phone and searched for the notes app. "You have an address for Monica?"

"It's probably not current. She moves a lot. You know that about her, right?"

He nodded. Monica had learned her lesson the second time he found her, back when she stayed at the love nest she shared with Christian. After that, she never stayed in one apartment for longer than a few months. Extended-stay motels and boarding houses became her choice of residence. "Just give me what you have and I'll go from there."

She hit some buttons on her smartphone and read the address out loud.

He typed it on his phone. "Where does she work? What's the nursing home called?"

"Serenity Gardens Care Center."

"It sounds like a cemetery," he said. "Who hired Monica?"

Silence.

He glanced up from his phone. "I won't get this person in trouble, I promise."

"Luzviminda Hidalgo. She's in charge of hiring and training caregivers."

Luzviminda was a distinctly Filipino name, which coined the three major islands in the Philippines—Luzon, Visayas, and Mindanao. He typed the name. "Who's the old lady...or ladies who are fangirling over Penn?"

"Well, she took care of several old ladies. There's Sofia, Galina, Evelyn...I'm pretty sure there were others. Yeah, someone named Hope, too."

"Great. So the geriatric crowd thinks Amaury Penn is hot."

"Apparently." She sipped her coffee.

He motioned at their waiter to bring the check, which he did. Domingo paid cash. "I got this, okay? My treat." After the waiter left, he said, "Anything else you wanna tell me about your friend?"

She shook her head. "Can you keep to yourself everything that you saw here and at Rockefeller Center? Please don't tell my family about this."

He raised his right hand, as though swearing an oath inside a courtroom. "My lips are zipped tight." He gulped his glass of water. "What makes you think Monica is missing? Don't tell me about your hunch. I want something close to evidence, if you've got any."

"Monica calls me two or three times a week. Without fail. She promised to call me right after her dinner with Amaury Penn. She didn't and hasn't called since. That was two weeks ago. I've been calling her, but her phone seems dead. It's one of those cheap prepaid, no-contract phones."

"Give me the phone number. I'll track it down."

After she did, he punched the numbers on his phone. The

young waiter came back with Domingo's change. "Keep it, buddy."

"Super!"

The kid's voice was high-pitched, which made Domingo wonder again about his age and whether the Labor Department allowed boys this young to work.

"I'm afraid something terrible happened to Monica."

Tess's anxious voice swept Domingo back to the conversation. "You gotta relax. Two weeks is not a long time for a tough woman like Monica. Maybe she just needs some alone time." In fact, the first seventy-two hours were crucial in a missing-person case, if indeed Monica was missing. Two weeks would be a cold case, but because an illegal like Monica was adept at hiding, he hoped she wasn't missing.

Tess scowled. "Remember when she almost died at the hands of her own father?"

"How can I forget?" *I was dumb enough to be complicit without knowing it.*

"Her own father had no reservation getting rid of her because she's illegal." She fidgeted with her table napkin. "People in this country think undocumented immigrants are dispensable...no more valuable than this piece of cloth they use to wipe crumbs off their mouths. I mean, this cloth is too luxurious. Illegal immigrants are more like cheap paper napkins. Hell, they're more like bulk toilet paper for wiping asses."

She pushed away from the table abruptly. The poor woman was all worked up. He couldn't blame her, given the DACA demonstration and her manhandling by Amaury's thugs.

He got up as well. "Not everyone in this country hates immigrants, so don't let the few bigots get you down."

More people arrived, taking up every inch of space. Domingo and Tess walked sideways to avoid colliding with the others.

Out in the sun-soaked sidewalk, they paused and tried to

catch their breaths. And then it hit him—the boy waiter was no boy! He was not a kid, but a grown-up transgender man, perhaps still in transition. Hence, no facial hair, high-pitched voice, and the excessive enthusiasm like someone overcompensating for something beyond his control. He glanced back at the glass door, but the waiter was not in sight.

"Thanks for lunch." Tess extended her hand. "And for your concern about Monica."

Domingo shook her hand. "I'm going to find her. Everything will be all right."

She bit her lip. She seemed to be blinking back tears. "She's undocumented—she doesn't exist. How can you be sure everything will be all right?"

Good point, but his sudden realization about the waiter's gender identity had boosted his self-confidence. He'd solved a small puzzle just by observing. The key to discovery, whether of information or people, was to look from every angle. Never accept anything at face value. Amaury Penn just gave him an opportunity to re-evaluate his theories about the Ghost. It fueled the chase and strengthened his resolve.

He rolled his shoulders back and stood straight. "You're right. There's no guarantee everything will be all right, but I know a thing or two about illegals. I sure as hell know how to find them."

20

THE PRESENT

Domingo walked Tess to her subway station. The hot breeze from the subway grates and the crowded mayhem greeted them down on the platform. He and Tess didn't speak, just looked around. A teenaged Cardi B wannabe was rapping, eliciting guffaws from her large group of friends. The conversations of non-English speakers overlapped and meshed together. He closed his eyes for a second, pretending to be amid a séance of people speaking in tongues.

When he opened his eyes, Tess was staring. "Whew," said Domingo "Where do you think everybody's going? It feels like all of Manhattan is here with us."

A smile flitted across her lips. "You don't have to wait with me. It might take a while."

"It's all right. Can I ask you a question? Then I'll be out of your hair."

"Okay."

"Are you sure there's nothing romantic between Monica and Amaury Penn?" Out of the corner of his eye, he caught a dude giving them a hot look. Jeans, dark polo shirt, sneakers. White. Perhaps fortyish, like Domingo. Average in build and looks except for the eyes.

Tess made a face. "Why would you think Monica is sleeping with Amaury?"

"I didn't say she's sleeping with him."

"Your tone certainly did. Why would you think that?"

"Because Monica is attractive, and Amaury goes through women like paper towels." He stole a glimpse at the dude. Yes, there was something wrong with his eyes, as though they didn't belong to the same face. The left eye looked away, but the right eye was trained on Domingo. Cross-eyed. *Duling* in Tagalog. Finally, the guy glanced elsewhere. He seemed to have controlled the misalignment of his gaze. He was only slightly cross-eyed. Good for him.

"I'm pretty sure Monica is not dating Amaury or anybody at the moment," continued Tess. "She's still trying to get over Christian."

"How about haters or enemies? Did she mention anybody?"

"No. She got along well with the old folks. She cares about them. You know how she is. She likes helping people."

"I know what you mean." Duling turned around, perhaps changing his mind about the train, which was indeed taking long. The teenagers hooted as Cardi B Wannabe entertained them with jokes instead of rapping.

The public address system crackled. "Ladies and gentlemen, we are experiencing delays on the F and E lines because of train traffic. We are sorry for any inconvenience."

Tess rolled her eyes in apparent frustration. "You should probably go. Who knows when the train will get here?"

"Yeah, okay. Call me if you hear from Monica, or if you think of anything relevant."

"Sure."

He weaved his way off the platform and climbed back up to the street level. If he were to fly to San Francisco within the next two days to investigate Monica's employer, he ought to visit Mamang now to keep the peace between them. His mother was becoming more and more like a child, throwing tantrums over dashed expectations and broken appointments. He also must book a flight to San Francisco, plus a hotel room. He debated whether to bother with renting a car. It was impossible to find parking in the city. Perhaps he would just hire an Uber or Lyft to get around. He also needed to trace Monica's burner phone.

He emerged from the steep stairs panting. The subway station for the train to the nursing home in Coney Island was a couple of blocks away. He hurried across the street. Damn it. He'd forgotten to ask Tess when she wanted to see Amaury Penn. He'd been serious about taking her to Penn's office, maybe before he flew to San Francisco. The guy wouldn't talk to them, but their presence in his office would remind him of Monica Reed, if indeed he'd met with her.

He bustled back to the station he'd just left. It would be faster than stopping to call or texting Tess. On the stairway, a middle-aged couple blocked Domingo. The woman wanted to go down the platform, but her companion, most likely her husband, thought otherwise.

Domingo waited patiently as the man tried to convince the woman to go back up the stairs. Down below, someone familiar was fidgeting with his phone. Duling.

The couple shuffled their way up the stairs, one arduous step at a time. Domingo sighed, wishing he could jump over their heads. The rumbling of an incoming train reverberated. He hoped it wasn't Tess's train, or he would miss her. All this hurrying back for nothing.

Duling glanced around, then back. He locked eyes with Domingo for but a second. The man barreled his way through the knot of commuters, as though wanting to get to the train first. How rude.

Finally, the couple cleared the stairs and Domingo ran down the steps. The train was not yet in sight, but it grumbled and strained as it came closer. He could see Tess, her back toward him.

"Yo, Tess!" The train noise drowned out his voice.

Duling lurched ahead, blocking his view of Tess. The train hissed louder. Someone screamed, but the deafening screech of metal on metal drowned it out.

"Stop that train!" a man yelled. "She fell on the tracks!"

People stampeded toward the front of the platform.

A ball of panic burned in his gut. It was impossible to spot Tess in the sea of heads. "Excuse me! Let me through!"

More commotion. He was pushing his way through the crowd now, eliciting cusses. The train had plowed to a stop. "What happened?" he asked nobody in particular.

Everyone around him was talking at once.

"Someone fell on the tracks..."

"It must be a homeless guy..."

"No, a woman got hit..."

The hot air remained still. He burst from the throng and gasped for breath. He'd reached the edge of the platform. Workers for the Metropolitan Transit Authority wearing orange vests hopped down onto the tracks. A subway cop pushed Domingo and the others back.

From where he stood, the nightmarish scene revealed itself. Tess lay still on the tracks. His heart clenched. The MTA workers swooped down on her, so only her shoes were now visible. Black leather flats.

Conversations around him swirled.

"I thought she jumped..."

"No, she fell..."

"She was pushed..."

"Someone pushed her?" asked the cop. "Who said that?"

A sudden realization cracked open, adrenaline rushing through Domingo. Duling! The motherfucking cross-eyed guy had reached Tess first and pushed her. He scanned the faces around him. No Duling. He pivoted around and moved as fast as he could without attracting the attention of the cop. He swept the sea of faces with another quick glance. The bastard was gone.

He scuffled back up the stairs and broke into a jog, looking around. Perhaps the son of a bitch was still around. He stopped only when he reached an intersection where cars zipped by. Duling was nowhere in the vicinity.

A sudden vertigo gripped him. Was Tess dead? Who was the cross-eyed man and who hired him? Why would anyone want to hurt Tess? Was it because of her connection with Monica?

The fear in his heart swelled into anger. He balled his fists. He would strangle the cross-eyed fucker when he got his hands on him. But first, Tess. Maybe she was still alive. He turned around and sprinted back to the subway station.

An MTA cop was blocking the entrance with yellow tape. *Do not cross do not cross do not cross.*

Domingo took a deep breath to collect himself. "Officer, can I go back downstairs?"

"No can do. Go to another station. We're dealing with an emergency." The cop plastered one end of the tape to the wall. He stretched another layer of tape across the subway entrance.

"I know the woman who got hit by the train," blurted Domingo. "I saw the guy who pushed her."

That got the cop's attention. He faced Domingo. "Come again?"

"Her name is Tess Chua. I was with her just a few minutes before it happened."

The cop shook his head, his eyes telling Domingo the bad news.

The humid, sour-smelling breeze assaulted him. His throat clamped in shock. All he could do was heave a sigh.

The police officer kept a hangdog look. "I'm sorry, but, yes... We're in the process of contacting her next of kin." He lifted the yellow tape. "Step inside and tell me everything you know."

21

July 2008

The third time's the charm. Three strikes and you're out. Domingo didn't know which was true when he walked inside the same damn hospital in Columbus, Ohio for the third time.

"Where are you supposed to meet Savannah?" He grabbed Max Gray's arm as they entered the outpatient surgeries wing.

"We need to get to pre-surgery," said Max. "It's across the hall."

"Hey, Max."

A woman's voice had stopped them. They both glanced back. "Oh. Hi, Jean," Max peeped.

A young brunette in floral scrubs. "What are you doing here? You hardly ever visit us." She flashed a big smile.

"I'm...uh...taking my friend to surgical services." Max's voice wavered.

"It's one floor down, silly." Jean eyed Domingo, a bit suspicious.

He tightened his grip on Max's arm: *Don't screw up.*

"I know that, but first, we need to go to pre-surgery."

"Oh, okay."

Domingo nudged Max, who blurted out, "Bye, Jean!"

They proceeded without glancing back. "No more chit-chat. Don't try any shenanigans," warned Domingo.

"She spoke to me first. It wasn't my fault."

Phones were ringing off the hook at the receptionist's station. In the waiting room, a few people milled about, while a couple of men in scrubs huddled over a clipboard.

"Attention, hospital personnel! We have a Code White." A man's voice on the intercom boomed. "All hospital personnel, please proceed with Code White procedures." A shrill alarm bell went off.

"What's Code White?" Domingo asked.

"Shit. It means an adult patient is missing," Max croaked.

All at once, men and women in scrubs dashed to the receptionist's counter. This time, it was Max who elbowed Domingo. "That way, quick."

The men's room—empty. Max let out a big sigh.

"What's going on?" Domingo blocked the door with his body.

"If we go outside, I would have to help look for whoever is missing. I'm an employee, remember?"

The dude locked eyes with Domingo. They both arrived at the same conclusion.

"Could it be the general's daughter?" Max's voice wobbled, his face flushed.

Domingo nodded. Maybe Monica had wised up and left. Maybe Christian Price had convinced her to ditch her father at the last minute.

"Someone fucked up," Max squealed. "Maybe I'm fucked, too."

"Shut up. You haven't done anything criminal, thanks to me." Domingo glanced at his watch: seven ten. Twenty minutes to find Savannah, in case it wasn't Monica who was missing. He opened the door to peek outside. Empty corridor. They couldn't stay inside forever. His predator instinct kicked in. *Keep moving.* He seized the dude's arm. "Let's go."

"Where to? There's nowhere to go."

Domingo didn't bother answering, just shoved him out the door. They walked side by side until they reached the gates separating them from the receptionist's desk, where people had gathered in an impromptu meeting.

Domingo's gaze swept the metal bars, which were not there only minutes before. "What's this?"

Max sighed. "I told you there's nowhere to go. The hospital is in a lockdown. That's Code White protocol."

"Let's go."

"Like I said, we're stuck here."

One of the employees at the counter turned her face toward them, making eye contact with Domingo. *Fuck.* He turned around, pulling Max by the arm. "We gotta get outta here."

They scurried down the corridor. A door left ajar caught Domingo's eye. He pushed Max inside and locked the door. They both gasped in relief. Something protruded from underneath the bed. Bare feet. Female.

A white sheet was draped over the bed, but not well enough to cover whoever was hiding below. Was this person dead or alive? Anxiety rose in his chest, blood humming in his head. He squatted down to take a look. "Monica?"

A squeak escaped. "Oh my God."

He reached in to pull her out from under the bed.

Monica Reed wiped her teary face with the sleeve of the ugly hospital gown she wore. Her hair stuck out in different directions like she'd been electrocuted. "What are you doing here?"

"I should ask you the same thing." He stepped back for a better look. Intravenous tubing hung from her right arm. "What's that? Are you okay?"

She shook her head and glanced at the tube in her arm. "The nurse at pre-surgery was going to start an IV line with this, but then another nurse came in." She peeled off the tape holding the tube. She dropped the whole thing in the trash can. "I overheard the second nurse complain about my father's transplant. She didn't understand why it's on fast track. She said it's against protocol—rules had been broken to schedule the surgery this morning because some people were in a hurry. I got spooked so I ran away. I've been having second thoughts. I discovered that Dad can walk! I saw him with my own eyes, but he's been using the wheelchair and pretending like he's too weak to walk. Why? Something's wrong. I don't want to donate my kidney anymore."

"Can I go now?" Max interrupted. "You guys don't need me."

Domingo almost forgot about him. He motioned for the lab technician to stand next to Monica. "Stay there and shut up unless I ask you to speak."

Confusion clouded Monica's face. "Who's this?"

"Nobody." Domingo and Max answered at the same time.

"Why are you armed?" Monica motioned toward Domingo's Glock, peeking from his waistband.

"It's part of my job." He pulled down the hem of his shirt to cover the gun and end her questioning. Better than explaining the conspiracy against her. "We've got to get out of here." He pushed Max toward the window. "Open it. We'll climb down that way."

"Climb down?" The dude's eyes widened.

"I meant jump. We're jumping, buddy."

"We're on the third floor."

"It's not that high."

A knock on the door. "Who's in there? We're on Code White. Open up." A man's voice, authoritative.

Domingo placed his forefinger to his lips to warn Max against yelping. Then Domingo himself unlocked the window as quiet as could be and slid it open. He motioned for Monica to climb first.

She hesitated. "I think we should hide."

"Where?" Domingo clenched his jaw. Fear had replaced his anxiety. What if they got caught? *I'll lose my job, plus Monica goes under the knife and dies under my watch.* "Should we hide underneath the bed like you did before?"

"There's no place to hide and no place to go. We're on a lockdown." Max was biting a hangnail. "That window is the only way out."

More rapping on the door. "Miss Reed? Monica Reed? Open up."

"Shit." Max flicked his gaze to Domingo. "They found us."

Domingo touched Monica's elbow. "We gotta go. You first."

More voices outside the room. A rattling noise. *Keys.* Movement, like someone unlocking the door.

"Shit," Max repeated. "I'm going. I can't be here." He hoisted himself up the window, one leg at a time.

As the door swung open, Max jumped out.

Domingo grabbed Monica's hand. Two security guards glided in like a pair of king cobras slithering up, their bodies straight, ready to bite. *No sudden movement or you're dead.*

"Please step aside, sir," commanded the guard in front of Domingo. The other one stayed by the door.

Savannah, the bitch, walked inside with a man in a lab coat.

"Miss Reed, you need to return to pre-surgery." Mr. White Coat spoke with deference.

"She's not going back there." Domingo clutched her hand tighter.

"Dr. Graham, I'm sorry. I've changed my mind." Monica's voice sounded small. "Dr. Hansen told me I'm free to change my mind anytime. The whole point of a living donation is that it's voluntary." Her ruddy cheeks and sheepish expression made her look much younger than thirty-five. Simple and innocent. The poor woman. What had she ever done to deserve an absentee father who only wanted her for her body parts?

"I understand." The doctor nodded, his hands behind his back. "I've paged Dr. Hansen so you can talk to her...go over any issues you have. We can delay the surgery, if you like."

"*Cancel*, not delay." Domingo released Monica's hand and stepped in front of her to block everyone. "She doesn't want to give away her kidney. Not anymore. Do you understand?" The hospital was colluding with the general when it was supposed to protect kidney donors like Monica. His blood frothed with anger.

Dr. Graham held up his palm. "Fine, fine. But Dr. Hansen will be here soon. It will be good for Miss Reed to talk to her. No harm in that."

Savannah threw Domingo a murderous look before sauntering past him toward the window. Everyone's eyes followed her. She peered down and shut the window. When she faced them, she shook her head. "Nothing there."

Max Gray had escaped—survived a three-story jump! *Good.* One thing less to worry about.

Dr. Graham inched forward. "Why don't we wait for Dr. Hansen in my office?"

Domingo spread his arms out wide to prevent the man from coming closer. "We're not going."

"It's all right." Monica set her fingertips on his arm. "I want to talk to my father." She tightened the ribbon ties of her blue hospital garb and squared her shoulders. "Please take me to my father."

"Sure. He's in surgical services." Dr. Graham gestured at the door and stepped aside.

Monica flounced out, Domingo at her heels. Everyone piled behind him like a procession.

Out in the hallway, Dr. Graham caught up beside Monica. The security gate rose and the doctor led the group to the exit door. They took the stairs to the second floor, where they navigated a series of corridors and passed by patients, doctors, and nurses.

Domingo felt like a rat in a laboratory maze. What was Monica thinking? Did she feel like a dead woman walking? If her father had his way, the hospital would be her death row.

At the entrance of the wing marked *Surgical Services*, a small crowd was waiting. Mary Reed, two women, another security guard, and a couple of guys.

"Thank you, Dr. Graham." Mary acknowledged the man with a nod.

Monica and Domingo paused before Mary. The rest of their entourage dispersed.

"I need to talk to my father," Monica repeated.

"Yes, of course." Mary led Monica to a room, Domingo trailing them. Before opening the door, she glanced back. "Your father's life depends on you." To Domingo, she said, "Do you mind waiting here, please? Let Monica and my husband talk."

"No." Monica latched on to his arm. "I'm not going inside without him."

By instinct, Domingo groped for his gun. He'd caught himself before he'd had a chance to pull it out. "Mrs. Reed, I'm going inside. I brought Monica here. This is my fault. I won't let your husband, Cutter, and Savannah kill her."

"What?" Monica jerked her head. She let go of Domingo's arm. "What are you talking about?"

Mary Reed stood there frozen, her jaw slackened just a tad. Did she know? Was she pretending to be innocent? Her family was the hospital's patron. She was the reason Leonard Reed had unlimited access and clout at the hospital. She was the instrument that allowed her husband to hatch his sinister scheme.

"Let's get to the bottom of this. We need to see the general." Domingo brushed past Mary, Monica behind him. He opened the door and pushed it wide—an operating room.

Leonard Reed lay still in a hospital bed, an arm hooked up to an intravenous pole. Two men in scrubs flanked him, so all Domingo could see was the old man's ashen face, eyes closed. Motionless. Rigid. Like death itself. Or evil just biding its time.

22

THE PRESENT

Dreamers and DACA
    My beloved readers, a good Filipino woman died in the subway a few days ago, just a few hours after joining a protest supporting DACA. I'm not saying her death is related to the rally. The case remains unsolved. What I'm saying is, I admire her courage. Hats off to my fellow immigrants who fight to be heard in this day and age of deafening intolerance and hatred.

So, what is DACA? Well, before DACA, there was the Development, Relief, and Education for Alien Minors (DREAM) Act, which was supposed to provide a path to US citizenship for children who had illegally crossed into the country with their parents. These children grew up in America. The bill meant to offer them a chance to build a life as bona fide citizens.

Guess what? The DREAM Act failed to pass Congress. President Barack Obama—bless his heart—offered an alternative called Deferred Action for Childhood Arrivals (DACA). The program doesn't grant citizenship, but offers temporary protection from deportation and allows DREAMers to work in the country legally. DACA is renewable every two years. A hassle, but better than nothing. The problem is, not all Dreamers are eligible. DACA covers only illegal immigrants who came to the country before 2007 and those who were fifteen years old or younger when they arrived. They must not be older than thirty-one in 2012 when DACA came into existence.

As if that weren't enough of a hurdle, the Republicans barreled into the White House in the worst presidential election in American history. Once in power, the Republicans refused to extend DACA, leaving about half a million young illegals in limbo. The DREAM turned into a nightmare. DACA became a political quagmire. And my memory of the Filipina who died in the subway will forever be associated with an immigrant's crushed hopes and dreams.

DOMINGO TUCKED the notepad inside the duffel bag on the passenger's seat of his car. He would continue writing this chapter at the airport. He had a few hours to kill before his flight to San Francisco.

When he looked up, one of the cops investigating Tess's death waved at him. Pete Ramirez, a detective from NYPD. The Transit Bureau had handed off the case to the detectives, thanks in part to information from Domingo. He'd told them about Duling, about Tess's friendship with Monica Reed, and his search for the latter. He'd answered all their questions, but declined the offer to file a missing-person case for Monica. He'd talked to Mary Reed, who believed in a benevolent universe and counted on Domingo to bring Monica home safely. Indeed, Mary was too ill to deal with the police or to risk attracting attention to General Reed's illegitimate daughter. The poor woman wanted only to settle her affairs and ask for Monica's forgiveness before the inevitable happened.

Domingo got out of his car and met Ramirez halfway. They stood under a tree, away from the grave site. A funeral was hardly the place for this meeting, but Domingo wanted to help out as much as he could.

"How long are you going to be in San Francisco?" asked Ramirez.

The cop was short like Domingo, so he liked the guy right away. He favored those he could see eye to eye with, literally, and hated those who looked down at him. Also, Ramirez, a Puerto Rican, spoke with a Spanish trill, which eased Domingo's embarrassment over his own thick Filipino accent. Two pluses right there for the detective.

"It depends on what I find out in California, but I'm guessing I'll be there at least two or three days." He smoothed down the front of his black sports jacket, too hot for the weather, but appropriate for a funeral. "Where's Lamont?"

"He's working on something else."

"You know on TV, it's almost like detectives are joined at the hip. They always go out in pairs."

"Wrong in real life. Each detective carries his own workload. Obviously, if I thought this funeral was dangerous, I'd ask him to come with me." He pulled his cell phone from the pocket of his pants. "I want to show you something. You're not going to like it, but here it is."

Domingo scooted beside Ramirez, and they watched a surveillance video from the subway station where Tess had died. A sea of heads. The grinding noise of the train. A blur of movement, which turned out to be Tess falling onto the tracks.

"From this video, it appears like Ms. Chua fell...or maybe jumped."

"Suicide?" Domingo shook his head. "No way. You've talked to her family and coworkers, right? They must have told you she had no reason to harm herself. She had a great life."

"All I'm saying is, the video doesn't show anybody pushing her."

"The video showed a commotion. That's how it happened."

"Unfortunately, it's not good enough as evidence."

"That's just from one camera. How about videos from cell phones?"

"Nothing has yielded anything useful so far. But we still have a lot of videos to go through."

Several people arrived and waited underneath a big tent beside the grave, but Tess's husband and sons were not there yet.

"About Amaury Penn...you got anything new on that?" asked Ramirez.

Funny how a bona fide detective was asking *him*, a mere bail enforcement agent, for information. He sympathized with Ramirez, who must be up to his eyeballs with work. Subway deaths fell into his lap because he used to be a transit cop. He'd become the default subway detective.

"I'm gonna try to meet with Penn when I get back. I'll let you know." Domingo glanced at his wristwatch. Probably another ten minutes before the people from the funeral Mass arrived. "There's something I wanted to ask you. It may be related to this case."

"Sure. Anything, bro."

Bro. That kind of goodwill from the coppers was priceless. It made his life easier, the very reason he shared information with them. He retrieved the yellow sticky note from his pocket and handed it to him. "This is Monica Reed's phone number. It's a burner. Tess told me it simply stopped working and she couldn't reach Monica anymore. That never happened before. Monica always gave Tess her number each time she changed disposable phones."

Ramirez took the piece of paper. "I'll see what I can do. You're aware that even the NSA can't track burners, right?"

"I heard they keep trying. Maybe they found a way already."

A convoy of cars arrived. Tess Chua's husband, Manny, emerged from the black limousine, the official funeral car. Their two teenage sons and an old couple also got out. They were met by a well-dressed woman who led them to the tent. Funeral director? Most likely.

"Are you gonna stick around?" Domingo asked Ramirez.

"I can't. I have to go back to the office." The detective squinted at the midsummer sun. The humidity rose like luke-warm soup. "I just need a quick word with Mr. Chua. How about you?"

"Me, too. I want to offer my condolences before I catch my flight."

They shook hands. He let Ramirez approach the family first while he talked to a couple of Filipino women who worked with Tess. The crowd had grown, everyone arriving at the same time.

As soon as the cop left, Domingo shuffled beside Manny Chua. He was about the same age as Domingo, a few inches taller, and a tad lighter in skin color like most Filipino-Chinese. Domingo extended his hand for a handshake. Instead, the man hugged him.

"You got no idea how sorry I am for your loss." Domingo tightened his embrace. His heart stung. If he hadn't left Tess at the station, she would still be alive. The cross-eyed monster got to her only because Domingo had let his guard down for all of twenty minutes. That was the amount of time he'd been gone before Duling made his murderous move. He, of all people, should have known that death could arrive faster than a train.

Manny broke their hug. "Detective Ramirez told me you've been cooperating with them. I appreciate it."

"I'm on my way to San Francisco. I hope to get more infor-mation about Monica."

"You really think this...this thing is connected to Monica?"

His eyes grew moist. He couldn't spit out the right word: *murder*. His wife had been murdered by parties unknown for reasons equally unknown. A husband's worst nightmare.

Domingo nodded. "I'm ninety-five percent sure it's not a coincidence. As long as I live, I will do everything in my power to find out who did this to Tess."

Manny's tears leaked. His voice quivered. "Tess loved Monica like a sister." He pulled a handkerchief from his trouser pocket and wiped his cheeks. "My wife would have done anything in this world to keep Monica safe. I hope she's okay. I hope you find her soon."

The priest arrived. They both turned toward the man, who nodded at them. The graveside ceremony would begin in another minute. Domingo shook Manny's hand and offered his condolences again before he left.

Domingo braced for the trip to California. He would be traveling from Newark to San Francisco, two of the busiest airports in the world. He would be flying from one zoo to another like a caged animal for seven hours of nonstop flight, but he'd prepared as much as he could to make it smooth-sailing.

Rule number one: don't check any luggage if you could help it. "Travel light" was his mantra. He skipped the check-in counter with just one carry-on.

Rule number two: no guns or weapons of any kind, though he was licensed to pack heat. If he needed one in California, he would tap one of his sources there. His duffel bag rolled through the X-ray conveyor belt, while he himself stepped into the booth-like body scanner without his shoes, belt, phone, or wristwatch.

No issues. He stepped out of the line, put on his shoes, belt, and watch, and picked up his bag. A TSA agent made eye contact, so he smiled. "Body scanners are definitely more efficient than a pat down. You're in and out and done."

Rule number three: be friendly with employees at airports, bus depots, and train stations. You never know when such a connection would come in handy. He'd made a career out of chasing fugitives, and they were bound to use public transportation at some point.

"Most people don't like it." The man spoke with the gravitas of a prison guard.

Transportation Security Administration agents were not law enforcement officers and had no power to arrest. Domingo understood the need for a grave demeanor to exude authority.

"Do you happen to know Bobby Alvarado? He's a supervisor here," Domingo said.

"I don't know him, but I've heard the name."

"He's a friend of mine. Tell Bobby Sunday says hi."

"Sunday?"

"Yours truly." He shook the man's hand and glanced at the ID card hanging from the agent's lanyard. "Nice to meet you, Rodney."

The alarm at the body scanner went off. The TSA agent dashed toward the line. A young woman stuck her tongue out to show the metal stud in her pierced tongue. She was removed from the line.

Thank goodness Domingo had already passed the checkpoint or he'd be stuck there. He strolled along the corridor of food kiosks in search of coffee. Afterward, he proceeded to his gate. His phone rang. It was Ramirez.

"Tell me some good news, detective." He sat down at the waiting area, the phone wedged between his ear and shoulder. He held the coffee with one hand and the duffel bag with the other.

"It's good news and bad news. Which one do you want to hear first?" said the cop.

"Hit me with the bad news. Get it over with." He put down the bag and held the phone. He sipped his coffee with his other hand.

"The burner phone is a dead end. I can tell you where and when Monica Reed bought it, but that's pretty much it. You want the info?"

"Nope. Thanks for checking, though."

"Now the good news."

"I live for it."

"The sketch for Ms. Chua's perp is finished. We're going to send it out to newspapers and TV stations today. I just emailed it to you. Check it out. Tell me if the artist did a good job. If you're unhappy with it, call me back. If you think it's close to what the perp looks like, just text me with an okay."

"Got it." They exchanged goodbyes, and Domingo hung up. He checked his email inbox from his phone.

He'd been taken to the NYPD Artist Unit on the same day Tess died. He'd described Duling as best as he could to one of the artists who churned out dozens of drawings of suspects and victims every day. He thought only suspects were sketched, but some victims suffered deaths so horrendous they couldn't be identified, or they'd been dead for a while so the artists needed to draw a face to add to the image of their skeletal remains. The woman who interviewed him had sketched his description by hand before she transferred it to the computer for an enhancement with software.

He opened Ramirez's message and the drawing materialized. Duling stared at him with his malevolent, misaligned eyes. Bingo! The artist had captured the full head of hair, pug nose, pointy jaw. He couldn't help but smile. The gift of a talented artist was nothing short of a miracle. He texted his approval to Ramirez.

The burner phone had brought zero information about Monica Reed, but the sketch turned out good and faster than he'd expected. He clung to the positive and set aside the setbacks. He picked up his coffee and took another sip, his confidence boosted by the day's developments.

23

THE PRESENT

Paths to US Citizenship: Naturalization of Spouses
  Marrying an American citizen out of love remains one of the best paths to citizenship. It's a win-win. The best of both worlds. A dream come true. A cliché, for sure, but you get the point.

  The problem is, you can't teach the heart to love, so sometimes you have to pay someone to marry you. I've investigated illegals who married "professional" husbands or wives. For the right price, a pro will marry you and pretend to live with you for at least three years, from the time you receive a green card by virtue of your arranged marriage to the day you apply for citizenship. That's the length of time required to prove your marriage. During that period, you and your hired spouse will share the same address, collect photos of trips to Niagara Falls, Las Vegas, and Disneyland, and produce utility bills and a bank account showing both of your names. After you obtain citizenship, you'll pay some more for the divorce proceedings before the professional spouse moves on.

Sometimes it works out. Other times it's fatal. A few years back, I hunted down a man who married an undocumented immigrant for fifty thousand dollars. The guy got carried away and became enraged after seeing his fake wife with another man. He stabbed her to death and disposed of her body in a dumpster. The murdering bastard saw the illegal woman not only as his means of livelihood, but as a piece of property he could discard on a whim.

But I digress. The point is, if you can find true love with a bona fide American citizen who will marry you for real, consider yourself very lucky.

TWENTY-FOUR HOURS after arriving in California, Domingo visited the nursing home where Monica last worked. He was sitting on a bench, scribbling on the notepad, when a most unusual sight distracted him. A young dude and his pug entered the spacious backyard of the nursing home. The beige dog, cute as hell, with large eyes and flat face, gripped a leather leash with his mouth, while the guy held the other end of the leash. *I'll be damned.* The dog was walking the guy.

The old folks milling in the garden swooned at the dog. "Hello, Boniva," they crooned at the same time.

The guy and the pug strutted along the paved path as though in a pet fashion show. They had come for a dog-walking-a-guy shtick. The senior citizens chuckled and applauded.

Luzviminda, the Filipino supervisor Domingo had been waiting for, emerged from the door with an old lady. Domingo got up and ambled toward the pair, but the dude and the dog beat him to it.

The guy kissed the old lady's cheek.

"Domingo—or is it Sunday? This is Evelyn, one of Monica's favorite residents," said Luzviminda.

"Hello, Evelyn." He raised a palm. "Call me Sunday."

"And this is Evelyn's grandson, Jonathan, and his pug, Boniva. Everyone, this is Sunday, who's come all the way from New York."

Evelyn smiled and proceeded to scratch the dog's ears.

"What kind of a name is Boniva? Does it have a special meaning?" Domingo tucked the notepad and pen in one of the pockets of his cargo pants.

"Boniva is a medicine for osteoporosis." Jonathan extended his hand. "Nice to meet you, Sunday."

"You named your pet after a drug?" Domingo chuckled as they shook hands.

"Her name is Daisy, but Grandma prefers to call her Boniva." Jonathan let go of the leash. Domingo had expected the pug to bolt, but it stayed by Evelyn's side as patient as could be. Jonathan leaned toward Domingo and whispered, "My Grandma has Alzheimer's. She kept confusing the names of my dog and her medicine. She has a tough time remembering new things."

"Ah. Sorry to hear that."

"It's okay. Daisy likes her nickname."

"Sunday wants to talk to Evelyn about Monica," Luzviminda interrupted. "Is that okay with you?" She touched the old lady's shoulder. "You don't mind, do you, sweetie?"

Luzviminda, also called Luz, wore floral scrubs like the aides. She was even shorter than Domingo and perhaps younger. Her one-inch acrylic nails painted in pink attested that, unlike the other immigrants in this nursing home, she didn't clean rooms or wash dishes.

Evelyn stopped petting the dog and straightened up. "I miss Monica. She used to come early so we could feed the birds before everyone's up. I loved our time together, that first hour in the morning when I didn't have to share her with anyone else. After that, she's just so busy helping the others." She locked eyes with Domingo. "Do you know where she works now?"

Evelyn's lucidity surprised Domingo. "No, I don't, but I'm hoping to find out."

Jonathan tossed a tennis ball across the lawn, sending Boniva panting after it. He followed suit.

"Let's take a little walk while we chat." Luz led the old lady by the elbow. "This is Evelyn's exercise time."

The Filipina exuded warmth and cheer, like one of those people persons who got voted employee of the month by her coworkers. She seemed cut out for her job.

"I don't mind a little workout myself." Domingo flanked Evelyn on the right side, while Luz was on the left. No wonder the residents were outside. Milling about passed for walking in the geriatric crowd. "Do you like watching *The Bull Penn* show? Did you and Monica watch it together?"

"Oh, yes. Every Sunday morning. I also listen to Amaury Penn on the radio."

"Was it your idea to write him a letter?"

"Not just me. We all wanted it."

They moved at a snail's pace, passing by clusters of white roses and colorful benches. Serenity Gardens Care Center turned out to be an oasis in Hayward's patchwork of neighborhoods. It thrived amid the city's graffiti-laden walls and parking lots with abandoned cars.

"Did Penn write back?" asked Domingo.

"Not right away, but Monica persisted until he responded. She even called him."

"Monica spoke to him?"

"Oh, yes. We were very excited about that." Evelyn broke away and inched closer to a wooden bird feeder in the shape of a house. It perched on a pole taller than Domingo. A brown sparrow pecked at seeds.

Luz and Domingo stayed a few feet behind the old lady. He breathed in the mild air. A summer morning in the Bay Area was as pleasing as a warm custard pie, golden and creamy. He would never be able to say that about New York, where he'd be steaming in humidity now if he'd been there.

"Evelyn remembers Monica pretty well," he said.

"There are days when she can't remember my name. You caught her at a good time. You better make your questions count while you can." Luzviminda glanced at her watch. "She's going to want some time with Jonathan and Boniva in a few minutes."

Domingo nodded. He stepped forward and stood beside Evelyn. "So, you were telling me about Amaury Penn...what did he tell Monica?"

"Oh, he's such a nice man. He agreed to see Monica so they could talk about his visit here."

"Really? Penn's planning to come here? You mean to visit you guys?"

"Yes! Just like Florence Henderson."

The name sounded familiar. He racked his brains until something clicked. "Is she the *Brady Bunch* actress? She played the mother, right?"

"Yes. Carol Brady came here and gave away signed copies of her book. She took pictures with us. Very elegant, very friendly. Everybody loved her."

The sparrow flew down to the base of the birdhouse. Both Evelyn and Domingo watched it forage for seeds that had fallen from the feeder.

"About Penn...when is he coming?" continued Domingo.

"Who's coming?"

"You said Amaury Penn is going to visit here, just like Florence Henderson."

Evelyn gave Domingo a faraway glance. "Oh, yes. Florence Henderson came here last month."

Domingo glanced at Luz. *Is that right?*

Luz shook her head. She mouthed, "It was three years ago." Luz held Evelyn's hand, and they started strolling again.

Domingo walked beside Luzviminda this time. He understood Evelyn's clarity had gone AWOL already. "Is it true that Amaury Penn is going to come here?"

"I don't think so," said Luz. "Monica would have arranged it since she talked to him. Without her, there's just nobody who's going to follow it up. Besides, Amaury Penn is not like Florence Henderson. He has no connection with us, while Florence was friends with the owner of this nursing home. She came here as a favor to our boss. Florence died in 2016."

"I see." They stopped at the edge of the green turf where Jonathan and Boniva played with the ball. "What did Monica say when she quit?"

"It was just a text. She apologized for the short notice and thanked me for everything."

"Isn't it curious that someone as thoughtful as Monica would quit by sending a text?"

"Not really. One employee left a Post-it note on my computer screen. 'I quit,' was all it said. She didn't even sign it," Luz scoffed. "Some people don't even bother to do *that*. They just never show up for work again. I hate to say this, but we're not talking about a high-paying job with retirement plans and bonuses. Employees come and go, and not everyone has the decency to give two weeks' notice."

Evelyn shuffled toward her grandson, who put an arm around her shoulders. They watched Boniva chew on the ball.

Luzviminda glanced at her watch again. "I should go back inside. Is there anything else I can do for you?"

"I'd like to talk to the other residents who were close to Monica." Domingo took out his phone and checked his notes from his conversation with Tess Chua. "Monica mentioned a certain Sofia and Hope, in addition to Evelyn."

"Sofia is away for a few days to be with her new great-grand-baby. You can talk to Hope, though." She waved at Evelyn and Jonathan, but only the dude waved back. The old lady picked up the ball and flung it for the benefit of the pug.

Luz raised her arm and tapped her wristwatch to indicate the time.

Jonathan nodded.

"Okay, let's go. Jonathan knows what to do. He'll take his grandma back inside when it's time for her medication." Luz turned around.

Domingo walked with her. "Do you know if Monica has any enemies here, anything suspicious? Any admirers?"

"You mean a boyfriend?"

"Boyfriend, admirer, stalker...anybody suspicious?"

"Do you think something bad happened to her?"

Domingo tucked his phone back in his pocket, buying a few seconds before responding. The NYPD had asked him to reveal information on a strictly as-needed basis. No point in scaring civilians like Luzviminda. "My job is to think of every possible scenario, so I can't rule out foul play. Would you give me Monica's home address?"

"I'm not allowed to do that."

"I really need your help."

She sighed. "You can talk directly to Sharon, Monica's roommate."

"That would be great. Sharon works here, too?"

"Yeah, but she's on the night shift. I can't give away her phone number either. So you'll have to come back later and catch her in person."

"Sure."

When they reached the door, Domingo opened it and gestured for Luz to enter first.

"You should know that Hope is very shy. Only Monica was

really able to draw her out. So please be patient with her." She stepped inside.

Domingo entered as well and shut the door. "That's not a problem, as long as her memory is better than Evelyn's."

"At least Evelyn is willing to talk to you." She glanced at him sideways. "That may not be the case with Hope. Keep your fingers crossed."

"I need to talk to Sofia, too. Is it possible to get her phone number?"

She stopped walking and faced him. They stood in a narrow hallway. She knitted her eyebrows. "*Bakit, may problema ba?*" Why, is there a problem? she said in Tagalog. He understood that, by switching to their native tongue, she wanted him to be candid in spite of the presence of the employees who walked around them.

He drew a deep breath and replied in Tagalog. "Monica hasn't contacted any of her friends in New York. It's been eighteen days since anyone has heard from her. She's never done that before. And five days ago, her best friend was killed in the subway. Someone pushed her, but I can't prove it just yet. There are a hundred pieces to this puzzle, and I'm sorting everything by color and shape. Every little help from you means a lot. If you know something and you prefer to talk to the cops instead of me, that's fine, too. Just do it sooner than later."

She gnawed on her lower lip. Her friendly expression had turned somber. "I can't give you Monica's home address, but I'll tell you how to get there. Just directions, not the address. Sharon should be home right now."

"I appreciate it."

"I'm not allowed to give you Sofia's cell phone number—"

"I just need to ask her—"

"However, I'm going to call her myself right now. And if you happen to be beside me and you just want to say hello to her… well, there's no law against that."

Domingo put his palms together, prayer position. "Thank you." With any luck, he could get more mileage out of this trip.

They proceeded to Luzviminda's office. She lifted the handset of the desk phone, but set it back down. "You know what? It did seem strange that Monica quit the day after she met Penn. She sent me the text early in the morning and just never showed up for work."

Domingo played devil's advocate to jog her memory. "Like you said, not everyone is decent enough to quit in person. Maybe Monica was in a hurry. I sometimes think of her as *Multo*. She's vanished like a ghost more than once. Undocumented immigrants are good at disappearing."

"I know that. I've hired other illegals before, but that's not what I mean." Her eyes widened, as though she'd just found something she'd lost. "You know what?"

"What?"

"Monica didn't even bother to tell the ladies how the dinner with Penn went. She could have at least called one of us to pass on that information. Maybe Penn stood her up, but she would have told the ladies what happened. She knew they were waiting for that news. Why would she crush the hopes of old ladies she cared about?"

Bingo. "That's a good question. Maybe Sofia can tell us something about that." He nodded toward the phone.

Luz lifted the phone receiver again and punched some numbers.

Domingo's chest rose in hope. Moments of discovery like this revved him up for the chase yet to come.

24

THE PRESENT

"**A**nchor" *Babies*

In the previous chapter, I talked about fake marriage as a way to get American citizenship. Let's face it, not all undocumented immigrants can afford to pay for a marriage. If they came here with their undocumented husbands, or if they fall for someone who could neither offer them marriage nor citizenship, they sometimes end up having children in less-than-ideal circumstances. They give birth in the great US of A. Their children are known as "anchor" babies. By virtue of the 14th Amendment, those kids are American citizens from the moment they were born.

Well, the bigots and the haters want to abolish the birthright citizenship in the 14th Amendment. They say anchor babies are not real Americans, but tools used by their undocumented parents to obtain citizenship. Maybe so. But let's stop and consider this argument for a moment. An illegal immigrant who gives birth in America must wait twenty-one long years before her American-born child could petition her citizenship.

Can you imagine waiting for more than two decades while cleaning toilets every day for less than the minimum wage, living in constant fear of deportation, and enduring harassment the whole time? Not to mention carrying the heavy responsibility of raising and supporting the child, who must also endure similar bullying, poverty, and the loneliness of being unwanted in this country. The person who thinks this is an easy path toward citizenship is a moron! It's the hardest way to become a citizen, so anyone who has lived through all that shit in immigration hell for twenty-one years has earned the right to become an American citizen.

By the way, kids of illegals are not "anchor babies"—but babies. They should not be punished for simply being born.

DAY THREE IN CALIFORNIA. Domingo shook off the thoughts of his book as he passed by the mansion on the corner of Jackson and Octavia in San Francisco's Nob Hill for the third time. *Private Property No Trespassing.* The warning appeared multiple times on the high gates and walls. Hedges as tall as a rampart surrounded the property. There must be security cameras somewhere. How many times could he circle the house without getting reported to the cops? He crossed the street to put some distance between himself and any cameras.

Amaury Penn owned the century-old mansion where he spent every other weekend and holidays with his current wife and their twin toddlers. Penn earned three-point-three million dollars a year for his live talk show on TV and radio. He made an additional two hundred grand from speaking engagements at conservative conferences last year alone.

Inday, back at the office in New York, had dug up the essential information about Penn. Social security number, income tax, and credit cards. The events he was scheduled to attend in the next two months and his social media presence. The bastard had five million followers on Twitter. He owned two houses, one townhouse, three cars, and a boat he never used. He had two ex-wives and a current trophy wife. A grownup son with Wife Number One. No kids with Wife Number Two.

So far, Domingo had interviewed the people at the nursing home where Monica worked, talked to her roommate, Sharon, and tried to meet with Wife Number Two. His efficiency had yielded scant results.

The old lady, Hope, at the nursing home had clammed up just as Luzviminda predicted. Neither the phone call with Sofia nor the visit with Sharon had amounted to anything. Monica no longer roomed with Sharon, though both women kept that fact from the nursing home. Monica lived with Sharon for only two weeks, but she retained Sharon's address for the record, as the official information she gave to Luz. Domingo had visited the long-term motel where Monica last stayed, but the manager said she checked out on July thirty-first, a week before her planned meeting with Penn. No forwarding address, of course.

Amaury's second wife, a lawyer for a prestigious firm in San Francisco, was in Europe. Penn's parents were both dead, but Domingo located their old address anyway. Nobody in the neighborhood told him anything significant.

He walked up and down the street across from the mansion. Compared to other uphill neighborhoods in San Francisco, this was moderately steep, and yet his heartbeat accelerated from the exertion like no treadmill could.

Not one movement in the big house. Nobody going in and coming out. He dared not contact Trophy Wife, a former fashion model twenty years younger than Penn. She would likely alert her husband, who would do everything in his power to block Domingo from snooping. He needed to investigate Penn from the periphery. It wasn't the right time to confront the man. He'd hoped to find a gardener or a housemaid working about, but the thick hedges blocked the view completely.

The sun blazed, but the breeze had dried his clammy forehead. The stop-and-go traffic hummed. He glanced at his wristwatch: 11:10. A half hour of aimless surveillance with no results.

He darted across the street and strolled along the sidewalk outside the mansion. Any security cameras would capture him for sure. He could get arrested for trespassing or loitering or soliciting or all of the above.

He circled the property. Still no movement inside. What now? Where should he go next? He ought to sit somewhere with a cup of coffee and check in with Inday at the office. Maybe she'd heard from Tess Chua's husband or from the NYPD. He could go back to the nursing home and try his luck with Hope.

He quickened his pace as he got closer to the fancy wrought-iron gates. He stopped before it, looking through the bars. The house, with its somber and solid architecture, could have been a museum. No cars in the driveway. Perhaps nobody was home. *Shit*. What a waste of time.

He raised his gaze up to the black box atop the brick pillar supporting the gates—a wireless intercom. It must be fitted with a camera, too. The front door opened and out came a woman. Bingo!

The woman was middle-aged, Caucasian. She scowled at him. "Sir, what's your business here?"

He'd counted on the hired help to be a person of color he could befriend. His ethnicity almost always helped when talking to nannies, assistants, and drivers, but not this time. The white woman had caught him flat-footed. He scratched his head, feigning ignorance. "I'm just looking around. Is this a house or a museum or something?"

"It's *something*, all right. It's private property."

"But I'm outside." He cast his glance down for emphasis. "Isn't this the sidewalk?"

"The last I heard, it's called a sidewalk."

"So, I'm not on private property."

"Sir, please leave if you have no business here."

"I'm just looking around."

She sighed, clearly exasperated. "I hate to have to call the cops again."

"Again? So, you get a lot of people standing outside your gate?"

"You're the second person in the last two days. The police know how to get back here in a jiffy if you insist on loitering."

Bingo again. He raised a palm in a gesture of *I'm cool*. "No need to call anybody. I was just looking, okay? I'm outta here. Have a nice day." He waved for good measure before turning on his heel. He'd gotten all the information he needed.

AT THE CORNER of Jones and Geary, Domingo sat in a cramped eatery that served traditional Filipino breakfast all day long. While he waited for his food, he got busy calling his contact at the San Francisco Police Department. He also called a PI and a bounty hunter in Oakland, all buddies he'd helped in the past. Quid pro quo. His career depended on it.

The cashier called out his name, and he picked up his order of sweet longaniza sausage, garlic rice, and fried egg from the counter. He sat down and attacked his meal. Halfway through it, his cell phone rang. He exchanged niceties with his friend at the SFPD and got down to business. "Boss, I could really use your help getting an ID. Someone trespassed at Amaury Penn's house in Nob Hill two days ago."

"Amaury Penn...the TV guy?"

"Yep, the host of *Bull Penn*. I'm very sure that SFPD was called. You must have it in your system."

"Has Penn hired illegal workers? Sunday, you should stop doing ICE's job. Let those guys deport their own perps." The cop chuckled.

"I wish those bums would do their jobs." Domingo had no time to explain why he needed the information. The background noise on the other end of the line got louder. The cop could get pulled at any moment, so he gave Penn's address and the date of the trespassing.

"Okay," his friend said. "I'll get back to you ASAP. *Mabuhay!*"

It meant *long live* in Tagalog. He smiled. "I'm impressed. Thanks, man." His non-Filipino friends sometimes surprised him with a Tagalog word or two they'd picked up somewhere. Out of the blue, they would say, "*Pancit!*" or, "*Bibingka!*" And he would wonder why they were greeting him by saying *noodles* and *rice cake* instead of hello. It always made him laugh, but also grateful they tried to speak his native tongue.

After finishing his food, he walked out of the eatery and bought a cup of coffee at a bistro. The text from his SFPD friend arrived while he sat sipping his java.

Michelle Lewis, 50, Caucasian. 101C Bryant St. Trespassing infraction.

That was fast. He made another round of calls to the PI, the bounty hunter, and Inday for much needed help. He asked them the same questions. Who was Michelle Lewis? Why did she trespass at Penn's house? What was her connection to him?

He knew from dealing with fugitives and criminals that a violation of trespassing in this state involved a few categories. He'd apprehended a dude from Turkey who served six months for trespassing charged as a misdemeanor. The Turk had done time for stalking a girl who had sought refuge in a shelter for battered women. The creep. If he'd threatened to kill the girl or if he'd actually touched her while at the shelter, the charge would have kicked up a notch as a felony punishable by up to three years in prison.

Michelle Lewis's infraction was a slap on the wrist, the lightest citation on the spectrum of trespassing. She might have been just a star-struck fan or a tourist who got lost. Anyone who had seen Domingo standing outside the mansion might have accused him of those things, too. But with any luck, this Michelle character could shed light on Penn. Just like him, she might have had a good reason for risking an arrest.

He gulped the last of his coffee, left a couple of bucks as a tip, and pushed away from the table. He glanced at his wristwatch: one o'clock sharp. He would try the nursing home one more time while he waited for his contacts to call back with the dirt on Michelle Lewis, whoever she was.

25

THE PRESENT

Domingo's job never failed to surprise him. Who knew he would one day be making his very own ceramic-tile coaster while looking for an undocumented immigrant? He sat at a table in the nursing home's activity room, sandwiched between Evelyn on his left and Hope on the right. It was Arts & Crafts afternoon. The tables hummed with cheery small talk while piped-in music played.

He couldn't afford to skip this exercise if he were to pry any information out of Hope. He braced himself for a snail-paced afternoon with the old folks. He couldn't complain since Mary Reed was paying him good money just to hang out.

He hadn't actually started working on his ceramic tile. His glance darted from Evelyn, who was painting hers, to Hope, who was reading the instructions from a flyer. Evelyn failed to recognize him today, just twenty-four hours after they first met. The poor woman. No need to bother her with his questions. It was Hope he needed. Luzviminda had advised him to try his luck by rolling up his sleeves and tapping into his inner artist.

He'd picked a tile that came with a stencil over it. All he needed to do was paint over the stencil. Evelyn brushed her tile with a bright blue.

"Should I start painting now?" he asked Hope. "Evelyn's going to beat me at the rate she's going."

"This isn't a competition. You don't have to do what other people are doing. This is your chance to create something unique," said Hope without looking at him.

That was the most she'd ever said to him. Her eyeglasses slipped down the bridge of her nose while she read the instructions. She'd picked a blank tile, which signaled her intention to draw something original.

"No can do," he objected. "No way am I gonna draw anything from scratch."

"Not from scratch. Here, take this." She handed him a shoe box filled with art supplies. "Pick a design you can trace or stamp. If you really want to use a stencil, at least choose something better than polka dots. This is supposed to be fun."

Wow, they were having a conversation now, whereas she'd declined to talk to him yesterday when she found out his job. He couldn't blow this chance. He picked a cardstock sunflower and traced its shape on the white tile. "Evelyn told me she and Monica used to feed the birds early in the morning. How about you, what was your favorite thing to do with Monica?"

"Scrapbooking." Hope cut out a letter M, about two inches tall, from a cardstock. "Monica helped me finish a scrapbook I was fidgeting with for two months. I thought I was running out of creative juice, but all I needed was a scrapbooking partner. We worked on it one hour each day until it was finished. Monica pressed some roses that my granddaughter Lily brought here and added them to some pages. It came out beautiful."

"Can I see it?"

"The scrapbook?"

"Yeah. I wanna see it."

She traced the letter M on her tile. "I gave it to Lily for her twenty-sixth birthday." She picked a tube of black paint and a brush and began filling the letter M with the color. "Why are you looking for Monica? Is she in trouble?"

"No, she's not. Monica's stepmother is very sick. She needs to come home before it's too late."

She paused without glancing at him. "She never mentioned a stepmother, but I'm sorry to hear that." She resumed her work.

"I heard you and the rest of the gang are fans of Amaury Penn."

"Gang? I suppose you could call us that." She picked a thin brush and a tube of yellow paint. "We've been doing things together long before Monica came here."

"So, you like Penn?"

A soft smile bloomed on her lips. "Yes. He's a smart man and easy on the eyes."

"Did Monica tell you how her dinner with Penn went?"

"She quit. How could she tell me?"

"She didn't call you after she quit?"

She shook her head, still not glancing at him. She painted tiny yellow flowers around the letter M without the benefit of cutouts or stamps. She was doing it with the gravitas of someone performing a surgery.

The shrill sound of a siren, perhaps an ambulance or a police car, distracted Domingo and Hope. They both craned toward the large glass window.

The other old folks whispered to each other as the siren got closer and louder. An old dude got up and raised the venetian blinds with a tug of the cord. Now everyone watched the ambulance pull up outside the window.

"Oh, my God...could it be John?" Hope rose. "I thought he was getting better—"

"No, he's not. He has a fever," said the man who'd opened the window blinds. "They should have taken him back to the hospital sooner."

"A little fever doesn't mean anything," snapped another man.

"What are you, his doctor?"

Everyone but Evelyn and Domingo had gotten up. Evelyn seemed oblivious as she continued painting. Boy, she'd finished one already and was starting on her second. Meanwhile, his sunflower remained half-traced. It was missing the leaves.

His cell phone rang. Inday's phone number materialized on the screen. He got up and sauntered away from his table. The conversation about John, who apparently suffered from pneumonia last week, swirled above his head.

"Hello, Inday? You gotta speak louder. I can't hear you."

"Lulu from the nursing home called about your mother..."

"What did she say?"

The Arts & Crafts enthusiasts, except for poor Evelyn, had gathered by the window, speculating about this John fellow and his health issues. Domingo proceeded to the back door and onto the garden. Nobody around.

"Sorry about that, Inday. There's something going on here—"

"Where are you?"

"At the nursing home where Monica worked." He dropped on a bench, facing the birdhouse. A lone blue bird perched on its roof. "So, what does Lulu want?"

"She said your mother isn't feeling well, so she made a doctor's appointment for her. She just wanted you to know."

"What's wrong with Mamang?"

"Heartburn."

"It must be some spicy food. She won't quit eating curry and stuff."

"It's really bothering her."

"All right, I'll call Lulu and find out from her. Anything on Michelle Lewis?"

"I found seven Michelle Lewises in San Francisco."

"Our girl lives on Bryant Street."

"That doesn't help. None of them live on Bryant Street."

"Just keep plugging away, okay?" They hung up at the same time. The blue bird burst into flight. An eerie silence descended upon the garden.

Where was Monica Reed? He'd caught her within twenty-four hours in 1998 and within three weeks in 2008. How long would it take to find her the third time around? She'd been missing for nineteen days, though he began his search only fourteen days ago. Whoever caused Monica to disappear had five full days of a head start. His spirits dropped.

An airplane droned in the distance, cutting across his thoughts. Maybe the PI and the bail agent found something about Michelle Lewis. As locals, they should have better information and contacts.

In quick succession, he called Lulu, who told him about Mamang's doctor's appointment in a couple of days, and then the bounty hunter, who didn't answer.

He rang the PI next—Arthur Pino, a Cuban-American by way of Miami, whom Domingo affectionately called *Pepino*, meaning cucumber in both Spanish and Tagalog.

"*Lechuga*! How are you?" Lettuce was Arthur's nickname for Domingo. The joke was that between the two of them, they could make a salad. "I will find this Michelle Lewis for you. No problem-o. How about a drink with me tonight? We got some catching up to do."

"Sure. And if you find out Michelle Lewis's connection to Amaury Penn, I'm paying for the drinks."

"Copy that, compadre."

Domingo returned to the activity room. The old folks had abandoned their work and continued to look out the window. To his surprise, Evelyn had joined them. Everyone seemed to know about John's every ailment, every hospital stay, and all about his good-for-nothing son who had gambled away John's pension.

"Is that *him*? Oh no!" gasped Hope.

The paramedics rolled out a gurney with a body covered with a white sheet. Poor old John had passed away. The old folks watched in stunned silence.

Hope sobbed into her hands.

Evelyn embraced her. "Now, now…please don't cry." She led her friend back to the table.

"I'm going to talk to Luz and find out what happened to John," announced the man who'd opened the blinds. Their de facto leader, the way everyone nodded. "Just hang tight and I'll be right back."

Domingo re-joined Hope and Evelyn at their table. They sat beside each other. "You ladies knew John pretty well? Did he watch *The Bull Penn* show with you?"

Hope removed her eyeglasses and wiped her tears away. "First, Galina. And now, John. We're dropping like flies." She put her glasses back on and blew her nose into the tissue.

Galina. It sounded familiar. He pulled out his cell phone and tapped the icon for his notes. And there it was—Galina Brooks was part of the Amaury Penn Fan Club at the nursing home. How could he have missed it?

"When did Galina pass away?" he asked. "Was it before or after Monica quit?"

Evelyn turned her face toward him, bewildered. "You know Galina?"

"No, I never met her, but I've heard of the name."

"July twenty-first. Friday morning," answered Hope.

"Galina didn't come down for breakfast. She won a game of Scrabble the night before—gone the following day. Just like that." Her eyes reddened, her voice quavered. "Those same paramedics arrived to take her body. And now it's John. Who's next?"

Evelyn draped her arm around her friend's shoulders. Hope sniffled, leaning her head on Evelyn's.

Domingo calculated in his head. July twenty-first and August sixth. Sixteen days passed between Galina's death and Monica's meeting with Penn. What happened during those sixteen days? He reached for a box of Kleenex from the table behind them and offered it to Hope.

"Thank you." She plucked one out and blew her nose.

"I'm sorry to hear about Galina. Were you close?"

"We were a gang, like you said." She sat up straight, breaking away from Evelyn, and gave him a forlorn smile. "Galina loved *The Bull Penn*. She got us watching the show and listening to Amaury on the radio."

He nodded, his head buzzing, the adrenaline kicking in. "Did Galina know Penn? Why did she like him so much?"

"Why does anybody like anybody? Galina just liked him." Hope shrugged. "She wrote so many letters to him, but it was Monica who got us results. Monica got Amaury Penn to talk to her. Galina would have been so happy about that."

"I'm surprised Monica pursued Penn even after Galina died. Why is that?"

Her eyes widened, as though he couldn't believe her ears. "You don't get it, do you? After Galina died, we wanted to contact Penn even more—all of us. We were doing it for Galina. That's the reason Monica persisted."

Bingo. "Tell me about Galina Brooks."

"What about her?" She balled the used tissues in her hand and tossed them in the plastic garbage can at her feet.

"Is there a Mr. Brooks? Did she have a husband? Any children?" He began typing notes on his phone. "Where was she from?"

"Sacramento," Evelyn blurted out.

"Sofia, not Galina, is from Sacramento," Hope corrected her friend. "Before Galina moved here, she lived in Richmond District in the house she shared with her husband, Christopher, until the day he died. Before that, she lived in New York, and before that...well, she lived in Moscow."

"Galina Brooks was Russian?" It never occurred to him that a member of the Amaury Penn Fan Club was an immigrant. The man abhorred foreigners, after all.

"Galina Duboff Brooks, as Russian as could be and proud of her heritage." She picked up her tile with the letter M. She appraised it.

Evelyn resumed painting her second tile.

Domingo's phone rang. It was Pepino. "Tell me some good news, man."

"I found the person who lives on 101C Bryant Street."

"Michelle Lewis—I was the one who told you that."

"Ay, Lechuga. Not Michelle Lewis, but Michelle *Lewis-Penn*."

"What?"

"Yep. She's Amaury Penn's first wife and the mother of their twenty-one-year-old son, Phil. She goes by Michelle Lewis, so that's what's on the trespassing citation, but her apartment contract is under her former married name. You want her phone number at the credit union? She's working today."

"Yes." No wonder Inday thought this Michelle character didn't live on Bryant Street. "Actually, I should go see her. You got her work address?" He picked a pen from one of his pockets.

"I do. If you move fast, you might be able to catch her before she clocks out at Golden Coast Credit Union. Are you ready to write this?"

"Hit me." He wrote the address on the sunflower cutout

he'd used for tracing. "Thanks, man. I'm definitely buying the drinks tonight."

After he hung up, he raised his gaze from the paper and found the two old ladies staring at him. They'd been listening to his phone conversation.

"Did you find Monica?" asked Hope.

"No, not yet. But I found another piece of the puzzle."

Hope handed him the ceramic coaster she'd been working on.

He didn't accept it. "What's this?"

She took his hand and placed it on his palm. He had no choice but to look at it—the black letter M staring him dead in the eye like a bad omen. The tiny flowers surrounding the solid letter appeared unfinished, just specks of the unknown, like the little information about Michelle Lewis-Penn, who might or might not be relevant to the Ghost's disappearance.

"It's for Monica." Hope's eyes grew teary again. "Please find her soon."

"I'm doing my best." He stuck the coaster in one of his many pockets, grateful for having worn cargo pants today. "I gotta run now. I appreciate the info about Galina Brooks."

26

THE PRESENT

Humanity swarmed Chinatown in San Francisco like honeybees in a hive. Tourists snapped photos at the Dragon Gate. Shoppers lined up outside a bakery. A girl thrust flyers at pedestrians. Domingo hopped out of the Lyft car and dashed toward the Golden Coast Credit Union.

Three women emerged from the storefront: two young Asians and a white, middle-aged woman. The Asians waved goodbye to the third woman, who was locking the glass door.

"Mrs. Penn?" Domingo stopped at the door, panting. "Hello, Mrs. Penn." He didn't know what the heck Michelle Lewis-Penn looked like, but she wasn't Asian, that was for sure. A bigot like Amaury Penn wouldn't have married her.

The woman wore a loose, ankle-length dress—a muumuu or maxi or whatever—and open-toed sandals. Her long hair was the color of dishwater.

She flicked a glance at him. "We close at four on Saturdays.

You'll have to come back on Monday at nine o'clock." She pulled the door handle, perhaps to make sure it was shut.

"Actually, I want to talk to you, Mrs. Penn."

A smirk appeared on her bare face. "If you stop calling me *that*, I might just talk to you."

"Michelle—I'd like to ask you a question, please."

The smirk broadened into a smile. "Now we're talking." She dropped her keys inside her bag and slung it over her shoulder. "Shoot."

"Two days ago, you got cited for trespassing at your ex-husband's house—"

"He's an asshole!" She strode away.

He stumbled into a half jog to keep up with her. "What happened?"

"He could have just answered my phone calls, but no, he likes to humiliate me. He called the cops. What a jerk! All I wanted was for him to talk to Phil. He's a good boy. He just needs his father." They weaved through the pedestrians and shoppers on Grant Street. The woman's venom surprised Domingo, though he welcomed the dirt on Penn. "I've been playing mom *and* dad to my kid all these years. This time I want the asshole to do his job as a father and talk to his son."

"What's wrong with Phil?"

"Nothing's wrong with him!"

"Okay. What I meant was, why do you want Amaury to talk to Phil?"

"Phil knocked up his girlfriend. They're babies having a baby. The boy has no father figure, no male role model."

"What did Amaury say?"

"Nothing. Just called the cops on me. He's an ungrateful son of a bitch. After everything I've done for him... When he was a nobody radio announcer, who do you think supported him?"

"You?"

"That's right. And after he made a name on the radio, who do you think convinced him to try television?"

"You?"

"Damn right."

"He owes his career to you."

"The son of a bitch left me—left us—just as soon as he made big bucks. Married a big-shot lawyer who helped him negotiate millions and millions. Divorced her, too, after a while. And now he's stuck with a third-rate bimbo." She glanced at him sideways. "Who are you? Why are you interested in the asshole?"

"I'm Sunday. Just trying to get some information."

"Are you a reporter?"

"Nope."

"Good. I hate reporters." She made an abrupt right turn on Commercial Street. He had no idea where they were headed, but her torrent was unstoppable. All he had to do was ride it. She entered a grocery store. He waited outside, where he could see her buy a pack of cigarettes. She was a regular here, judging by the banter with the cashier.

She emerged from the store and lit up in a hurry even as she walked on the sidewalk. He trailed her. So Penn was in town just two days ago. Could he still be here today? Was Penn at home when Domingo had talked to the help? There had been no cars in the driveway, no sign of the bodyguards. Nope, Penn hadn't been home, but he could still be in San Francisco.

Michelle Lewis led him to a sprawling wall painted with a colorful mural of Bruce Lee. She stood against it, leaning right below the gigantic head of the fierce green dragon threatening to swallow Lee. It must be an homage to *Enter the Dragon,* Lee's last film and his greatest.

"Wow, this is awesome," he muttered. "I'm a big Bruce Lee fan."

"Isn't it something? This is my favorite mural." She took a deep drag and exhaled smoke with evident pleasure.

Her face colored. One of those women with natural rosy cheeks and no need for make-up. She must have been a looker once, still was, despite the extra pounds. Hence the loose dress.

"I like coming here, especially with a smoke. You want one?" She raised her hand with the cigarette.

"No, thanks. I don't smoke."

"Good for you. My son-of-a-bitch ex-husband tried to stop me from smoking. I'd rather smoke and die of lung cancer than get rich off bigotry. In this country, it pays to be an anti-immigrant loudmouth asshole." She looked him up and down, not hostile, but curious. "Amaury would build a wall with his own hands, if he could, to stop people like you from entering this country. What do you want from him? This is about him, right?"

He nodded. "Yeah. A Filipino woman who met with him on August sixth seems to have disappeared. She's illegal."

"Is she pretty?"

"Yes."

"He probably fucked her. His cock wouldn't know legal from illegal. He's the biggest hypocrite I know."

"Why does he hate illegals so much?"

"It beats me. What I *do* know is he's a user. He'll use you and then leave you. He did it to me, his second wife, and everyone else. Even to his adoptive parents, who were the kindest people I've ever known."

"Amaury Penn was adopted?"

"Not that he wants it broadcasted," she scoffed. "He doesn't know where he came from. He keeps a very tight lid on his childhood. Do you wonder why he hasn't written a memoir while every two-bit celebrity out there is doing it?" She took a puff and let out a smoke ring. "The asshole refuses to admit his own mother gave him away. Somewhere out there is a woman who didn't think he was worth keeping."

Indeed, he couldn't remember finding anything about Penn's family on the internet. Inday had dug up the names and the old address of Penn's parents from public documents, though she hadn't known Penn was adopted.

"Well, Sunday, it's nice talking to you, but I have to go to work." She dropped the cigarette butt and stepped on it.

"You just got out of work."

"Some of us have to work a second job to make ends meet. We were renting a studio apartment in the Tenderloin when the douche bag dumped us. It was right before he signed his first six-figure deal."

He pulled out a business card from one of his pockets and handed it to her. "If you ever go to New York, give me a call. Or if there's anything I can do for you, ping me."

She studied the card. "Immigrants Bail Bonds? What do you do exactly?"

"I locate undocumented immigrants."

"Like the pretty Filipino woman who disappeared."

"Right."

She put the card in her purse. "I hope you find her." She hoisted the bag over her right shoulder. "I hope she has some dirt on Amaury Penn and blackmails him. I wish the asshole would fall down hard." She turned on her heel.

27

July 2008

When Leonard Reed opened his eyes, he appeared startled to see Domingo, who should have been long gone by then. After all, Cutter had already terminated his services. Domingo's presence in the hospital signaled that something had gone awry.

"Gentlemen, may I have a moment with my daughter, please?" The general's voice wobbled, though his gaze remained sharp.

Gentlemen meant Domingo as well. The two scrubs-wearing men piled out of the room, but not Domingo.

"Very well...if Sunday must stay, so be it." Leonard struggled to sit up. He wore a similar blue hospital gown as Monica, his bony hands folded on his lap. He trained his eyes on his daughter as though they were the only two people in the room. "What happened, Monica?"

An accusation, not a question.

"Something doesn't feel right. There's something you're not telling me. You've been using the wheelchair even though you can walk. You're pretending to be sicker than you really are. This kidney donation was scheduled so fast even the nurses were surprised by it. I can't go through with the surgery." She faced him, her right hand clutching the side of her hospital gown.

"So you've already decided not to do it." His gaze moved from his daughter to the chair nearby, though he didn't offer it. Courtesy seemed out of the question.

Monica inched forward. "I want to know."

"What happened to *Dad*? I like it better when you call me Dad."

"I want to know! Don't change the subject." Her voice cracked then.

The old man's gaze flitted through the bright room with the glaring overhead lights and the smell of strong disinfectant. How Domingo hated to be a fly on the wall, but he stayed put. He couldn't leave Monica alone with her father.

"Do you believe in purpose?" At last, Leonard gestured at the chair. "Please sit."

"Yes, I suppose." She perched on the chair while Domingo stepped back.

"Every person, every animal, every organism in this world has a purpose. It's a belief as old as Aristotle. A tree grows to bear fruit, the fruit grows to feed animals, and the animals are there for man to eat, and so forth and so on." The general's eyes were sunken, his pallor cadaverous. If he were a place, he would have been a desert where nobody survived and nothing ever grew. "As for me, I believe that my purpose in life is to be a *great* fighter pilot—to fight for my country. I did that. And I would do it again in a heartbeat if I could. No question about it."

His breathing rattled. He sucked in air before he continued. "And you? What's your purpose in life?"

"There was a time when I would have said my reason for being is to find you. All my life, I wanted to be with you. Now...I simply don't know."

The old man nodded. "I was in the Philippines for a reason. In a rather circuitous way, I ended up there because I was fighting for my country and fulfilling my purpose in life. You understand?" He turned his eyes abruptly to Domingo. Hostile.

Domingo kept his expression as neutral as possible.

The general panted when he continued. "But my affair with Solina was an aberration. It was my fault. Her pregnancy was an even bigger mistake. None of these things should have happened."

He meant Monica, the unwelcome result of the unwanted pregnancy.

"But all these things *did* happen. And you...you could have stayed in Manila." He waved a hand airily, chest heaving. "And I would have never known that you existed. But you came to my door. I tried to get rid of you—there's no way to say it politely, and I won't apologize for it—but you stayed in my country illegally. Why?"

Monica took a deep, shaky breath. She opened her mouth, but her father wasn't finished with his tirade.

"Then I became very ill. And you're all I have." Leonard's stare didn't waver. "When Sunday found you for the second time, I realized that what seemed like random mistakes were neither random nor mistakes. They were meant to be. Your purpose is to save my life."

Monica scraped her chair back, as though about to jump up. "You don't care if I die in this surgery."

The old man's eyes widened, his mouth tightened. "Do you think the thought of dying stopped me from fighting in Vietnam? Did the fear of getting pregnant out of wedlock stop your mother from having you? Do you think a fruit can stop itself from growing for fear that it will be eaten?" He breathed out with great effort. "The thing about purpose? Well, you just do it, no matter what. Whether you live or die hardly matters. What's important is you fulfill your purpose."

In that moment, Leonard Reed had regained his power. His every word was law. Everything about the man—his military career, marriage, mistress, daughter—fueled the power inside him. Monica was but an appendage, a healthy kidney and heart, to the general.

"You want me to die," Monica muttered. Her voice, though barely a whisper, rang out like an alarm clock going off. "You want me, the aberration in your life, to die."

The general smirked.

Monica rose, her hands balled into fists. "Your life is not more important than mine. It's not up to you to decide when or how I die."

Leonard rested his head back against the pillow. Though he'd been just a shadow of his old fighter-pilot self, he wore his arrogance like skin itself. "What's your purpose, Monica?"

"I won't die for you."

Her audacity swept through Domingo, made him wince. She didn't even know the whole truth, the plan to harvest her heart in addition to her kidney, but her instincts saved her.

The old man's sneer had turned into a wan smile, his demeanor like air being let out of a tire. *Deflated. Defeated.* He clenched his eyes shut. He must have realized that his body, once a powerful instrument with the bones and muscles all working together according to an inherent mechanical law, had broken down forever. No new kidney for him, certainly not a new heart. *Game over.*

When at last he opened his eyes, the smile had faded, the imperiousness gone. "Go, Monica. Go find your purpose in life."

Her face contorted, but no tears. Did she expect him to apologize? And then she turned around and shouldered her way past Domingo, the door slamming in her wake.

The general locked eyes with him. "You knew, didn't you?"

"I found out this morning."

"If I could have a kidney, why not a heart, too?" His eyes flashed with something akin to wonder. "You understand my desire to live, don't you?"

"No, not really. It's not desire. It's greed. You think you can get a heart transplant at your age?"

"Yes. At sixty-four, my doctors pronounced me fit enough for it. I tried, that's all. I would have gladly accepted my daughter's sacrifice of life and considered it a most precious gift."

"Does Mary know about your plan?"

"Ah, Mary." Leonard flicked his tongue over his chapped lips. "Of course, not. My wife's a saint."

"If anyone finds out how you and Cutter connived with hospital personnel to murder your own daughter, you'll bring Mary down with you. She doesn't deserve that."

"No one got murdered and nobody's going to talk. Not Monica, because she's illegal. Not Cutter or the nurse and the others, because they've all been paid up properly. Not even you, because that would make you an accomplice. You were responsible for bringing Monica to me."

Domingo swallowed the revulsion rising in his throat. He'd been used and duped.

"Do you believe in purpose, Sunday?" Leonard asked with a contemptuous smile.

"With all due respect, General—fuck you." He turned on his heel without a glance. It was all he could do to contain his fury. All his life, he'd tried to do good. Some people served by becoming scientists or priests or soldiers. Bounty hunting happened to be his vocation. He was serving his adopted country by catching criminal illegals and deporting them.

Wasn't that as honorable as fighting a war in Afghanistan or rounding up gang members in the inner city? To make the word *immigrant* honorable was his purpose in life. He never counted on working for someone like Leonard Reed, who subjugated and terminated anyone who got in his way.

At the door, he stopped and glanced back. "You know what? In spite of all your medals and money and prestige—today you lost. General, you're going to die a loser."

Amid the humming, clicking, and whirring of gadgets in the hospital room, Leonard held Domingo's gaze for a long time. His insolence had cooled down to sadness. The general's expression was one of resignation, the calm of accepting death.

Domingo left the room and vowed to forget this episode of his life.

28

THE PRESENT

Birth Tourism

    Crazy rich Chinese women have found a way to buy American citizenship for their children. They've single-handedly created "birth tourism" in California. Travel agencies in Beijing, Shanghai, and Shenzhen openly sell the chance to give birth in the great US of A for upward of sixty thousand dollars. Why does a country that calls itself Communist—born out of an ideology that advocates for a classless society—have a capitalist-style one percent? China has more billionaires than the United States. Business and political corruption are closely intertwined in China; its parliament is known as the Billionaire's Club. And for this new wealthy class, the sky is the limit. These people pay to give birth in America as easily as they would buy a Rolex or a Ferrari.

    How do I know all of this? I apprehended one such Chinese woman, the daughter of a bigwig in Beijing, and her boyfriend. They entered the country with valid tourist visas through Honolulu, where airport officials are more lax than in Los Angeles or San Francisco. She'd come when her stomach didn't show yet to avoid any questions. The couple proceeded to Los Angeles, where they rented a house for ten thousand dollars a month and hired a driver and a maid. But their story didn't end happily ever after.

The girl's politician father was enraged when he found out the young couple couldn't marry because the boyfriend was already married. To make a long story short: the couple's cash flow dried up, their tourist visas expired before she could have her baby, and they'd pissed off their landlord who reported them to ICE. So, the courts got involved, bail was made, mandated court appearances were violated, and that's when I entered the picture.

What's the point of this story? Well, there's a gaping loophole in American immigration law. There's nothing illegal about traveling to the United States for medical reasons. A pregnant Chinese woman could come to California to give birth just as a Frenchman could travel here for heart surgery. Both of them would be granted tourist visas, but only one of them is deceiving the US government by hiding her real motives and her pregnancy. Do you see what I'm saying? While the dumbasses in this country are obsessing about building a wall to stop illegal immigration, the rich communists are busy taking advantage of our legal loopholes.

DOMINGO SAT on the steps outside the Catholic church near the Serenity Gardens Care Center in Hayward. He could have attended Mass since he'd been brought up Roman Catholic, but he'd rather use the time to catch up on his writing. He attended Mass only when Mamang demanded it.

The church stood out amid one-story houses in a residential neighborhood. Sunlight glistened off the hood of a white pickup truck parked across from the church. The air carried the solemn silence of a Sunday morning, perfect for contemplation. He scribbled more notes for his book.

Bells pealed from speakers—a recording. The church had no bells. Without a bell tower, its nondescript architecture blended with the neighborhood. Mass must be over. He got up and stuck the notepad and pen in his pocket.

He crossed the street and positioned himself beside the truck, facing the church's front door. If Luzviminda left through one of the side doors, he would still be able to see her. He'd scoped out the church before the Mass. She would leave through one of the three doors. He guessed she would walk home since she lived just a few blocks away.

The front door swung open. A man in a dark suit kicked the door's latch to prevent it from shutting. The priest stood by the door, saying goodbye to churchgoers as they streamed out.

Luz, in a striped dress and strappy sandals, bounced down the steps with a girl of about ten or eleven. Domingo waved at the Filipina, who waved back. He'd told her he would catch her today, though they didn't specify the time and place.

He crossed the street to join Luz, who introduced him to her husband, the little girl, and another girl, maybe sixteen or seventeen. The guy and the girls were Caucasian. Luzviminda's husband had kids from a previous marriage. Monica's roommate had shared all of this information and even revealed Luz's address.

"Sorry I had to catch you in church," he said. "I'm not sure how much longer I'll stay in town."

"No problem. It must be quite easy for you to find out where I live or which church I go to," she teased. "My life is an open book."

They all stopped on the sidewalk, letting other people ease around them.

"If you don't mind, I'd like to walk with you and just ask a couple of questions about Galina Brooks."

"All right." She pulled out a pair of sunglasses from her shoulder bag and put them on. She turned to her family. "You guys go ahead. We'll be right behind you."

The two girls linked arms and sauntered away, their father trailing. Domingo and Luz watched them for a moment before she said, "Okay, come on. What do you want to know about Galina?"

"I understand her husband passed away several years ago, and they had no children. Do they have any family members still alive?"

"I doubt it. Galina left everything, including her personal effects, to a nonprofit organization."

"Which group is this?"

"Jewish American Immigration Program. It's based in New York, but it has an office in San Francisco."

"Was Galina Jewish?"

"I'm pretty sure she wasn't because she had a crucifix in her bedroom. Of course, she could still give her assets to a Jewish group even if she wasn't Jewish."

"True. Tell me everything you know about Galina."

They strolled without hurry, passing by a school next to the church. A traffic jam had ensued as cars from the school's parking lot, where the churchgoers had parked, snaked onto the street.

"Galina immigrated from Moscow to New York in the 1960s. She was a refugee who escaped Moscow through East Berlin. She didn't talk about it much."

"Did she say why she left Russia?"

She shook her head. "I assumed it was to get out of poverty."

"What else did she say?"

"Galina taught English to her fellow Russian immigrants in New York. Later on, she married an American, Christopher

Brooks. He was an engineer from San Francisco. After they got married, they moved back to the city."

When they reached a stop sign, they stood behind Luz's family as they all waited for cars to pass.

"You should talk to JAIP. Check out its website and you'll find the San Francisco address and phone number."

Jewish American Immigration Program. He pulled out his notepad and pen and jotted it down.

"When you call, ask for Jacob Grossman. You can mention my name if it helps. He was a friend of Galina's. I personally gave him her belongings."

Traffic had cleared, and Luz's family crossed the street. Domingo exchanged goodbyes with her before she followed suit.

He shoved his notepad and pen back in his pocket and walked toward the church, the way he came. Why had a refugee like Galina been so enamored by a xenophobe like Amaury Penn? Why not obsess over Ryan Seacrest or Pat Sajak? Was it just because of Amaury's good looks? It didn't make sense. And just where would he find Jacob Grossman on a Sunday morning? He was still processing the bits of information he'd gotten from Michelle Lewis-Penn. His mind resembled a junkyard, unrelated facts piling atop one another. He needed to sort things out.

His foot got caught and he nearly tripped. *Damn it.* He glanced down. The sidewalk bore a lengthy crack. He followed the jagged line, which led him to an offset curb. Someone could trip and break their skull. It was a lawsuit waiting to happen.

It hit him. He was in Hayward, as in Hayward Fault, one of the most dangerous earthquake zones in the world. If the ground were to shake at this moment, the crack could open wider and swallow him. In the same breath, the thought of Galina struck him. How a cracked sidewalk jolted his sixth sense was inexplicable, but he knew something was amiss.

In the 1960s, Russia didn't produce refugees the way Syria and Afghanistan did today. Very few managed to escape as defectors. He'd watched *White Nights* and *The Hunt for Red October*. They were all he needed to understand how the Soviet Union gripped its population with a stranglehold back then. His gut tingled. Galina Duboff was no refugee, but a defector.

29

THE PRESENT

Domingo was not a fan of social media. The selfies were too narcissistic. The memes and emojis too silly. Yet his heart swelled with gratitude for Facebook when he spotted the crimson façade of The Red Victorian, a historic building circa 1900s turned bed-and-breakfast.

Who knew today was the annual Haight-Ashbury Street Fair? The entire neighborhood pulsed with music, laughter, and commerce. Vendors peddled anything you could think of at booths and tables, from hats and T-shirts to donuts and dog treats. He weaved through the crowd toward The Red Victorian.

Inday in New York had no trouble finding Jacob Grossman on a Sunday morning. One visit to the Jewish American Immigration Program's Facebook page told her where the man was likely to be at this hour—outside The Red Victorian, at the popular street fair, where dozens of civic organizations conducted community outreach every year.

Three people manned a table bearing the JAIP sign. Two elderly guys were chatting, while a young woman handed flyers to passersby.

"Hello. I'm looking for Mr. Grossman," Domingo interrupted. He had no idea what the man looked like and whether he would, in fact, be here. He knew only that Grossman was old. He could think only of his own desperate need to locate Monica Reed. Every day, every hour she was missing was a step toward the unthinkable.

"I'm Jacob Grossman. How can I help you?"

Jacob was thin as a whisper and looked as old as The Red Victorian. In a sea of hipsters and hippies clad in jeans and tank tops, shorts and tube tops, he stood out in his pressed khakis and white button-down dress shirt.

Domingo extended his hand. "I'm Sunday." They shook hands. While he was at it, he also exchanged a handshake with the other man, Lucas.

"I was referred to you by Luzviminda Hidalgo at Serenity Gardens Care Center," said Domingo.

"How's Luz?" asked Jacob.

"She's fine. I saw her a couple of hours ago. We talked about Galina Brooks. She suggested that I speak with you about Galina. Do you have ten minutes to chat?" He pulled out a business card from his wallet and handed it to Jacob.

"Immigrants Bail Bonds." The old guy squinted at the card. "I forgot to bring my reading glasses. What does a bail enforcement agent do? If you don't mind my asking."

"No, not at all. I'm a bounty hunter." Though he hated the term, it was still the fastest way to explain his job.

"Of immigrants?"

"Only if they're criminals."

Jacob stared at the card and stroked his chin, his fingers

trembling. "How interesting. How can I help you?" He spoke and moved like a black-and-white film in slow motion.

"I'm hoping you can tell me a little bit about Galina Brooks and how she came to this country. Was she a refugee?"

"Yes, Galina Duboff chose to be a refugee."

"Chose? I'm sorry...what does that mean?"

"She checked off the refugee box on the customs and immigration form. Because of that, she was referred to our organization. I was her case worker. I handled most Russian-speaking Jewish émigrés."

"Was she Jewish?"

"No, she wasn't Jewish, but she was Russian-speaking, so I was happy to help." He tucked the business card in his shirt pocket. "May I ask why you're interested in Galina's past?"

Before Domingo could answer, Lucas interjected. "You want a hot dog? I'm going to get one."

"Sure." Jacob turned to Domingo. "How about you? Would you like a hot dog?"

He shook his head. "No, thanks."

Lucas shuffled away. A couple popped in and read a flyer. Did JAIP help refugees from other countries? Did the group accept donations in kind? The couple fired away while the young woman answered with a smile.

Jacob turned to Domingo. "Where were we? Ah, Galina. She was so young when I first met her. She was very scared. We were all so young during the Cold War." He appraised Domingo in his slow-motion way. "This was before you were born."

"I was born in 1977."

"Galina and her husband came to this country in 1962."

"I thought she was married to an American engineer named Christopher Brooks."

Jacob's eyes narrowed, his expression shifting from eager to suspicious. "You haven't told me why you're interested in Galina."

Domingo could kick himself for opening his big mouth. He should just let the old man talk. Luckily, Lucas returned and handed Jacob his hot dog and a can of Coke. There were no chairs, so they sat on the pavement, a few feet away from the JAIP table. Lucas wolfed his lunch while standing at the table. The young woman continued to talk to the couple. More people had joined them. Laughter rang out from the next booth.

"You don't mind if I eat?" asked Jacob. "It's your turn to talk anyhow. You were about to tell me what brought you here."

"I'm looking for a Filipino woman who used to care for Galina at Serenity Gardens. She's undocumented. She seems to have disappeared."

"Shouldn't ICE be looking for her?"

"Well, no. Her stepmother, who's very wealthy, is very sick. She's made her stepdaughter her heiress, and that's why I'm looking for her. She won't remain illegal for long. About Galina's husband—"

"What's Galina got to do with the Filipina?" At last, he began eating. The unwrapping of the hot dog alone had taken ages.

Domingo told him about Galina's interest in Amaury Penn, the fan club she started at the nursing home, and Monica's dogged persistence in contacting the talk show host for the benefit of Galina. He managed to tell Monica's story without naming her.

Jacob pecked at his lunch. He gripped the hot dog with both hands. Still, the tremors showed. Parkinson's disease? The little that Domingo knew about it came from reading about the actor Michael J. Fox.

Jacob caught him staring. "There's no cure for Parkinson's, but at least there's medication for my symptoms. It's really not bad. I just pretend my fingers have a life of their own. Right now, they want to have a little fun." He chuckled, followed by coughing.

Domingo opened the Coke can. "You want your drink?"

Jacob nodded and set down the hot dog on his lap. He slurped the soda. He paused and coughed. Drank again. More slow-mo. Time stretched and suspended every movement. A homeless dude wandered to the JAIP table, but saw right away the lack of edible freebies. He tottered to the next booth and the next. Finally, a bowl of free candy. The table bore the sign of a real estate company. The guy scooped a handful.

"Are you okay?" Domingo asked Jacob.

The man nodded and resumed eating, the Coke by his feet. "You were telling me the connection between Galina and the Filipina."

"I don't know yet if there's a connection. That's what I'm trying to find out."

"When did the Filipina disappear?"

"August seventh was the last time anybody heard from her. She texted her resignation, which in itself is suspicious."

"The resignation or the text?"

"Both."

"Galina died on July twenty-first and then the Filipina quit. It seems to me there's no link between the two."

"Another Filipino woman, the best friend of the Filipina who's missing, died on August twentieth. Someone pushed her into the path of a train in Manhattan. I have a bad feeling about all of this."

"Who's missing again? And who's the friend who died? What are their names?" He shook his head. "I'm not following."

He sighed. "Okay, the missing woman is Monica. Her friend, Tess, might have been murdered."

"Monica?" Jacob's eyes grew wide. He swallowed hard. "The missing illegal woman is Monica Reed?"

"Yes. Did Galina mention her?"

Jacob nodded. His hands shook. He set his hot dog back on his lap. "Galina was very fond of Monica. Every time I called her, it was always, 'Monica said this and Monica did that.' I didn't realize she's undocumented. No wonder they bonded."

Domingo's phone rang. He pulled it from his pocket and glanced at Inday's name on the screen. She could wait. He turned off the ringer. "You mentioned Galina immigrated with her husband? Did I hear you correctly?"

"I meant Galina's *first* husband, Bogdan Minsky. He hanged himself six months after arriving in New York. Most likely he was murdered."

The hair on Domingo's arms prickled. This, more than anything else, told him Galina was no ordinary immigrant. "You said Galina checked off 'refugee' on a form. Are you saying she wasn't a refugee?"

Jacob gave him a knowing smile. "Well done."

His heart pumped faster, as though they were playing Hot & Cold and he was getting warmer. "There were no Russian refugees during the Cold War, right?"

Jacob nodded. "Mostly defectors, and only a few survived."

The phone in Domingo's hand vibrated. Inday again. He ignored it. "Luz told me Galina taught English to her fellow Russians after she arrived in this country. I'm surprised she knew English enough to teach others."

Jacob's eyes glittered. His tremors persisted. Did they get worse when he was agitated?

Domingo continued, "If Galina spoke good English, I'm assuming Bogdan was just as good."

"Bogdan taught Galina. He was a man of many skills."

"Were they spies?"

"Bogdan was a spy, but he changed his mind, so he took his young wife with him and fled." Jacob re-wrapped the half-eaten hot dog. "They escaped from Moscow to East Germany through the trash."

"What do you mean?"

"They hid in trucks that hauled off trash, going from truck to truck until they reached Sonneberg. You see, even when borders are sealed, the trash still has to move. Even hardcore communists couldn't stand the stink."

Domingo smiled at the wisdom of his remark. "I'm not familiar with Germany. So, why Sonneberg?"

"It divides East and West Berlin. The fields were lined with fences, watch towers, and landmines."

"How did they escape all that?"

"By paying off a guard, who led them through a tunnel. They had some near misses with landmines. Lucky they got out alive."

Domingo's phone vibrated again, nonstop this time. "Sorry, I have to take this. I'll be quick." He rose and answered the phone. "Hello, Inday. What's going on?"

"It's your mother!" she squealed.

"What's wrong?" He moved away from Jacob.

"Remember she was having chest pains yesterday? It wasn't heartburn, more like a heart attack—maybe."

"What? Is it a heart attack or not?"

"We don't know yet. An ambulance took her to the hospital thirty minutes ago. Lulu is freaking out. She wants you to come back home."

Oh, Mamang. Fear pinched his chest. "All right, all right."

"So you're coming home now?"

He glanced back at Jacob, who sat on the pavement with a placid expression. Perhaps a lifetime of service gave him such peace inside. He helped Galina, Bogdan, and countless immigrants, refugees, and defectors. Wasn't everyone a refugee in the end? Even Domingo himself and Monica Reed and Mamang, too. They were all refugees of their past, leaving a core part of themselves behind in their old countries.

"Yes, I'm coming home," he'd decided out loud. "Tell Lulu I'm catching the next flight." He ended the call, shoved the phone in his pocket, and went back to Jacob.

"Are you okay?" Now it was the old man's turn to ask after Domingo.

It made him smile. "Yeah, I'm fine, but I need to fly back to New York today."

Jacob gazed up with an expectant expression. "Does it have anything to do with Monica?"

"No. It's something personal."

Jacob nodded. "I guess lunch break is over."

Domingo extended his right hand. "Need help?"

When the old man nodded, Domingo helped him up. He grabbed Jacob's leftover hot dog and soda from the ground. "Can I ask you one more thing?" He gestured at the plastic trash bin and inched toward it.

Jacob lumbered beside him. "Of course."

"So, Bogdan hanged himself. Why do you think he was murdered?"

"Because Bogdan warned Galina his handler would kill him. Besides, he went through all the trouble of escaping Russia precisely because he wanted to live. A man like that wouldn't kill himself."

"And Galina? How did she cope with his death?"

"The only way a scared young woman like her would—by marrying. She became Mrs. Galina Brooks of San Francisco, no longer a refugee, but an American wife."

They stopped before the plastic bin. Domingo dropped in the food trash. "Is there anything else I need to know about Galina?"

Jacob shrugged. He smiled encouragement at him. "What do you want to know? You ask. I'll answer."

So, they were still playing Hot & Cold. And now Domingo had grown cold. There was something odd about Galina's story, but he couldn't put his finger on it. Either that or he'd wasted his time. He was back to square one. There was no connection between Galina and Amaury Penn and between Penn and Monica. He was very cold indeed.

"I have to go. I appreciate you talking to me."

"It was my pleasure."

They shook hands. He turned on his heel, navigating his way through the boisterous crowd of hippies, hipsters, and homeless. Live music played in the distance. And yet, he felt the weight of Jacob's stare. He stopped to glance back.

The old man hadn't moved. His face lit up, as though he'd expected Domingo to look back all along. His words rang in Domingo's head. Galina married an American man to reinvent herself and to bury her past. *The only way a scared young woman like her would cope.* But it wasn't the only way, and not every fearful woman took refuge in marriage. Monica Reed was a scared young woman like Galina. Monica had escaped death from her own father's designs, but she hadn't married. No, something else compelled Galina to wed Christopher Brooks.

His pulse skittered in his wrists, his face warmed by the thrill of realization as much as the high sun. He strode back to Jacob. "I have one more question."

Jacob beamed. "Of course, you do."

In their Hot & Cold game, Domingo was warm again. "When and where did Galina meet Christopher Brooks?"

"They met in New York, shortly after Bogdan's death."

"She moved on that fast? Her husband was murdered."

Jacob smiled. Domingo was getting warmer still.

"Was Galina pregnant with Bogdan's child? Is that why she married Christopher Brooks?"

"You answered your own question." Jacob patted Domingo's shoulder. "Well done." His fingers hadn't trembled this time.

30

THE PRESENT

Birthright Citizenship
Remember I said in another chapter that the bigots in this country want to abolish birthright citizenship in the 14th Amendment? It's xenophobia in its purest form—the fear that immigrants would change America forever for the worse. What the haters forget is how and why the 14th Amendment and birthright citizenship came into existence. Anybody who knows how to use Google will learn that it was passed in 1868, three years after the end of the Civil War. It was meant to ensure that all African Americans born in America were recognized and protected as US citizens.

Birthright citizenship is sacred, paid for with the lives of those who died in the Civil War. It tells the world that being an American is not by blood and not an inheritance you gain. Being an American is more inclusive than that. Birthright citizenship empowers America itself, the land where the blood of countless willing and unwilling *immigrants—from the African slaves in the seventeenth century to the undocumented immigrants today—has been spilled.*

As it turned out, Mamang hadn't suffered from a heart attack, but angina. She had chest pains due to partial blockage of an artery. Domingo learned this during the trip back home —four hours of waiting at the San Francisco International Airport, seven hours on a red-eye flight, and very little sleep. At least he'd been able to scribble a few pages for his book during the lull.

By the time Domingo got to the hospital the following morning, his mother was already preparing to undergo coronary angioplasty. The cardiologist was possibly Indian or Pakistani, very soft-spoken, just a trace of an accent. "I will make a small incision in her leg and insert a long tube all the way to the partially blocked artery. To clear the blockage, a tiny balloon will be inflated and a stent will hold the artery open," he explained. "It's a common procedure. Nothing to worry about."

Domingo sighed. "How long will the procedure last?"

"A couple of hours. But she needs to stay overnight so we can monitor her condition."

"May I talk to her?"

"Of course." The doctor motioned toward Mamang's room. "You have a few minutes."

Domingo proceeded inside. His mother was lying on a bed, her arm hooked up to an intravenous drip. She shared the room with another old woman who was sound asleep.

"Hello, Mamang." He slid closed the curtain dividing the two beds for privacy.

Her withered face lit up. "I thought you were in San Francisco."

"I'm here now." He kissed her forehead. "I flew back as soon as I found out."

Her moist eyes told him she expected nothing less.

"How do you feel?"

"Okay, I guess." She lifted both arms to show the patches. "What are these for? I got some on my chest, too."

"I think they're EKG patches. It's for your heart...to monitor it during the procedure."

"Can I go home tonight?"

"No. The doctor said you have to stay overnight."

"I thought I was going to die."

"You're not going to die. You're gonna be fine."

"I wish you would find a nice girl and get married."

"Where did that come from?" He plopped on the chair beside the bed. His bones still ached from sitting in a cramped seat on the plane for seven hours. No matter what he and his mother talked about, everything led back to his zero love life.

"That's the first thing that entered my mind yesterday." Her voice wobbled. "What if I die? You're not even married. You're going to be alone."

"Mamang, please. Can we not talk about this?" He leaned toward the counter and plucked a tissue from a box. He handed it to her. "You need to stop worrying about me, especially right now. Let's just think about your procedure."

She dabbed her teary eyes with the tissue. Luckily, a nurse arrived, and he was spared further drama.

"It's time. Are you ready, Mamang?" asked the woman.

His mother nodded sheepishly. She introduced herself simply as Mamang, so that every stranger called her Mother. She endeared herself to everyone that way without trying.

He kissed her forehead again before he left the room. "I'll be here when you wake up. And I'll stay overnight if they let me."

He headed to the elevators. *Good Lord*. Mamang would

never stop nagging about his love life until the end of time. How exasperating. How could he explain that his heart wasn't free though he had no girlfriend? His mother considered love to be black and white. Either you're single or not. Either you're married or you're gay. No room for the gray area of unrequited love and lost opportunities. Did she think he enjoyed his love-lessness? That marriage never crossed his mind?

The elevator bank was packed. He climbed down three flights of stairs before he found a coffee vending machine. His cell phone rang just as he reached for his wallet. Couldn't he just grab a cup of java in peace? He'd never felt so tired. His knees seemed ready to fold on their own.

He pulled the phone from the pocket of his jeans. He stared at the caller's ID. Manny Chua, Tess's husband. He'd talked to him four days ago at the cemetery.

"Hi, Manny." He moved away from the vending machine so the woman behind him could use it. "How are you? What's going on?"

"I'm fine. I'm wondering when you're returning to New York."

"Actually, I just got back. I'm in Coney Island Hospital. My mother is undergoing a procedure." He leaned against the wall in absence of any chairs.

"Sorry to hear that."

"She's okay. She'll be good as new after this. What's up?"

"I received a manila envelope in the mail from Monica."

Domingo's heart lurched. He sprang to attention. "What's in it?"

"I haven't opened it. I'm having a hard time... It's addressed to Tess."

Silence. Followed by sniffles. Was Manny crying? "Are you at home or in the office?"

"At home. I'm on leave."

Domingo rocked on his heels. Why did Monica send the

envelope? Nobody wrote anymore. Nope, it wasn't a letter. A manila envelope meant more than just a letter. "How about I come to your house now so we can open the envelope together?"

"That would be great, because I can't do it."

The poor man sobbed. His wife had been dead for only eight days, after all. To be reminded of that fact by mail from the Ghost must have been too much to bear.

Domingo said goodbye and ran to the parking lot where his car awaited him. At last, a solid lead on Monica Reed's whereabouts.

31

THE PRESENT

*D*earest Tess,
        I can't believe I'm writing this letter. It's just like before, when we wrote to each other after you moved to New York and I was dreaming of following you—LOL (: I'm writing this because I'm a little scared. Remember I mentioned that Galina Brooks died last month? She was my favorite resident at Serenity Gardens. Perhaps her death hit me most because she entrusted me with her biggest secret. You could say that she entrusted me with her memories and her love for her son.

        So, here's the lowdown. Galina Duboff came to this country in 1962 from Russia. She came with her husband, Bogdan Minsky. He was found dead, hanging from the ceiling, less than a year after they arrived in New York. Galina believed he was murdered before the perpetrator hanged him. Get this—Bogdan was a KGB spy! After spending time in England and France, he had a change of heart. He and Galina escaped from Moscow. She was pregnant when he died.

In this envelope, you will find the birth certificate of Moris Minsky, Galina and Bogdan's son. After Bogdan died, Galina married Christopher Brooks, but they gave up Moris for adoption. She feared for her and her baby's life. If the KGB wanted to target her, she could, at least, spare the boy a similar fate. She wanted Moris to have an American life and to never find out about his Russian roots.

Today, the world knows Moris Minsky as Amaury Penn, the famous host of **The Bull Penn.** *You once asked me why I watch Amaury's crap. Now you know! An American couple adopted Amaury and gave him an all-American name and upbringing. It was a private adoption, so only a few people know about it. The Penns told Amaury he was adopted, but that's it.*

Galina had been content to watch Amaury on TV and to stay anonymous. But in her old age, especially after Christopher died, she was increasingly disturbed by Amaury's hatred for immigrants. She wanted to let him know that his birth parents were once illegal immigrants pretending to be refugees. Bogdan stole information in foreign countries in the service of a murderous regime. He once thought of defecting by surrendering the secrets he'd stolen to the U.S. Embassy in London. But the KGB would have killed Galina back home in reprisal. They had to leave together. Bogdan invented a story that they were part of forced labor sent by the Brezhnev regime to Tashkent (capital of Uzbekistan). They entered the U.S. illegally by showing fake papers and passing as refugees to seek asylum. Galina always felt guilty that they'd deprived some legitimate refugees under the quota system.

She was forever grateful for the generosity of Americans who helped her, no questions asked. That was the America she knew. Why couldn't Amaury be a good American and do the same? If he didn't have it in his heart to help immigrants, then, at least, he shouldn't fan the hatred for them. She tried to reach him many times, but to no avail. When I arrived at Serenity Gardens, she told me everything and asked for my help. She wanted Amaury to get to know her and his Russian heritage.

How could I say no? I, myself, had spent many years looking for my father. Galina and I shared that deep desire to be known and to be validated by the one person we held dearest in our hearts. And so I helped her.

I succeeded where Galina had failed. She tried to reach out to Amaury with her loving letters, while I sent him an email telling him outright that his biological parents were Russian immigrants. OMG, I was so brazen that I wrote, "Your Parents Were Illegal" on my email's subject line! That got his attention!!! LOL! I did this only after my first six emails went unanswered. By then, Galina was gone. She wouldn't have allowed me to do it otherwise. Anyway, Amaury responded and even invited me for dinner at The Cliff House in San Francisco.

A few days ago, I realized he might have seen my email as an attempt to blackmail him. Will his fans continue to worship him if they found out his birth parents were "filthy" Russian immigrants? Amaury describes ALL immigrants as filthy, lazy parasites. Maybe he invited me to dinner to stop my attempt at "blackmail." Maybe he'll try to buy his birth certificate from me to make the evidence of his Russian roots go away. Maybe he'll make me, the bearer of bad news, go away! Tonight is the night I'll meet him at The Cliff House. That's why I'm writing this letter and sending you Amaury's birth certificate and adoption papers. Please keep them safe for me. Don't worry, I'll take them back eventually.

When you receive this, call me, and I'll tell you everything you want to know. But if you receive this and I'm dead or somehow missing, then you'll know it's because of Amaury's secret, which has become my secret, and which could get me killed!!! Okay, I'm being morbid, so I'll stop now. We can laugh about this later (:

Love,
Monica

∽

DOMINGO SAT on Manny's couch with Monica's letter in his hands. He stared at the curly handwriting and multiple exclamation points. He read her final words again. Sunlight streamed through the glass windows. A car started next door, its noise overpowering the low hum of the air conditioner in the living room.

He was holding the definitive piece of evidence connecting Monica's disappearance with Amaury Penn. Postmarked August seventh from San Francisco. Monica must have mailed it late on August sixth, and the post office had processed it the following day.

He set the letter down on the coffee table and skimmed through the birth certificate and adoption documents. Monica was indeed missing and not hiding. All at once, the weight of this realization fell upon him. The tears rolling down his cheeks astounded him. They burned his eyes and stung his heart. He loved Monica. There—he finally admitted it, if only to himself. He'd suppressed his love all along and never told a soul, least of all Monica. How could he when she loved Christian Price? Her beauty was the kind he could admire only from afar. She was a distant country he visited only in his dreams, the one place he dare not to cross in reality, the impossible love of his life. Now gone forever.

"Domingo?"

Manny's voice pulled him back to the job at hand. He wiped his eyes with his fingers. He couldn't remember the last time he cried. "You know, I used to think of Monica as *Multo*."

"A ghost?" Manny carried two mugs of coffee and offered him one.

He accepted it. "Yes. Because she could disappear and reappear unlike anyone I've ever known."

Manny sat in an armchair across from him, nursing his coffee mug. "I'm sorry about Monica. I had no idea... It just never crossed my mind that you, uh..."

"I was always a little in love with her from the start," he blurted out.

Manny's face brightened. Domingo had spared both of them further awkwardness with his confession.

"The first time Leonard Reed asked me to deport Monica, I found her within a few hours at the Greyhound station in Pittsburgh. I set her free that same night. Did you know that?"

Manny nodded. "I was puzzled that you just let her go."

"Well, now you know." All these years, he'd slept with women he paid or picked up at bars. They satiated his lust and kept his longing for Monica at bay. True love, though it might never be expressed or requited, was a gift. It gave him hope and kept him grounded. So, what now? The pang of his loss crept back in. He tasted the coffee, still too hot, as he eyed the letter. "Did you get this today?"

"No. It's been here all along, buried in a pile of manila envelopes that Tess meant to tackle at some point. A bunch of envelopes from Aetna and Charles Schwab. Insurance and investments, the two things Tess dislikes—" He frowned. "*Disliked*, past tense. She sets those types of documents aside until they're as high as a mountain and she has no choice—*had* no choice but to tackle them. Shit! I'll never get used to talking about her in the past tense." His eyes grew teary, and he set his coffee down on a wooden coaster.

The coaster reminded Domingo of the ceramic tile Hope made for Monica, which he would never be able to give to her now. "At least you found the letter. That's what matters."

"Collin almost threw out the entire pile."

"Where's Collin? And Bernie?" It was safer to talk about the kids or Manny might sob, which was how Domingo found him earlier. If Manny cried again, he wouldn't be able to stop the floodgates of his own emotions. "When does school start?"

"Right after Labor Day. They're both working this summer. Collin works at Queens Center at the food court there."

"How about Bernie?"

"He volunteers at the public library."

"Cool. Your kids are great."

Manny picked up his cup and took a sip. They drank in silence. Two men grieving, clinging to the smallest joys of life: a fresh-brewed cup of java, the comfort of a quiet room, generous sunlight from the windows.

Domingo gazed at the family pictures lining the top of a bookshelf. A gilded mirror adorned the wall instead of a painting. The leaves of the bamboo plant atop a side table sprouted like long, delicate fingers.

By the time Domingo finished his coffee, a plan came to him, and scenarios churned in his head. He replaced Monica's letter and the other documents inside the envelope. "If you don't mind, I'd like to borrow this for twenty-four hours."

"Okay." A blank expression on Manny's face, like someone who just woke up from sleepwalking. The poor guy. "What about the detectives? What should I tell them?"

"Nothing. At least, not right now. Just let twenty-four hours pass without saying anything."

"Okay."

He glanced at his wristwatch. Not even noon. The day remained intact with the urgency of his work still ahead. He would hunt down the people who harmed Monica Reed, even if it took him forever. He rose, clutching the envelope.

Manny glanced up at him. "What are you going to do?"

"I'm going to find Amaury Penn."

Tears pooled in Manny's eyes again. "You think he did it?"

"I hope I'll have an answer in twenty-four hours. If not, I'll give you back this envelope. We'll call Detective Ramirez and let him handle it."

Manny nodded, tears leaking from his eyes.

"Do you have a scanner? I need to make a copy of everything in this envelope."

"Let me do it for you." Manny scrubbed his tears away with the heels of his hands. "How do you do it, Domingo?"

"Do what?"

"How do you switch off your heart and just go back to work?"

"I don't know about my heart, but my mind is built for crisis."

"I wish I could say the same thing. I can barely function right now."

"What you had with Tess versus what I never had with Monica are not the same. You need time to heal, man."

His heart clenched. In another minute, the layers upon layers of regret from years of unexpressed love for Monica might just unravel. But his job propelled him regardless of the circumstances. He hunted down illegal criminals and murdering fugitives. He would have gotten himself killed a long time ago if he hadn't learned how to survive in the face of danger. Whenever a badass beat him up or shot him, he couldn't afford to wallow in self-pity. He fought back or he ran for dear life. Either way, he moved fast. No time for brooding. Not ever.

He gave Manny a small smile and tapped his right temple. "This works best when everything's going wrong and nothing makes sense."

"Like right now?"

"Yeah, like right now. Where's your computer?"

Manny let out a big sigh and dragged himself out of the chair. Domingo followed him.

32

THE PRESENT

Finding Amaury Penn was easy enough, thanks to social media. The Legacy Foundation, a conservative think tank, lit up Twitter, Facebook, and Instagram with promotions for a fundraiser where Amaury was speaking today.

By the time Domingo arrived at the Hilton Hotel in Midtown Manhattan, the fundraising luncheon had ended, but Amaury lingered in the ballroom, hobnobbing with supporters. Domingo could see him through the open doors, yet he wouldn't barge inside and risk getting thrown out by Amaury's thugs who stood behind their boss. These were the same guys who had kicked Tess out of the gym. Would they remember him? He hoped not.

He headed for the elevator and down to the lobby. He'd called the hotel earlier and learned that guests arriving by car could park only through valet parking at seventy dollars a pop.

No self-parking allowed, so he parked at a nearby garage. He expected Amaury to be whisked away by his bodyguards through the front doors, where the valet would drop off Amaury's car. Domingo waited at the entrance.

He could have handed Monica's letter to the NYPD, but he needed to look the man in the eye. This was more than a job. His wounded heart laid open. Unlike Manny, he dealt with his loss through action. He would never be able to bring Monica back, but he sure as hell could make Amaury Penn pay.

Now he waited at the hotel lobby like someone who'd just been robbed, all his senses alert and aware of the one thing stolen from him. The night he first located Monica nineteen years ago burned in his memory. Beautiful dark eyes blazing, hard-as-diamond determination behind the innocent face. It was midnight at the Greyhound station, and she'd yawned when he introduced himself. How could he have known her sweet insouciance would leave an indentation in his heart forever? He'd fallen for her at first yawn. Now the memory wound him tighter and tighter. Of course, he needed to confront Penn.

The tractor-like bodyguard, Mr. John Deere, led the entourage. Two women followed, then Amaury in a crisp gray suit, chatting with an old guy. Sasquatch, the big and bearded thug, protected his boss from the rear. A mini procession in the hallway.

Adrenaline rushed throughout Domingo's body like the onset of a fever. He crossed the lobby in three big strides. "Mr. Penn, where's Monica Reed?"

His sudden appearance brought the group to an abrupt halt. But just for a second. The bodyguards immediately flanked Amaury Penn with arms extended in a protective cordon.

Domingo stood before the triangle formed by the two men in front with Penn behind them. "On August sixth, you met a

Filipino woman named Monica Reed for dinner in San Francisco. She's been missing ever since," he said as loud as possible. The more ruckus he created, the better.

Everyone in the lobby ceased movement, as though time itself had stopped. All eyes on Amaury Penn.

"Excuse me, who are you?" asked John Deere.

Domingo flashed his fake badge. *Swoosh!* So fast, nobody had a chance to blink. "Where is Monica Reed, Mr. Penn?" Up close, Amaury's eyes were a startling blue, sharp and cold as a blade. Not a hint of shock or distress.

"I don't have the foggiest idea who you are or what you're talking about." Amaury, a head taller than Domingo, cut him down to size with just one look. "You may have a badge, but I don't see any warrant." He strode past Domingo. His entourage followed.

"The security video at The Cliff House showed you with Monica," yelled Domingo.

Amaury glanced over his shoulder and raised a palm. "Talk to the hand!"

Both bodyguards pivoted toward Domingo, but to his surprise, Amaury flicked his fingers. The attack dogs scowled, but heeded their master and caught up with the group.

The surprise element of Domingo's ambush was gone. Now they knew that *he* knew. They would forever remember his face. Perhaps Amaury even recognized a fake badge, but he could not have known the bluff about the surveillance video. Truth was, he hadn't heard from Pepino, who'd promised to look into the matter. He just wanted to see Amaury's reaction.

Although he'd become vulnerable by revealing himself this way, Domingo maintained a distinct advantage. Nobody but Manny knew that he possessed Monica's letter and a copy of Amaury's birth certificate.

He hurried out of the hotel to get his car. Time to get back to the hospital before Mamang woke up from the procedure.

The satisfaction of ambushing Amaury in public warmed his veins like wine. He'd locked eyes with the man and caught the malice in his steely gaze. Most of all, he'd rattled the bastard good, or he wouldn't have called off his thugs. Those dudes got paid to take care of intruders like Domingo, and yet Amaury stopped them outright.

Talk to the hand? That was the best zinger he could spit out? Domingo couldn't help but smile. Yes, he'd shaken up the son of a bitch.

33

THE PRESENT

Everything You Need to Know About the Green Card
What's a green card? It's literally a greenish ID card given to a permanent resident in the great US of A. If you possess the card, you can live and study and work in America forever —as long as you don't commit a crime. You'll enjoy pretty much the same benefits as a citizen except you won't be able to vote. Considering the disastrous results of the 2016 presidential election, most green-card holders I know would kill to be able to vote and make sure bad history doesn't repeat itself.

So, how do you get one of those coveted green cards? Let me count the ways: through marriage with an American citizen, through sponsorship by an immediate blood relative who's a citizen, through sponsorship by an American company that needs your services, or through a major investment or entrepreneurship that makes you a valuable addition to this country.

When you get your green card, take care of it like you would an heirloom crystal bowl. You wouldn't believe how easy it is to lose your legal status. Take the following people: the gangbanger who killed two people during a drive-by shooting, the old-timer who had given false information in his immigration application, and the soldier who got busted for pot possession. Uncle Sam revoked their green cards and kicked them out of the country.

In America, only American-born citizens truly have irrevocable rights. For everyone else, the privilege of taking up precious space in this precious land is conditional. Naturalized US citizens can be de-naturalized and permanent residents can be reduced to transients overnight if they commit a crime. Never ever forget that your green card is as fragile as a glass. Don't break the rules. Don't blow your chance.

ON THE FIRST day of September, Domingo found himself at the back of a line of tourists at the corporate headquarters of PepsiCo. He read what he'd just written in his notepad, the beginning of a new chapter for his book. Not bad at all.

Amaury Penn and the executive producer of *The Bull Penn* were meeting with the bigwigs of PepsiCo, an important sponsor. For the last four days, Domingo had tailed Amaury around New York City and all the way to Atlantic City and Washington, D.C. The TV host was a busy man indeed. When he was off the air, he spoke at conferences and fundraisers or visited big advertisers just like today. Rumor was Amaury's unfettered bigotry increased his ratings but soured his relationship with advertising sponsors.

The line moved. Domingo tucked his notepad and pen in one of the many pockets of his cargo pants. Two PepsiCo employees gave a perfunctory check of purses and backpacks.

Domingo had none, so they herded him and other tourists without bags to the Sculpture Garden.

At least PepsiCo was only a forty-five-minute drive away from Amaury's Manhattan digs. This was easy-peasy compared to flying to and from Washington or driving more than two hours to Atlantic City. Inday had scoured social media and the internet to put together Amaury's schedule. Domingo had been following him in the hopes of discovering more about Monica's disappearance.

Manny Chua had agreed to hold off on contacting NYPD detectives and let Domingo borrow Monica's manila envelope for a little bit longer. Once Domingo gave the evidence to the police, he would no longer be part of the case. The coppers would take their sweet time in approaching a famous celebrity like Amaury Penn for fear of bad press. They would have to convince a judge to issue a warrant first. Who knew how long that would take?

She's undocumented—she doesn't exist. That was how Tess had described Monica. She was right, too. Nope, Domingo needed to continue his surveillance until he could hand over a case tied up in a neat little bow to the NYPD detectives.

The tourists oohed and aahed over the sculptures in the garden. A bronze grizzly bear. Towering totem poles. What looked like a bright red, three-headed giraffe titled *Hats Off.* The women beside him praised the sculpture of people removing their hats. Seriously? He was no art enthusiast precisely because he didn't understand art.

He kept an eye on Penn's thugs, appraising a giant trowel. These same guys had been traveling with their boss for the past four days. They fetched water or coffee, escorted him every-where, and carried his bags. The oddest thing—even when Amaury hadn't stayed overnight in Atlantic City, he'd brought a carry-on luggage in addition to a laptop bag. Was the man so vain he needed a suitcase for his moisturizers and hair gel?

Mr. John Deere mumbled on his cell phone. After a moment, he shoved it in his pocket and whispered something to Sasquatch. They veered away from the giant sculpture and exited the garden.

It must mean Penn was ready to leave. Domingo followed them to the entrance where a limo waited. Domingo jogged to the faraway parking lot for the masses. By the time he'd gotten in his car and out of the parking lot, the limo was nowhere in sight. *Shit.* He guessed Amaury was en route to the city, either to the network's office in Rockefeller Center or to his posh townhouse in Greenwich Village.

An hour later, Domingo trudged along Fifth Avenue, hoping to see any signs of Amaury's black Lincoln limo and the silver SUV that followed him around. One bodyguard with him, plus two more in the SUV. On Friday afternoon before the long Labor Day weekend, Midtown Manhattan's stop-and-go traffic worsened by the minute. Tourists were arriving for the holiday and New Yorkers were fleeing for the same reason. No sign of Penn's entourage.

Domingo drove to the West Village and pulled up at a private parking garage a couple of blocks away from Amaury's home. He slapped a baseball cap on his head and put on his sunglasses. Just another pedestrian in the tree-lined neighborhood, one of the priciest in the city. Movie stars Sarah Jessica Parker and Matthew Broderick and an assortment of high-tech and Wall Street billionaires lived here.

Amaury's building, a red-brick, four-story Victorian, circa 1840s, loomed ahead. A quick sweep of Domingo's surroundings yielded nothing of interest, just a Lyft car dropping off a passenger on the curb and women pushing strollers. He kept on going until he found a bench outside a boutique on Greenwich Street.

He perched there and called Pepino in California. The PI was about to enter a courtroom to testify in a client's case, a nasty child custody battle. They spoke briefly. Bottom line: no surveillance video existed showing Amaury or Monica, certainly not both of them, at the restaurant.

Next, Domingo returned Detective Ramirez's call. He'd been procrastinating to avoid having to lie about Monica's manila envelope.

"The sketch of the perp is finally paying off," Ramirez said.

"The cross-eyed guy? You got him?" Domingo's heart jumped in anticipation. Seven days had passed since the artist's sketch had accompanied news sound bites aired by local TV stations. In the scheme of things, it wasn't big news, and part of him hadn't expected any results, but this was a pleasant surprise.

"No, we don't have him yet, but three people caught the image of the cross-eyed man with their cell-phone cameras. He was in the subway station just minutes before and right after Tess Chua's death."

"What happens now?" asked Domingo.

"We're checking on those three leads."

"Any possibility of a police lineup?" Domingo held his breath. He would never forget the face of the son of a bitch.

"We have to identify the guy first."

"And then?"

"We have to convince him to voluntarily come in for a lineup. That's not easy, especially if he's guilty. So it's going to take a while. Just hang tight, okay?"

"Right."

"What's the scoop on Amaury Penn?"

Domingo swallowed hard. He hated lying to Ramirez, who treated him as an equal. "Come again? It's noisy here. I can't hear you."

Indeed, a car alarm rang in the distance. Someone was talking to Ramirez in the background. The detective said goodbye after Domingo promised to update him if he found any Penn connection that was relevant.

He exhaled a big sigh. Time to go back to Amaury's town-house. He waited from across the street, like someone looking for a taxi. A humid breeze wafted in, remnant of the long, hot summer. He looked up to Penn's building, at the windows with white shutters. No movement at all, though he'd seen the twins, their mother, and the nanny arrive two days ago, perhaps commuting from San Francisco.

When he lowered his gaze, the black Lincoln glided into his view. Amaury's car! The silver SUV appeared out of nowhere, and both Sasquatch and John Deere hopped out. With military precision, the guys opened the passenger doors of the black limo. From the side closest to the street, Amaury stepped out. From the other door, Trophy Wife emerged. No kids, just the couple. Where did the wife come from? Amaury must have picked her up or met her in the city.

The limo and the SUV were double parked, but the entourage showed no regard for the small traffic jam they'd created as other cars were forced to wait.

Penn and wife climbed the few steps to the front door. John Deere handed a laptop bag to his boss, who hoisted it over his shoulder. Domingo pulled out a compact pair of binoculars from one of his pockets and zeroed in on the target. Black bag with gray monogram—*LV*. Louis Vuitton. Yep, the same bag from this morning and every morning for the past four days.

The door slapped shut with Amaury and Trophy Wife safe inside. The bodyguards strode back to the SUV, and both cars pulled away. The traffic returned to normal.

Domingo replaced the binoculars in his pocket. A tall woman in black leggings and a white T-shirt stared at him from across the street. She stood before a crosswalk, as though waiting for the cars to pass. And yet, even after the traffic cleared, she lingered there. She was dressed like a jogger or a power walker, a CrossFit type of person. Had he seen her before? Only one way to find out.

He dashed across the street and ambled toward the woman. He wanted to lock eyes with her, maybe even say hello. She glanced to her left and right before crossing the street in a hurry. She jogged without looking back.

Ha! The thing about following people for a living was that he'd developed a heightened sense of awareness of his surroundings. He knew when he was being watched, and Miss CrossFit had spied on him.

She had disappeared from his view, so he proceeded to the parking garage to get his car. Would Amaury use a woman to tail him? Why not? Indeed, the stranger appeared physically capable of kicking Domingo's ass.

He drove his Pontiac GTO and paid for parking at the machine on the way out of the garage. On the Brooklyn-Battery Tunnel, the traffic moved slowly but at a steady pace. From his rearview mirror, a red car behind him shone like a fresh apple waiting to be picked. The headlights glared. Impossible to see the driver, and yet a faint recollection came back to him. Yes, it was the car from the garage. He'd pulled over at one payment machine while this car stopped at the next machine. Well, red sedans were common enough.

The image of slick-haired Amaury Penn in a crisp suit returned to him—something about Penn's routine bugged him. What was he missing? His thoughts whirred, facts bumping against assumptions and suppositions.

At last, he emerged from the tunnel. From the corner of his right eye, the red car materialized as it lined up at one of the toll booths. Thanks to the E-Z Pass mounted on his car's windshield, he breezed through the queue. *Adios, amigo.*

He gunned the Pontiac. As traffic eased up, he listened to the news on the radio. A nap for an hour or two at home would be nice before visiting Mamang at the nursing home.

She was recovering well from the coronary angioplasty four days ago.

After Domingo merged onto I-278, he hit a traffic gridlock, forcing him to slow down. He turned off the radio, letting this morning's events replay in his mind.

Something was missing, but he couldn't place it. John Deere had carried the laptop bag for his boss, while Amaury had gripped a small black suitcase. This little detail stood out in Domingo's memory because the man didn't seem the type to carry his own luggage. After all, he had two bodyguards. Why couldn't the thugs carry both bags? The suitcase looked ordinary, about twenty-four inches long and sixteen inches wide— something that would fit in an overhead bin in an airplane.

Also, why had Amaury needed a suitcase just to go to a meeting upstate? He'd been gone for only six hours. And now, he had returned home without it. Where was the suitcase? A slight thrill prickled in his scalp. An idea popped into his head.

He glanced at the rearview mirror—the red car. *Again.* Not right behind him this time. A white Audi stood between his car and whoever was tailing him. Could it be Miss CrossFit? No way. She hadn't been in the parking garage. His chest tightened and his mouth dried. He'd forgotten to bring bottled water.

When the traffic flowed again, he weaved out of his lane, prompting irate honks. *Shit, shit.* He crept onto the left lane and rolled for about a half mile. The red car's tires squealed as it changed lanes in pursuit of Domingo. Who the fuck was this? Without the headlights blinding him, he could see now that it was a sports coupe.

Just as the freeway split into two directions, he stepped on the gas and barreled through the exit ramp for *Prospect Expressway.* The coupe, several cars behind him, sped up. Fast, but it missed the exit. No turning around on the freeway.

Now Domingo entered Brooklyn using the side streets. Whoever was stalking him most likely expected him to go home. It could only be one of Amaury's mercenaries. Intimidation, not elimination, was Penn's goal. Otherwise, a drive-by or a sniper shot would have been more efficient and expedient.

Domingo pulled up at the first paid parking lot he spotted. He would break his routine and visit his mother now. Better to leave his Pontiac here and get an Uber instead. No need to take the sucker tailing him along to the nursing home.

34

THE PRESENT

The Labor Day parade inched along the main drag of Foresthill, an exuberant Connecticut town sixty-eight miles north of Manhattan. Domingo had followed Amaury Penn from New York City and now stood on the sidelines in his ridiculous long-hair wig, beanie hat, and sunglasses —his idea of channeling Johnny Depp. Outdoor surveillance put him on the spot now that Penn and his thugs knew what he looked like, hence the disguise.

After the spooky encounter with the red car and Miss CrossFit three days ago, Domingo avoided loitering near Penn's home. For today's surveillance, he'd mounted a tiny battery-operated security camera on the tree outside the townhouse at the crack of dawn. He'd stayed within Wi-Fi coverage a block away and watched Amaury and his entourage leave the house. The camera transmitted the entire scenario to his phone screen via an app.

He noted that Penn brought a duffel bag and the Louis Vuitton laptop bag. This morning, Amaury had carried the no-name-brand bag. Domingo asked Inday to capture the security-video image and convert it into a still picture. Would the TV host return home without the duffel bag? Domingo intended to find out.

The good folks in Foresthill had invited Amaury to be the parade's grand marshal and keynote speaker at a luncheon sponsored by a conservative group. He'd already scoped the Royal Hotel downtown where Amaury's speech would be held.

Kids in their Sunday best waved from the public library float with big cardboard sculptures of books and the sign *Libraries Rock*. Domingo waved back.

The float for a farmers' association followed. Huge baskets of fresh tomatoes, pumpkins, and apples adorned the platform. A banner said, *Eat Local! Thanks for Your Support!*

Domingo expected the grand marshal to be the first in the parade, but no. Five floats had passed by. At last, the man of the hour—Penn waved from a Mustang convertible with the top down. The crowd applauded, hooted, and called out his name. He probably made fifty thousand dollars, at least, for this event alone. What an overrated, overhyped bullshit artist.

Sasquatch and John Deere flanked the slow-moving Mustang. Domingo cast his glance down to avoid eye contact. As soon as the convertible passed by, he ran for his own car two blocks away. Time to lock and load.

At the Royal Hotel, he went straight to the kitchen. He'd already laid down the groundwork with the head chef. A friend of a friend at the police department introduced him to the dude, whom he'd paid for the opportunity to borrow a waiter's uniform and deliver food to Amaury Penn's suite. Although Penn wasn't staying overnight, he required a room for his administrative assistant, Roxanna, who took care of fans seeking autographs and photos.

Domingo had ditched his Johnny Depp disguise since Roxanna had never laid eyes on him. Dressed in the black-and-gray uniform of a server, Domingo knocked on the door. A young woman opened it. "Yes?"

Who the hell was this? Roxanna was middle-aged, while this girl could have been her daughter. It threw Domingo off. Inday's research about Roxanna, down to her latest income tax return, was for naught. Was he even in the right room? "I have a fruit platter and water for Mr. Penn. Is this his suite?"

The woman glanced over her shoulder. "Did you order something?"

Domingo peeked inside. He smiled at the sight of Roxanna, who sat at the desk with a laptop. He was in the right place, after all. The young woman must be a local, probably an employee of the organization sponsoring Amaury's speech. She had not traveled with the entourage from New York.

Roxanna didn't even glance up. "Dan must have ordered it. Just take it. Amaury will be here any minute. He might want to eat a little something before his talk."

The girl appraised Domingo and then the serving cart, as though deciding whether to pick up the tray herself. Thank goodness she motioned for him to enter the room. He pushed the cart inside.

Roxanna was typing with vigor while the young woman unwrapped the plastic cover off a roll of tickets, the kind used for a raffle.

The suite had a mini kitchen, so Domingo laid out the platter, small dishes, silverware, and napkins on the table there. All the while, he eyed the black duffel bag and the Louis Vuitton satchel sprawled on the couch. So close yet so far.

He picked up the big bottle of Perrier and stacked glasses and brought it to the coffee table. While bent down to set the water and glasses, he pulled the tiny GPS tracking device from his shirt pocket and dropped it in the pocket of the duffel bag. When he raised his gaze, Roxanna was scowling at him.

He scratched his head, giving her a sheepish look. "You don't want the water here? Where should I put it?"

"It should go to the dining table where the food is?" It wasn't a question, but a declaration of his stupidity. He took advantage of his brown skin in moments like this. White folks assumed he spoke little or no English. And when they heard his thick Filipino accent, they warmed up to him out of pity.

"Okay, sorry about that." He transferred the bottle and glasses to the table in the kitchenette. Though he kept his head down, he felt the weight of the woman's stare. His heart bounced faster; his palms turned clammy. Time to vamoose. He left the empty serving tray near the sink for the benefit of the real waiter who would collect the dirty dishes later. He pushed the cart out the door in a hurry.

"Hey!"

Shit, shit. He didn't look back.

"Hey...please stop!"

Could they have discovered the tracking device? So soon? Slowly, he turned around. The young woman sashayed toward him. "Here's your tip." She handed him a five-dollar bill.

"Oh." His chest loosened up. He accepted it with a nod. He turned on his heel and fled.

AT NOON, an overweight guy in a dark suit took to the podium for an introductory speech. Domingo, wearing a poor man's Johnny Depp disguise again, lurked at the back of the ballroom.

"Today, in honor of Labor Day, we will tackle one of the most important topics we ought to be discussing in our community—are undocumented immigrants stealing American jobs?" said the speaker, a John Goodman look-alike back when the actor weighed four hundred pounds. "Somehow we have relegated this topic to the liberal factions of our society. We haven't spoken clearly and loudly in this important public discourse. As a consequence, we are passive recipients and witnesses of the liberal agenda!"

Oh boy. Domingo shrank back. He was in hostile territory for sure.

The audience, including Amaury, applauded. According to the program in Domingo's hands, the TV host would deliver his keynote speech at one o'clock, after the luncheon.

Penn sat at a table closest to the podium with Roxanna and a bunch of middle-aged men. The girl who gave Domingo the tip sat at another table, while Sasquatch and John Deere stood near a side door, about twelve feet from their boss. No duffel bag or Louis Vuitton in sight.

Domingo's cell phone vibrated in his pocket. He pulled it out and stared at a text message. *Location of Device 55VM013 has changed*. He looked around. Everyone in Amaury's entourage was inside this room, yet his duffel bag was moving. Could the driver be loading it into the limo? Already? Amaury had neither eaten lunch nor delivered his speech yet.

A message popped up on the phone's screen. *Retrieve location*. He tapped it. The map of Foresthill materialized. A green dot blinked, right on the street where the hotel was located. Whoever carried the bag was outside the hotel, but still on the premises.

The parking lot? Excitement swelled inside him. Let the real chase begin! He scrambled out of the ballroom.

35

THE PRESENT

At the parking lot, Domingo ditched the Johnny Depp wig and beanie and got behind the wheel. The green dot on his cell phone's screen was moving. He'd barely mounted the phone on the dashboard when he heard tires peeling out. He turned his head toward the noise—the red coupe, the same car that had tailed him last week.

He nosed out of the parking lot and accelerated until he caught a glimpse of the coupe again. Traffic in downtown Foresthill flowed smoothly. He kept a safe distance. After all, the driver didn't know Domingo existed.

Under the cloudless sky and out in the open, he got a better view. It was a Chevy Corvette, flashier than his GTO. It shone with menace, its red paint resembling blood. Most surveillance cars were black, the very color of Domingo's car. But this perpetrator flaunted the brightest color in a vehicle.

The coupe entered a ramp to the freeway and merged with

other cars in a hurry. The green dot on the phone confirmed the duffel's location—just ahead of Domingo. Where was the perp going with the luggage?

The traffic opened up, relaxed and steady, unlike the manic contact sport in New York City. He'd been following the coupe for about eight miles when it hopped two lanes to the right. The perp must be getting off the freeway soon. A mile later, the car glided into the exit lane. Domingo did the same.

A landscape more urban than Foresthill greeted him: fast-food restaurants, motels, and strip malls. On these side streets, he allowed a distance of three cars between him and the perp. Still, he risked being discovered.

The coupe pulled into a gas station beside a pump.

Oh shit. Domingo hadn't expected a stop so soon. He kept going until he spotted a supermarket where he parked. He would wait here and keep an eye on his phone. Within a minute, the coupe passed by. The perp did not gas up after all.

Domingo rolled back onto the road, with just one truck between him and the red coupe. Too close? The answer to his question came when the sports car pulled an abrupt U-turn, prompting a loud honk somewhere.

Fuck. The perp knew he was being followed. The most prudent thing to do was to abort this surveillance, but the way his gut tingled and his scalp prickled told him no. The questions in his head looped without a beginning or an end. Who was the perp? Why was he carrying Amaury's duffel bag? Where was he going with it? What was in it?

Domingo maneuvered a quick turnabout and pursued the blood-red car. It sped up. *Now we're talking.* He lived for the chase. He should have been a NASCAR driver or a pizza delivery guy. With his 2006 Pontiac GTO, he sometimes felt like a race-car dropout turned delivery man. He drove the last GTO model ever made, which fell below the aesthetics of sports cars. No matter. It looked as boring as a sedan, but it ran twice as fast

as a cheetah. He pressed on the accelerator, tailgating the
Corvette. He was no longer hiding, so why not have a little fun?

At an intersection, the perp swung to the right without a
turn signal. Domingo careened to make a hard right. The coupe
zipped past slower cars. A dude on his bike shook his fist and
yelled a curse. The traffic light turned red, forcing Domingo to
a screeching halt. The son of a bitch got away.

No problem-o. The tracking device would tell him where to
go. He exhaled, not realizing he'd been holding his breath. The
traffic moved again and he followed the pulsing dot on his
phone. Five miles of trailing something unseen made his palms
sweat and the steering wheel sticky. He blasted the AC. The
green dot stopped blinking.

Was the phone frozen? It happened sometimes. He pulled
off onto the shoulder and scrutinized his phone. It worked fine.
The green dot was stationary because the Corvette was parked
somewhere.

He shot back onto the road. After another five miles, a sign
emerged on the horizon. The white arrow pointed to the New
England Environmental Park. The signal from the tracking
device remained strong, so he kept going.

What kind of a park was this? The open gate beckoned. He
entered and drove on the paved pathway, passing by a patch of
greenery. Not a soul in sight. The rank odor smacked him hard.
Even with the car windows shut and the AC on, the foul stench
clung to his nostrils. He should turn around, but the green dot
on his phone stared him down. Also, a warehouse loomed up
ahead, complete with a parking lot. Yellow front-end loaders
occupied most of the lot and, yes, the red coupe was parked
there, too.

He pulled up to the curb. The tractors were idle because
nobody worked on Labor Day except for him and the perp.
Under the mild September sun in a remote place with no
witnesses around, anything could happen. He took out the

Glock from the glove compartment and tucked it in his belt. He climbed out of the car.

The dot on the phone led him to the warehouse, except it wasn't a warehouse. The sign said, *Landfill Transfer Station.* From ten feet away, he could see the trash through a garage-door type of opening. That explained the smell. In an instant, the stink of Manila's port area came back to him. It had been nineteen years since he'd endured worst odors—rotting fish, dead rats, and polluted water—at Manila's Harbor where he'd worked as a stevedore for years.

The phone confirmed the duffel bag was inside. He slipped the phone into one of his pockets. No use pretending he was trespassing just for fun, so he pulled out the Glock, released the safety, and went in.

The interior was just a vast concrete floor. The middle was empty, while mounds of refuse lined the walls. The fluorescent lamps in the high ceiling were off, but the feeble light from the open door helped. He held the gun out in front of him, swept the far-left corner, then the right. A man stood with his back to Domingo. Several inches taller than him, but not a big guy.

"Don't move or I'll shoot!" He crossed the space of about fifteen feet between them in huge strides. The floor underneath him creaked, telling him this part was not concrete. The gloomy sunlight cast the perp in a shadow. No sign of the duffel bag, or rather, it was impossible to tell if the bag was in the garbage. "Turn around. Let me see your face!"

The man lurched forward, pressing his palm on the wall. A loud cranking noise ensued—a panel of the wall rose. No, not the wall, but a back door. The perp broke into a run.

Worse, the floor underneath Domingo's feet opened up, sending him and a pile of waste down a pit. He landed on his ass amid wet cardboard, ratty sneakers, dirty diapers, gooey stuff, and all kinds of crap. He gagged from the stench. He clutched the gun with his right hand and covered his nose with his other. He got up and hopped out of the trash, shaking off whatever clung to his hair and clothes. He rubbed the sole of his shoe against the ground to remove something sticky.

He glanced up and around, trying to make sense of his surroundings. Domingo had plunged a few feet into some kind of a pit that stretched like a tunnel. It was wide enough for a large truck to pass through.

The floor above probably stored garbage until filled to capacity. A worker would then open the trapdoor, except the trash was not meant to be dumped into the pit/tunnel, but into a truck that would transfer everything to the landfill. The perp had opened the trapdoor just before Domingo arrived. But he could only guess.

On his far right, the afternoon sun winked. He followed the light at the end of the tunnel, literally. No doors or gates here, reinforcing his impression that this was a drive-through for trucks hauling off refuse.

He emerged from the tunnel gulping fresh air. The odor weakened the farther he plodded away from the building. He tucked the Glock in his belt and checked his phone. The green dot was moving. *Shit*. He followed the signal, sprinting toward another warehouse-type structure. Its sign: *Material Recovery Station*.

The dot kept moving. He jogged along, passing by bales five deep of flattened plastic. *Recovery* must mean recycling or something.

He pressed ahead, past idle compactors, cranes, and golf carts. Workers probably used the carts to navigate the "park." The green dot stopped.

He crouched and crept behind a compactor. The perp must be nearby, though he couldn't see him. He waited. Ten seconds flew by. Thirty seconds. Sixty seconds. He stared at the dot, which still hadn't moved. It hit him—the perp had ditched the bag.

He jumped up. *Ping!* The sound of a bullet hitting metal. He dropped to the ground, face down. His heart slammed hard against his chest. The motherfucker just missed him and had struck the tractor instead. Before he could even raise his head, another shot rang out, and another. Where was the perp? He was panting, as though breathing through a mask. He stared at the phone. The green dot remained still.

He couldn't hide forever. A mountain of discarded rubber tires lay ahead, about thirty feet away. Could the bag be in that pile?

He crawled behind the loaders and the cranes. A series of *pop-pop-pop*s erupted. Gunfire. The noise came from the heap of tires. The bastard and the bag were both behind it, and he was shooting blindly. The perp must consider the bag's contents a matter of life and death, or he would have tossed it by now.

Domingo squatted behind a tractor to compose himself. Though the shots had ceased, phantom noise rang in his ears. He waited. Nothing happened. What to do? He didn't want to fire randomly the way his attacker was doing. If he could equalize the situation and remove guns from the equation, he would have a fair chance.

His glance darted from the dot on his phone to the tires stacked about eight feet high. He secured the phone in his pocket, tucked his chin to protect his neck, and dashed to the mountain of tires like a wild bull attacking a matador.

He slammed against the rubber pyramid hard. It collapsed on him and the perp both. The bastard's gun flew, but he was unscathed. No duffel bag. Domingo got up and tossed old tires from his path. Face-to-face at last. It was Duling, the cross-eyed monster who pushed Tess in front of the train. He lunged at Domingo.

They collided and rolled onto the dirt, Duling on top, while

Domingo lay flat on his stomach. "You dirty immigrant!" He straddled Domingo in an improvised half nelson, one arm encircling Domingo's neck, while the other hand pinned his right wrist. "I'm going to make you regret you ever came to America."

Duling gripped him so tight that Domingo's lungs clenched. He inhaled short, fast breaths through his mouth as his heart galloped. Strangulation. Suffocation. One hundred percent possible. The pure animal instinct to survive took over and everything he ever learned about wrestling came back to him. He planted his left palm flat on the ground as Duling continued to rant, "Go back to where you came from, cocksucker! This isn't your country! This is *my* country!"

All that rabid energy on useless talk helped loosen the man's hold around Domingo's neck, just enough for him to bring his free elbow in and push himself up into crouching position. With all his might, he arched his back to disentangle himself from the attacker and peeled the bastard's hand off his right wrist. His arms were free! He slammed his elbows against the man's chest.

Duling hit the ground backward. Domingo jumped back up on his feet and kicked him in the ribs. The man doubled up, but stood back up. His agility surprised Domingo. A split second to decide. Not enough time to take out his gun, so he leapt forward and grabbed him by the neck, pulling Duling's face into the crown of his skull for a brutal headbutt.

Duling crumpled to his knees. Domingo pulled the Glock from his waist and struck Duling's head with the gun's barrel. The man dropped, the wind knocked out of him.

Domingo released a big sigh. The best butthead and pistol whip he'd ever done. He unbuckled his belt and knelt down to tie Duling's hands together.

He checked his phone. The green dot remained in the same spot. He scoured the refuse and flung tires out of his way. The duffel bag revealed itself like a miracle. He grabbed it, squatted, and unzipped the bag.

It was stuffed with men's undershirts, jacket, sweatshirt, jeans. He sniffed them. He'd been chasing a bag of smelly clothes? What the fuck?

Until he got to the bottom of the bag, and an odor of rot escaped. *Jesus*. Bile rose to his throat. *Oh God*. His heart turned cold. A little sob escaped from him before he jumped up to his feet and staggered away. He vomited in one tremendous heave.

36

THE PRESENT

By the time Domingo got back to the hotel ballroom, the main event was over. Luncheon had been consumed, judging from the waiters serving coffee, tea, and water.

Amaury Penn stood before an enthralled audience answering a question. It meant he'd finished delivering the keynote speech. The emcee, the John Goodman lookalike, passed the microphone to an elderly lady.

"Hello, Mr. Penn. My name is Juliet Pembroke. I'm a big fan!" she squeaked.

"Thanks, Juliet." Amaury flashed a toothy smile and straightened the tiny microphone clipped to his lapel. "You have a question for me?"

"Yes, sir." She cleared her throat. "Last year, I hired a Mexican house cleaner, a sweet gal, but she could barely speak English. I fired her when I found out she was undocumented."

The crowd murmured. "It wasn't my fault! I didn't know she was illegal." Her expression changed from personable to defensive. "With her broken English, communication was so hard. I misunderstood her. Now I'm afraid she'll bring all of her relatives to America. I heard that's what these people do...bring their entire families and live off welfare. Is that what you call chain immigration?"

"That's right." Amaury stepped forward, closer to Juliet, who remained standing. "Chain immigration means *endless* immigration of foreigners. When an immigrant is granted citizenship, that person can bring members of his immediate family—his wife, their children, his parents, and his siblings. Before long, those people are bringing other relatives—the sibling's children, the children of those children—and it becomes a never-ending chain of people we don't want! Remember, we accepted only that *one* immigrant, but now we've opened the floodgates to all of his relatives."

Amaury paced slowly, locking eyes with the people around him. A moment of introspection hung. The eye contact made it seem like he cared about every individual in the room. The son of a bitch was a great bullshit artist, all right.

Domingo stood at the back for now. Without his Johnny Depp disguise, he stayed as far away as possible from Penn's bodyguards who kept watch in front. After his foray into the environmental park—aka garbage dump—he wanted nothing more than to shower, but it was impossible. He glanced at his wristwatch. Another fifteen to twenty minutes of waiting.

"The original immigrant might be a good US citizen, a productive member of our society, but what about his extended family?" Amaury continued.

Scenes from the last hour rewound in Domingo's mind like an out-of-control home movie. Mounds of trash in the warehouse. The face of the cross-eyed fucker now safely in police custody. The duffel bag. A pair of severed arms inside the bag

—the hardened skin had turned black. Each arm wrapped tightly in plastic like beef foreshank bone. *Oh, Monica.* He bit his lower lip to control the pang in his heart. The cops needed a DNA test to confirm the identity of the victim, but Domingo knew in his heart.

Penn stopped pacing. "The extended relatives of the original immigrant could be thieves, rapists, or murderers. But once they're in America, there's no way they're leaving." He gazed out at the audience with a little smirk. "Not when they can get free money! I'm talking about scholarships for their kids, food stamps, Medicaid, Medicare, disability, workers' compensation, social security payments. Why, they've hit the jackpot. They live in the Land of Free Money."

The crowd exploded in a booming applause. The TV host nodded, appearing very pleased with his performance.

Juliet raised her hand. "The system is obviously broken. What's the solution to this problem?"

"Well, what do you think, Juliet?" answered Penn. "If the president were to ask you, 'What should we do?' What would you say?"

She shrugged. "I guess I'd say, 'Let's not accept those other relatives.'"

"That's right. Let's *end* chain immigration—now!"

The audience rose to its feet in a standing ovation. Someone yelled, "Build the wall!" Amaury basked under his supporters' admiration with a little smile.

Domingo glanced at his watch again. He had ten minutes left, maybe. He conducted a quick mental inventory: Tess's confrontation with Amaury in New York, which led to her death in the subway. Now he was certain Tess had been murdered because of her connection with Monica. The ambush of Amaury in the Hilton lobby, the short business trips, the red coupe tailing Domingo. His gamble had paid off. He'd rattled Penn into making a fatal error. The bastard was forced to get rid of the body, one piece at a time. Hence, the generic luggage during every trip. He couldn't entrust the bags to Sasquatch and John Deere, and yet he'd trusted Duling. Too bad for him, Domingo fought better than the cross-eyed motherfucker, whose identity remained a mystery. The man's driver's license and car registration were phony. The cops were still trying to find out.

The applause persisted, and Amaury nodded, as though he wanted it to last forever.

Domingo drew a deep breath. *Here we go.* He strode toward Juliet. "May I?" He extended his hand, but she hesitated, so he snatched the microphone. It was now or never.

Juliet flinched, whether from the surprise of Domingo's action or from his stench, he couldn't tell. She sat down without a peep.

He tapped the mic to make sure it worked. "Mr. Penn, the first lady herself got her parents into this country through chain immigration." A shot of fresh adrenaline flooded him. He paused to compose himself.

Penn appeared stunned. Of course, he recognized Domingo.

"So, if we're going to end chain immigration, we should start from the top—at the White House," he continued. "Let's stop the first lady's Slovenian relatives from entering this country, because how do we know they're not thieves or rapists or murderers?" Domingo swept the ballroom with a glance. Everyone gaped, like *who the hell is this guy?* "But I digress, Mr. Penn. I'm here to tell you that I found your duffel bag. I've hit the jackpot!"

Penn's face bloomed a bright red. He turned to his thugs and flicked his fingers. The attack dogs swaggered toward Domingo.

"Mr. Penn, my name is Sunday, and I'm a naturalized US

citizen. I'm here to warn you that you have about five minutes before you get arrested for the murder of Monica Reed."

Sasquatch and John Deere halted at the mention of *murder*. They exchanged bewildered glances.

Domingo continued. "Does the name ring a bell? Monica was the woman who told you that your biological parents were once *illegal* immigrants." The crowd buzzed. The John Goodman lookalike rose, but someone pulled him back down. "Your name is *not* Amaury Penn, but Moris Minsky. Your parents, Bogdan Minsky and Galina Duboff, were Soviet citizens who benefited big time from the asylum program by pretending to flee an oppressive labor camp. Your dad was actually a spy, who eventually got his comeuppance and got whacked, but that's another story entirely. My point is...you're a man who hates *all* immigrants, but you're the son of Russian immigrants whose lies deprived two legitimate refugees their chance at citizenship. Did you know there's a quota for asylum seekers? Imagine a cookie jar with only ten cookies for ten very hungry orphans. Your parents, who were neither hungry nor orphans, stole two of those precious cookies. So your immigrant parents were kind of like thieves. Or thieves, actually."

Mortification spread over Penn's face as he balled his fists. Domingo braced for a scuffle, but the TV host wasn't even looking at him. He followed Penn's gaze. The door was open— held by a cop. The police lieutenant Domingo met earlier entered, followed by several officers.

"Okay, I lied, Mr. Penn." He couldn't help but grin. "You don't have five minutes because your escorts have arrived. Good luck in prison—watch out for your cornhole! Have a nice day, everyone." He dropped the microphone in Juliet's lap and waved at the lieutenant, who nodded in acknowledgment.

Sasquatch and John Deere scrambled to protect their boss. They could do nothing but flank him as the officers surrounded Amaury. The rest of his entourage huddled around Roxanna, who was barking on her cell phone. Yeah, she ought to be calling her employer's fancy-pants lawyers in the Big Apple for help.

The copper who held the door asked everyone to leave. "Ladies and gentlemen, this way, please. The meeting is over. Proceed this way...thank you."

Domingo joined the stream of people getting out. He needed to return the call of a San Francisco detective. The guy had a hell of a job—finding out how Penn got rid of Monica. How did the bastard take her from the West Coast to the East Coast? He'd met her somewhere in San Francisco and ended up lugging her decaying arms to Foresthill.

He sighed. Every time he thought of Monica, a jagged pain hit him. He burst out of the ballroom, trying to shake off his enormous loss. First things first: new clothes and the nearest motel for a quick shower. New York was too far just to clean up, especially because he was wanted at the police station ASAP. He was the number one material witness in a murder case against Amaury Penn.

37

July 2008

Domingo was whistling while making scrambled eggs in his tiny kitchen. He glanced at the oven clock. It was seven o'clock in the morning. Monica was still asleep in the guest room after the long drive from Ohio yesterday. He still hadn't revealed to her the full story about her father's failed scheme to harvest her heart in addition to her kidney.

She'd asked him about it just once, but when he kept mum, a moment of understanding had passed between them. It was best to leave it alone. He'd offered to let her stay in his house overnight, while she thought of what she would do next. She'd accepted. After that, they'd driven in silence for the most part.

The wooden floor creaked, telling him Monica was approaching. She stood in the kitchen doorway.

"Want some breakfast?" he asked.

"It smells great."

She wore the denim Bermuda shorts and plain T-shirt they'd bought from Target yesterday. She'd left her belongings in her father's house in their haste to leave town.

"It's chow time." He motioned for her to sit down at the table. The kitchen was so small there was space for only two stools at the table. He set up the plates, silverware, and napkins. He poured coffee in two mugs.

"I'm starving." She eyed the food: fried garlic rice, chorizo, scrambled eggs, and sliced tomatoes.

A genuine Filipino breakfast. She smiled her approval. They both ate eagerly, without talking. He needed to be in Manhattan in an hour. He was already running late.

She took a sip of coffee and said, "I'm going back to New Jersey. I'll take the subway to Port Authority."

So, she meant to return to Christian's love nest. She had nowhere to go. "I'd feel better if you stayed here until I get back this afternoon. Let me check things out first. I want to make sure Cutter is not waiting for you in New Jersey."

"What if he comes here?"

"He doesn't know where I live. And even if he does, he won't dare come here."

"Are you sure?"

"You should have seen the condition I left him in two days ago." *That* didn't come out right, like he was bragging. Whatever. He shoved a piece of sausage into his mouth.

The sudden trill of the telephone mounted on the wall interrupted their conversation. He answered the call, then returned to the table. "That was Mamang."

"Does your mother know you have a house guest?"

He shook his head and slurped his coffee. If Mamang had known, she would have jumped to a wrong conclusion. She would start planning Domingo and Monica's wedding.

"My father asked me what my purpose in life is." She was fidgeting with the napkin. She'd finished her food.

"Forget about him, Monica."

"It's a good question. I've been thinking about it. How about you, what's your purpose?"

"Me? To catch the motherfuckers who ought to be kicked out of this country."

She winced, whether at the cuss word or the idea of deporting illegals, he couldn't tell.

"Forget about your father," he repeated. "I mean it. Family, blood relations, whatever...it's overrated. You don't need him." He finished his coffee. "I gotta run. Traffic's going to be a bitch at this time." He rose, grabbed the dirty plates, and stacked them in the sink.

She got up as well. "Just go. I'll wash the dishes."

He went to the foyer and collected his cell phone and keys from a small basket on the console table. She stood a couple of feet away, glancing around. His stepfather's house was too dark, with its small windows, narrow hallway, and the gloom of its sixty-plus years of history. Mamang's faded silk flowers on the coffee table and the old plaid couch contributed to the overall sadness. What a lonely thing to be living alone in an empty house.

He turned around to face Monica. "Here. Take this spare key for the front door, in case you want to take a walk."

She stepped forward and accepted it.

He opened the door. "Call me if you need anything."

"You know what my purpose in life is?"

"You gotta stop thinking about Leonard Reed. He's not worth it."

"No, no...this is actually good. I owe it to him that I finally found my purpose."

"Which is?"

"To never quit."

"Okay. You didn't strike me as a quitter to begin with."

Her eyes smiled even though her lips curled into a small frown.

"I'll try to be home around six. I'll drive you to New Jersey, if you like."

She nodded. "*Bahala na.*" Come what may.

The national motto of the Philippines if ever there was one. He stepped outside and shut the door. The weak sun made a pinhole in the sky.

The world praised Filipinos for their resilience and their ability to endure earthquakes, floods, poverty, dictatorships, revolutions, and hundreds of years of colonization. What some people called resilience, he called resignation—the ability to not quit and say, "*Bahala na.*"

He got into his car and started it. He glanced at the house. Monica was peering out the window, watching him. He raised his hand in a half wave and drove away. In his heart, he knew she'd be gone by the time he returned tonight. He would never see her again.

38

THE PRESENT

L ist of Undocumented Immigrants

Monica Reed
25
Philippines
Father seeks deportation
10/1/1998-10/1/1998
Last seen in Irwin, PA

35
Philippines

Father needs kidney donation
7/7/2008-7/16/2008
Last seen in Brooklyn, NY

44

Philippines
Stepmother seeks reconciliation
8/12/2017-Deceased

DOMINGO SAT in Mary Reed's living room, gawking at the cathedral ceiling, thinking of the list of illegals in his laptop in the office. Three weeks after he busted Amaury Penn, Monica Reed's case remained open. A DNA test had confirmed the severed arms in the duffel bag belonged to her, but Penn had not been indicted. Authorities continued to search for the rest of the body.

Domingo called Mary soon after the incident in Foresthill and asked her to end his contract. He wanted no more of her money after he'd failed to bring her stepdaughter home alive. Mary insisted on paying him, including this trip to Columbus.

Rosie pushed Mary's wheelchair into the living room. Mrs. Reed wore a sunny dress with a white cardigan. The headscarf matched the color of her dress. And yet, the happy colors failed to brighten her up. Her face appeared as faint as a shadow, a mere trace of the beauty long faded. Had it really been six weeks since she hired him? Too fast and yet too slow.

He rose. "It's good to see you, Mrs. Reed."

"Same here." She extended her hand, elegant and courteous as ever.

They shook hands. Her fingers seemed too fragile under his touch.

"Are you up for a walk?" she asked. "I could use some sunshine this morning."

"Sure. I'm happy to take you outside." He glanced at Rosie. "May I?"

Rosie nodded. "Give me a holler if you need anything." She lumbered toward the door and opened it.

Domingo pushed Mary's wheelchair out onto a ramp that circled the house, all the way to the vast backyard. A man he'd never seen before was trimming the bushes. They exchanged a nod.

The size of the Reed property amazed him anew. It stretched far beyond what he remembered from a decade ago. The small guest house loomed up ahead. The rock swimming pool with the fake waterfall sparkled. He doubted anyone used it, but Mary must enjoy it for the view and the soothing sound of crashing water.

"How's your mother?"

He'd mentioned Mamang's procedure the last time he called, used it as an excuse to delay coming here. "She's good. She's doing so well she's been talking about traveling to Manila. Fat chance. Twenty hours of flying is too much for her."

She shaded her eyes from the sun with her hand. "And you? Don't you want to visit Manila?"

Mary's question surprised him. The Philippines lay in the past like the mist of dawn. It evaporated under the full glare of the sun. "You know...I've never thought of it."

"Not even a short vacation?"

"I'm afraid I don't have time for a vacation."

He pushed the wheelchair on the paved pathway. A flock of birds formed a massive black cloud against the bright sky. In the distance, a lawn mower growled.

Mary pointed to the guest house. "Monica liked living there."

"Yes, I remember." They paused outside the white, dollhouse-like cottage. "She told me you built this guest house using an architectural design dating back to 1800. Is that right?"

"Yes, indeed. Somewhere in Virginia, there was once a house that looked exactly like this. We used an original blueprint, a collector's item."

My very own digs. That was how Monica had described it. He'd helped her move in. His anger from long ago blew like a cold wind, making his skin ripple in goose bumps.

"Sunday?"

"Should we keep going? Sorry." He resumed pushing the wheelchair.

"Gary told me Amaury Penn has lost his TV show. But why isn't he in prison?"

Mary's lawyer handled her dealings with the NYPD, the SFPD, and other authorities. The murder of Monica in California and Tess's death in New York meant a complex, interconnected investigation. Domingo himself got his information about the case from Manny Chua and, sometimes, from Detective Ramirez.

"The DA in San Francisco is being very careful," he said. "Instead of just filing a case willy-nilly, he wants a grand jury to indict Amaury Penn. That's an extra step he's taking so the case will stand up to public scrutiny. There's too much publicity involving Penn. The guy has millions of fans who think he's being bullied by left-wing prosecutors and cops. They think it's a conspiracy."

"What about that man...the man you caught carrying Monica's...?" She shook her head, unable to continue.

She meant Duling. "They nailed him, all right."

"What's his name again?"

"Hank Loserby."

"*Loser*-bee? That's his name?"

Domingo chuckled. "The most appropriate name, too. The

guy has a rap sheet dating back to 1999. He's active in the Build the Wall circles. He's an avid fan of Amaury, and he'll do anything for the guy. Hank violated his probation on a previous charge of assault and battery, plus he's the key suspect in Tess Chua's death, on top of transporting a murder victim's body parts across state lines. He's staying in prison for sure."

Mary glanced back at Domingo with a squint. The sun had climbed higher. He wheeled her underneath a tree. "Is this okay?"

She nodded. "This is nice."

He pulled the chair's brake lever down before perching on the bench beside her. They fell into silence and just stared at the islands of flowers around them. The pink roses appeared sturdy, but the sunflowers drooped like little soldiers who'd surrendered to autumn.

Mary sniffled. She was crying.

"Mrs. Reed? What's wrong?"

"I was too late. I could have saved Monica." She pulled an old-fashioned handkerchief from her dress pocket and wiped her tears. She barked a dry cough.

"It's not your fault. You have nothing to do with Penn's bigotry or the fact that he didn't want the world to know his biological parents were Russian immigrants and that his dad was a KGB. He's making millions of dollars based on his all-American image, a success story of an upstanding adopted boy who rose from humble beginnings. That illusion means everything to him. Even as we speak, he's claiming that the documents from Galina Brooks are fake, and that the cops are lying."

"If I'd taken in Monica after Leonard's death nine years ago, she'd be safe and sound today. We could have been a family. But, no, I was too proud and selfish."

"Mrs. Reed, do you know Jon Bon Jovi?"

She shook her head and tucked the handkerchief in her pocket.

"You're kidding me! You've never heard of him? You have to listen to my playlist sometime. Here's my best Bon Jovi, okay?" He took a deep breath before he sang and played air guitar. "Nooo regrets for things I've done...nooo regrets...la-la-la-la... hey, hey!" He grinned like an idiot because he couldn't remember the lyrics, but at least Mary smiled. "I haven't been to a karaoke bar lately, so I'm a little rusty. Anyway, there's no point in blaming yourself or holding on to regrets. That's what I'm trying to tell you." He blew out a breath and admired the well-manicured lawn and garden. The overripe scent of tumbling roses mingled with the whiff of dry leaves. Mother Nature's fall potpourri.

"Sunday?"

"Mrs. Reed, no encore of my Bon Jovi, okay? We should probably go back in." He rose.

"Tell me how Monica died."

He'd been dreading this moment, though he knew it was the reason Mary had asked him to come here. No amount of levity would distract her from this part of the conversation. He sat back down and rubbed his chin. "At this point, everything's just a theory. The cops are still trying to get to the bottom of the story. We should wait for the facts."

She placed her hand on his. "Please tell me."

He heaved a sigh. "The detectives think Penn met Monica in San Francisco with the intention of paying her off in exchange for his birth certificate and her silence about his biological parents. Unfortunately, Monica didn't have the birth certificate because she mailed it to her friend, Tess, for safekeeping. All Monica wanted was to relay the message of the old lady, Galina Brooks...that she loved her son, that she was sorry she gave up Amaury for adoption. But maybe Penn thought Monica was playing games with him or trying to blackmail him or whatever. Who knows? He must have snapped. And he hurt her."

"How?" Mary squeezed his hand. "How did he kill her?"

Oh man. The word *kill* pierced his heart. "It's only a theory."

Her eyes grew teary, begging him.

"Most likely she rode with him in his car. She must have thought a celebrity like him wouldn't do anything stupid because he had so much to lose. The SFPD thinks Monica never went to the restaurant with Amaury, and that's why the surveillance cameras didn't capture any images of her or him."

She leaned her head on his shoulder.

He listened to her huffing breaths, like a runner after a long race or someone exhausted beyond description. This was the closest he had ever been to Mary Reed or any client. They relapsed back into silence. What he knew for sure was Monica had been alive in San Francisco, and he'd found her severed hands in Connecticut. How she got from the West to the East coast was anyone's guess.

According to SFPD, Penn owned a beach house in Southampton with an old chest freezer, which he'd placed in a storage unit out of the blue. Very convenient for hiding a body, but hard to prove until the cops found the rest of that body. Duling had confessed to disposing the duffel bag for Penn in a landfill, but claimed no knowledge of any murder, certainly nothing about Tess's death.

That Duling had ended up driving to a waste transfer station instead of a landfill told Domingo that his unexpected appearance had led to the bastard's critical mistake. The fucker probably thought a recycling center was just as good as a landfill, except he hadn't known a tracking device had been planted in the duffel bag. Domingo would have found it regardless.

Mary sat up straight and fixed her headscarf.

"Mrs. Reed, let me take you back in." He stood up.

She gazed up at him with grief in her blue eyes. "What are you going to do now?"

"Me? From here, I'm flying to Los Angeles for my next case. I'm hunting down a Cambodian perp. It should be interesting."

"That's not what I mean."

Of course, not. He bowed his head and stuck his hands in his jeans' pockets. How many times had he met Mary? Five or six times, tops, in a span of nineteen years. Yet she understood him, saw the tiniest fissure in his façade. From that crack, his sorrow flowed like water.

At last, he met her eyes. "I always loved her, but I kept it to myself. I wasn't good enough for her. Now she's gone. My loss is so big it's like a black hole. It could swallow all of me right here, right now." His breath hitched, and he sucked in air with a small groan. If only he could scream. He brushed the hair out of his eyes and looked away, his gaze landing on the gardener crossing the lawn with the hedge trimmer.

After a moment, he turned back to Mrs. Reed. "You think you're too late? Well, me, too. Even more so, and I'll never forgive myself."

Mary's eyebrows creased together in a soft frown. She looked twice as worn out than only fifteen minutes ago. "Don't say *never*. It's a cruel word. Besides, it's not true. You're young, and someone else will come along, and you'll move on. And when that happens, you'll think of Monica with fondness. In the meantime, you have Bon Jovi to remind you of the most important things in life. No regrets, remember?"

"You got me. Good catch." He managed a smile, comforted by the warmth of her camaraderie. They had lost Monica, the bridge between them, and yet they remained connected. "You know why I like that song?"

"Tell me why."

"Have you ever danced when you thought nobody was looking? Maybe you're making coffee and toast in the kitchen with the music playing in the background, and you start singing out loud? Before you know it, you're twerking without a care and shaking your booty like crazy. That song's gonna make you dance like that."

She let out an unexpected chuckle, perhaps imagining herself doing a little jig. Then they both laughed until she started coughing.

"I better take you back inside or Rosie's gonna kick my ass." He got behind the wheelchair and unlocked the brake.

"Yes, I better turn in. I get so tired so fast."

He held the push handles and swiveled the chair in the direction of the house. They passed by the guesthouse, which would always be Monica's digs in his mind.

Leaves floated on the swimming pool. A small puddle formed on the ground where a fine spray from the pool's manmade waterfall hit. Was the waterfall ever turned off? What a waste. Anything wasted was lost and anything lost might never be recovered. That pretty much summed up the essence of his life.

He glanced down. Mrs. Reed's eyes were closed, her chin down. Poor Mary. The sight filled him with tenderness and brought back a childhood prayer, not for himself, but for her.

Now she lay down to sleep,
I pray the Lord her soul to keep,
May God guard her through the night,
And wake her with the morning light.

Mamang would be so proud to know that he remembered the prayer. On second thought, his mother better not find out that he still prayed sometimes, or she would tell her besties in the nursing home, including the old lady who wanted to touch his gun. Leila, with the whitest dentures he'd ever seen.

At the front door, Rosie waved. He waved back. A mild breeze rustled the leaves on the tall trees. The sky promised a full day of autumn goodness.

As soon as he landed in Los Angeles later today, he would find the nearest Best Buy or Target and buy the Bon Jovi CD for Mrs. Reed. He doubted she or Rosie had ever heard of Spotify. He would have to send it through overnight mail. No time like right now to say *you're not alone.*

ACKNOWLEDGMENTS

In 1995, I wrote the first draft of a manuscript that became *Multo*. It was my first attempt to write fiction. I was a green-card holder at the time. I was keenly aware of how lucky I was compared with the 3.5 million undocumented immigrants in the U.S. back then. They were top of mind for me when I conceived the character of Monica Reed. That was how *Multo* began.

Today the number of undocumented immigrants in the U.S. is estimated to be around 10.5 million. Sadly, immigration reform is as elusive as it was in 1995.

I became a naturalized U.S. citizen on Sept. 9, 2000. I don't take my citizenship for granted. I am and always will be grateful for finding a home and acceptance in America. I'm equally grateful that Agora Books gave *Multo* a publishing home. I want to express my heartfelt thanks to:

• Maria Napolitano of Jane Rotrosen Agency for taking a chance on me and shopping Multo under the most difficult circumstances at the height of the COVID-19 pandemic.

• Chantelle Aimée Osman for acquiring Multo and amplifying my voice through the novel.

• Jason Pinter for establishing and growing Agora Books and Polis Books and giving marginalized writers a place in traditional publishing.

• Flavia Viotti, founder and CEO of Bookcase Literary agency, for your utmost attention and support for Multo.

• Dana Kaye, Eleanor Imbody, Angela Melamud, and Hailey Dezort of Kaye Publicity for your expertise and unwavering enthusiasm.

• Corinne DeMaagd, author, editor, and friend, for your insights, which made Domingo stronger.

• Georgia Morrissey for the fabulous book cover.

• The Crime Writers of Color for the wonderful camaraderie and community.

Last but not least, thank you Vincent and Nina for just being you.